I

Valerie

Valerie

Joan Smith

ROBERT HALE · LONDON

© Joan Smith 1981
First published in Great Britain 2007

ISBN 978-0-7090-7922-4

Robert Hale Limited
Clerkenwell House
Clerkenwell Green
London EC1R 0HT

www.halebooks.com

2 4 6 8 10 9 7 5 3 1

Typeset in 11/15pt Souvenir
by Derek Doyle & Associates, Shaw Heath
Printed and bound in Great Britain
by Biddles Limited, King's Lynn

Chapter One

In defense of my reputation, let me deny at the outset the odious rumor that I went to Troy Fenners to nab a husband. That there chanced to be a few eligible gentlemen running tame at my Aunt Loo's house was mere coincidence. That was not why I went at all. When one has, however, an aunt possessed of a staggeringly large fortune and no children, she is not tardy to accept an invitation to visit. Add to that the fact that Papa is not at all high in the stirrups, that he has not less than four of us daughters to see matched, that life at Kent had sunk into a dismal business of hearing hints I was destined for the shelf, add to that three bickering sisters, and you will, I hope, believe that I went for the adventure and the simple pleasure of a change of scene.

My Aunt Loo, for Louise, is a dear, zany creature, *totally* unlike her brother, my papa. She is rather plump and fiftyish. She spends a great deal of her money on perfectly ugly outfits that run from the peculiar to the downright bizarre. She is a frustrated actress at heart, usually playing some role in her mind for which she unfortunately costumes her body. Having recently fallen amongst spiritualists, she brought with her a great many flowing, pale, vaguely ghostlike ensembles on her last visit home. It was while she was with us that she asked me to return with her to Troy Fenners, her estate in Hampshire. I said, 'Yes, please and thank you,' before her words were hardly out of her mouth.

'You will do very nicely,' she went on, running her bright blue eyes over my anatomy. Aunt Loo's eyes tend to protrude more from their sockets than other people's, giving her an air of perpetual surprise. It is a look that is quite familiar to me.

There is plenty of the anatomy she was examining. Five feet and ten inches of it, to be precise. I go beyond Junoesque. No one has ever referred to me as a ladder either; the frame is well filled. My sisters are kind enough to call me a Percheron, but I like to think of myself as more of a lioness. I have hair of a lionish shade, eyes that are topaz in color and somewhat the shape of a feline's eyes. I try to manage my large frame with catlike grace, though I cannot claim complete success in this endeavor. It is hard to be graceful when one must bend not only the head but also the shoulders to converse with other people. Then too the furniture makers scale down their sofas and chairs to accommodate smaller ladies. I am most at home in a man's stuffed armchair.

I never adopt any posture of apologizing for my size. There is nothing so pathetic as to see a large woman trying to shrink down to match her escort by buckling her knees, bending her head, or wearing childish flat-heeled shoes. I walk tall with my head high and my shoulders back, proud of my body. Cringing and groveling are not for a lioness. Just why my particular sort of body would 'do very nicely' for my Aunt Loo was not clear to me at the time. I soon learned her meaning!

Mama had a few reservations on the scheme of a visit. 'You are not used to being away from home, Valerie,' she reminded me. This loomed as one of my chief desires, the change, but I could not like to tell her so.

'I'll write every week, Mama. Twice a week, and the girls will write to me.'

'Hampshire is so far away,' she went on, with a worried frown. Mama, dear Mama, is the only person in the world who still sees me as a helpless little thing.

'Loo is lonesome,' Papa pointed out in an encouraging way to my mother.

'You must let me have her,' Loo implored. 'Just for a month. A month will be long enough.'

The question *would* just arise – long enough for *what*? Being so eager to go, I only smiled and nodded. 'Just one month, Mama. I'll be back for your birthday in July.'

'I hope so, my dear. My fiftieth – we plan a large party you must know.'

Lest you take the notion that, being the eldest daughter, I am verging on some such ancient age as twenty-five or thirty, let me point out that I have two brothers, both older than I am. I am twenty-one, and still consider myself very nubile, whatever my younger sisters may say. If ever I find a man I like who is over six feet tall, and providing of course he feels the same way about me, I shall have him. I have had several offers from midgets, and have been in love a few times with nonmidgets who failed to return the compliment, but till the present, I and my true love have failed to meet.

My sisters, excepting Sukey who is only fifteen and my favorite, were perfectly happy to see me go. Elleri's so-called beau has lately been showing some symptoms of turning into a cat-lover (the cat in question being me), and Marie was never perfectly happy having to share a room with me. Marie is a martinet; her belongings are on hangers and in drawers within a second of leaving her body. Mine have the inexplicable habit of falling on to floors, and hanging off chairs, even landing on beds, sometimes Marie's. I daresay I am a thorn in her side, but I am the one who actually *cleans* the room. She only *tidies* it. I am very particular about cleanliness, even if I am a little messy. What I crave, in my deepest heart of hearts, is a woman of my very own to pick up after me, and tend to the thousands of stupid chores women have to cope with. Mending, sewing, making hideous little flower arrangements – they are *women's* work, not fit for a lioness.

When Papa is in favor of anything at our house, it is done. I was allowed to accompany my Aunt Loo home to Troy Fenners, and went with no notion in my head what she wanted me for, but only the determination to have a wonderful time. We were two days and two nights on the road, for despite her elegant chaise and her team of four, she did not make a wild dart through the countryside. We stopped at the finest inns, dined on exquisite food, with my rich aunt picking up the bill for the whole. The first evening, we stopped over at Tunbridge Wells. As the clientele at our watering hole were well into their sixties and seventies, I made no demur when we retired to our rooms early, nor even when she handed me a novel to read, to while away the evening. It was an ersatz Mrs Radcliffe gothic book, entitled *Search for the Unknown*. I never cared much for gothics. Elleri and Marie eat them up like bonbons. I skipped through twenty pages and set it aside.

'Don't you like it?' she asked, disappointed.

'It's fine. I am rather tired from the trip. That's all.'

'Read a little more, just to please me,' she begged.

I read on, trying to become interested in an insipid heroine who fell into a fit of hysterics every ten pages or so. When she began receiving bumps on the head in the dark, threatening messages, and most particularly when a dashing gentleman entered into the story, my simulated interest became more genuine. I read half the book at the inn at Tunbridge Wells and finished it the next night at Horsham. The heroine's uncle was the villain; her dashing hero uncovered the plot, for Debora hadn't the wits to know even that she was in love with him, or he with her.

'How did you like it, Valerie?' she asked eagerly as soon as I closed the cover.

'Very much. Do you have any more by this writer? What's her name? Ah, Mrs Beaton. I don't recognize her.'

'No one does,' she answered, with a sly look on her face. She was trying to narrow those little pop eyes, which had the strange effect of pushing them out farther.

'What do you mean?'

'Oh, nothing,' she said, with elaborate nonchalance, pulling a fold of pale pink chiffon over her knees.

'You know Mrs Beaton. Who is she, Auntie? Do I know her?'

She could contain her marvelous secret no longer. 'It's me!' she squealed, then threw back her brindled head and laughed in pure glee. 'I am *so* glad you like it.'

It was not necessary to do any playacting. I could not have been more surprised had she told me the incredible events in the story were true. I made all suitable exclamations of surprise and congratulation.

'Oh, good, then perhaps you won't mind helping me,' was her reply.

She had chosen poorly. Writing, like sewing, is one of my more pronounced aversions. Marie was the one she ought to have brought back with her. When Marie is not tidying her room, she is making up lists of good resolutions, of her belongings, of things to do and read, anything to give her a reason to sit at a desk writing. A lengthy book to be copied out in copperplate would be a boon to Marie.

Before I had time to begin making my excuses, she went on, 'The thing is, you see, I want to murder someone, and as soon as I saw what a great, strapping, strong girl you are, and so very bold, I realized it could be done very easily.'

'Oh! But really, Auntie, I – I am not much good at – *murder?*'

'You can do it if you put your mind to it.'

'Who is the victim?'

'Mr Sinclair,' she answered promptly.

My aunt's married name is Sinclair. Of course she was a Ford, like Papa, before her marriage. The intended victim was not her husband; he had been dead for ten or more years. Sir Edward Sinclair was his name, some kin to the noble St Regis family. A first cousin to Lord St Regis I believe was the kinship. Just which relatives she planned to dispose of was unclear, but the whole idea was of course repulsive.

'Papa would never allow me,' I told her, my tones rising to strange heights. My normal voice is low-pitched.

'He shan't know a thing about it, dear. How should he? I would not tell him for worlds. It will be our little secret. I have it all planned out. You must climb up the trellis outside of his window, after first entering in the afternoon and making sure the window is not locked, then you raise the window, crawl in, and – well, I have not decided whether to shoot or strangle him. Maybe a dagger would be nice,' she said, setting a finger to her chin to ponder this detail.

I was beginning to think a straitjacket was what was called for. 'Yes, but it is illegal, you must know, to go killing perfectly innocent men.'

'Innocent?' she demanded, the eyes shooting forward. I feared they would depart from their sockets entirely. 'It is nothing of the sort. He is the foulest villain ever darkened the countryside.'

'What did he do?' I asked, my interest soaring.

'As to that,' she said more mildly, 'I haven't quite sorted the details out. But he is to be the very blackest sort of villain, who will stop at nothing. He is after Gloria's money, you see. I think he will have a wife already stashed away in a corner, while pretending to make love to Gloria.'

'Auntie,' I said, weak with relief, 'is this your next *book* we are discussing?'

'Mrs Beaton's next,' she laughed merrily. 'I had thought to call it *Madness Most Discreet*, from Shakespeare of course, but wonder if *Tenebrous Shadows* is not scarier. Walter will advise me; he is excellent at titles.'

'Walter – who is that?'

'A friend, a neighbor of mine. He is the one gave me the idea a mere female could not perform the feats required of Gloria in killing off the villain, but as soon as ever I saw how *huge* you are grown, and so bold, my dear Valerie, I knew perfectly well it could be done. I shall make Gloria *you*, you see, like I have made the villain Mr Sinclair, and if *you* can do it, she can. Only of course I shan't call her Valerie, because her name is already Gloria, which is a much prettier name. I am a little famous for my exactness of detail, if I do not puff myself off unbecomingly to say so. They may praise Mary

Brunton to the skies all they like, *I* think *Self-Control* was a vastly overrated piece. How should it be possible for the heroine to escape in an Indian canoe down a wild, treacherous river in America? I doubt it could be done, and I'll tell you this, Valerie, if Mrs Beaton were to have written it, she would have tested it out first.'

'Elleri liked the book,' I was so foolish as to say.

'Walter Scott liked *my* book!' she retaliated. 'As to Elleri, *I* never saw her open any book but the fashion magazines the whole time I was at your place. I had a most kind note from Mr Scott, forwarded to me by my publisher. I wish he would have showed the book to Lord Byron instead, but he don't care for novels. It may work its way into his hands yet. I know Byron's has got into the hands of the butcher, for I got a flitch of bacon wrapped up in 'Childe Harold,' which I thought *ever* so miserable an end for it. The *poem*, I mean, for the bacon ought to have been honored.'

'What else does Gloria do?' I asked, to stem the tide of useless details from Auntie.

'She jumps her mare over the tollgate booth, which I am sure you can do very well, for it is only five or six feet high. The gate you jumped at home is not much lower.'

'Yes, but the gate at home is not five feet *wide* as well.'

'I shall procure you an excellent jumper for the occasion, my dear. I have already arranged for that.'

Any scheme that put an excellent jumper under me was not much argued. 'We shall see. What else?'

'You have to carry your hero for a mile over the wildest terrain in all of England. Devon, or possibly Cornwall. I have not quite settled on the locale. Which do you think more frightening, moors or rocks?'

'Moors. How much does my hero weigh?' I asked, wondering if this too must be put to the test.

'Sixteen stone. One hundred and sixty-eight pounds.'

'Who is the hero in real life?' I asked with some interest.

'Jeremy Welles, our local solicitor. He is a handsome fellow. I never *could* understand why he married that ugly patch of a wife, but he is to be a bachelor in our book, of course. He weighs sixteen stone; I asked him, in an innocent roundabout way so he would not know why I wished to know. If you can carry him across the meadow, I shall know it is all right, and if you cannot, then the hero must lose a good deal of weight while he is in prison. We can put the weight back on him before the book's end. I would not want Gloria to be marrying a scarecrow in the last chapter.'

'I wager Gloria would not like it either.'

'I wonder if I should change Gloria's hair color,' was my Aunt's next irrelevant remark, while *I* wondered what was to be the pretext for me to carry Mr Welles across a meadow. She was smiling fondly on my lionish locks. 'I had her a blondhaired beauty, but as she is to be rather more vital than I originally intended, perhaps I shall brighten up her hair. And give her those strange yellow eyes you have got. Yes, I think Gloria may sparkle a little more than Debora.'

Debora was the young lady in search of the unknown, you will recall. It would not be at all difficult to sparkle more than that watering pot. I encouraged this scheme strongly. 'Oh, but I do not want her brassy, Valerie,' she declared, when I mentioned that more backbone would not go amiss. 'She must rely on FitzClement to rescue her in the end. It would not be at all the thing for her to rescue herself. There would be no romance in *that*.'

I soon understood, from further discussion, that this Amazonian heroine was to decline into a rasher of vapors in the end, like Debora, which I thought a great pity. Already I had managed to change her hair and eyes, and had some hazy intention of doing a similar switch on her personality before the book was all written. For the meanwhile, there was a little zest added to the visit in having to perform these feats of strength and daring. I am not a lioness for nothing. If I cannot clamber up a trellis, pull open a window, stab a victim, and haul a sixteen-stone carcass across the moors, I will be much surprised. I confess the jumping of the tollbooth raises an unworthy premonition of a vapor. We shall see.

Chapter Two

*T*here is French blood from the days of the Normans in the Sinclair family. The name of the estate, Troy Fenners, is a corruption of *Trois Fenêtres*, which is presumably the number of windows in the original home. There are considerably more than that in the present building. I counted eighteen on the facade alone as we drove up to it. But before we get through the park, let me say that the setting was ideally gothic. Mrs Radcliffe might well have been describing the place in any of her gloomy word pictures. There were ancient oaks and elms to distribute the requisite tenebrous shadows, with a stand of willows to droop forlornly behind the house. The dark yews in front of the windows would do a good job of stealing light within, and the upper windows were being invaded by ivy to prevent a surfeit of daylight. The soaring lancet windows, the battlements, gargoyles, finials, the aging stone, the general spooky atmosphere were very evident in daylight. When evening shadows stretched, the place would be enough to frighten a witch. The whole of it was blasted with antiquity. Living in this house might well have incited my aunt to write her novels. It lacked only an uninhabited wing with mysteriously locked doors containing deep, dark secrets to be a perfect model of a haunted castle.

'Uninhabited wing? Why, no, I live in the whole place. There are no locked doors, but only a secret passage, and of course the oubliette in the cellar.'

'You mean – a dungeon?' I asked, enraptured.

'A horrid old place, full of mice and spiders, with irons and chains rusting in the walls. I would like to have it all cleaned up, made into something useful, but it seems a waste of good money.'

My aunt had plenty of good money, so the redoing of the oubliette must have been a passing whim, no more. Her staff, who lined up to welcome us, were distressingly modern and normal. There wasn't a saturnine butler or a dour housekeeper in the lot. A squinting parlor maid was the closest we came to it, and she was not at all sneaky-looking, but only rather ugly. It was quite a disappointment. The house was dark and gloomy, however, with a long-case clock that had a haunting way of wheezing, emitting quite a human sound before it struck the hour. I suspected that on a windy night the chimney would belch smoke and distort the wind to a nice eerie pitch. The stairway too creaked, and the ivy tapped mysteriously at my windowpane. The canopied bed was done up in funereally dark shades of green, while the clothespress was of the proper size to hide a body or two.

When I began putting my things away later, I discovered to my dismay that it held nothing but clothes hangers and two dry orange pomander balls, without a bit of scent left to them. They were as hard and brittle as porcelain. They rattled when shook, from the dried seeds within and the dried cloves outside. Soon the press contained my clothing too, not through my own efforts, but – joy of joys! – through the good offices of a servant assigned to my own particular service. It was the squinty-eyed girl who came tapping at my door, sent by Aunt Loo to tend me. I saw, all of a sudden, that the girl was not at all disfigured by her poor squinting eyes. If she proved a good worker, I would be finding her beautiful before too long. Her name, she told me, was Hester Pincombe, but she was commonly known as Pinny.

While Pinny performed for me those duties beneath a lioness, I went below to dine on a meal fit for my species. Aunt Loo's cook did her proud; one did not eat at Troy Fenners one dined. What a marvelous difference, and without Elleri and Marie there to count how many refills my plate and glass had too. I lost count of the latter myself, but I was by no means staggering when we retired to the paneled saloon. Aunt Loo, eager to get to her work, reverted to the matter of killing off our villain.

'I *do* like the notion of a dagger, dripping with blood, and perhaps dropping a few spots on your white gown, Gloria,' she began. So wrapped up was she in her melodrama that she assigned to me the heroine's name. 'When you climb up the gate-house trellis for me, you must experiment and find the most convenient way of holding the dagger. The teeth would do, or stuck into your waistband, which means you must wear a suit, for these new empress gowns are not good for concealing or carrying a weapon at alt.'

'The teeth, definitely, which means it must not be too large a dagger,' I advised.

'I have just the thing. I'll get it and let you try if you can hold it in your mouth. Mrs Brunton's Laura was not at all credible in her adventures. I don't mean Gloria to make such a cake of herself.'

I sat contemplating what would be a suitable gown for murder while she ran off to find the weapon. When she returned, she had not only a pretty bone-handled knife with a carved blade in one hand, but a bulky sheepdog of a man at her side. 'This is Doctor Hill, Valerie. You have heard me speak of Walter. And this is my niece, Valerie Ford, Walter. She has agreed to come home with me and try out those feats you claimed to be impossible for a mere lady.'

'Miss Ford, a pleasure,' he said, shaking my hand as though I were a gentleman. I like shaking hands, much prefer it to the simpering curtsey usually practiced by my sex. You can tell something about a person by the grip of his hand. Dr Hill had a firm, indeed a crushing, grip. But then he was a big man. I had to look *up* to him. His general appearance was that of a country squire. There was no elegance at all in the man. His grizzled hair had been allowed to grow to a countrified length without aid of professional barbering. His outfit for an evening call was not the sort seen in finer homes, but a slightly spotted brown afternoon jacket and faun trousers, with dusty Hessians on his feet. He looked like someone's father.

'Very happy to make your acquaintance, Dr Hill. I would not have taken you for a medical man,' I added, for something to say.

'Just what I always tell him,' Aunt Loo laughed. 'But he is one of the best. He had a very fashionable Harley Street practice before he retired here to Hampshire.'

'I could only tolerate London for a decade,' he confided. 'Perhaps it was the address did me in. I ended up prescribing hartshorn and laudanum for bored ladies, so decided to gather up what few resources I had and return to the country to practice *real* medicine.'

'He means prescribe hartshorn and laudanum for *me*,' Loo translated. 'I have a touch of rheumatism and a twinge of the migraine and insomnia from time to time. Not enough of anything to be interesting, but my maladies keep me amused.'

'You look too healthy ever to require my services,' the doctor said to me as he passed to reach the sofa. It was his professional way of mentioning he had noticed I was a little larger than most females.

'In the normal way, I don't see a doctor for years at a time, but the activities my aunt has planned for me may provide you a patient,' I told him.

'I do not suggest jumping the tollbooth,' he said bluntly. 'As for the rest of it, I come to see Lady Sinclair has found just what she requires – a lady to do the impossible.'

The discussion that ensued showed me Dr Hill was a bosom bow of my aunt. He was privy to not only her alias of Mrs Beaton, but to all the details of the forthcoming *Tenebrous Shadows*. He was even slipping into my aunt's habit of calling me Gloria at one point in the discussion. He was a local man, who had kept his cottage in the neighborhood for a holiday retreat while practicing medicine in London. His association with the family went back into history and continued up to the present. He was aware of certain aspects of her domestic arrangements that she had failed to mention to me.

'Is Pierre not back yet?' he asked, after a half hour's talk.

'Who is Pierre?' I asked.

'Why, he is my late husband's cousin, my dear,' she told me. 'He has been staying with me these six months. Pierre St Clair, from the French side of the family. He was smuggled out of Paris as a very infant during the reign of terror, and raised on a farm in Normandy. He was schooled in a Jesuit seminary and sent to England last year to wait out this horrid business of Napoleon. When he goes back, he will be a *comte* or something of the sort, but meanwhile he calls himself plain Monsieur Pierre St Clair. He is a pretty boy; he will be some company for you while I am writing during the day. I write in the morning while I am fresh. I used to lie in bed till noon, but Walter says this is much healthier for me, to be bent over a desk.'

'What I said, Miss Ford, is that it is good for your aunt to have a hobby, an interest in life. Well, the money does not go amiss either, for that matter.'

My surprised stare was due to a hint that money was required in this house of opulence. The doctor was sharp enough to notice it at once. 'We can all use a little spare cash,' he added, then hastened on to change the subject. 'So Mr Sinclair has taken Pierre to Wight. He will like that. It will be a nice trip for the boy.'

'You never mentioned a word about Pierre St Clair to us at home, Auntie,' I said.

'I was afraid your mama would dislike your coming when I had a young fellow staying here at the house. She is a trifle old-fashioned in her ways, and Pierre is French, to make it all the worse. He has found an English strain in his background now and insists he is English, but he is very French, and I did not like to mention him to your mama. He slipped my mind once we got back home and discussing my book. The other fellow we are speaking of is Welland Sinclair, the fellow you are going to murder for me.'

Dr Hill smiled at her strange way of speaking. 'Mr Sinclair is staying at the gatehouse, then,' I mentioned, knowing my victim's lair by this time. 'Is he also a cousin of your late husband?'

'Yes, some relation. He only came a month ago. He lives in Hereford, stays right at Tanglewood with Lord St Regis. St Regis wrote asking me if I had a private, quiet spot he could put up in. He is a scholar, Valerie, writing up a treatise on ghosts.'

A surprised laugh escaped my lips, at the incongruity of a scholarly ghost treatise. 'On the occurrence of ghosts in English literature over the centuries,' Dr Hill explained.

'Like Hamlet's father,' I said, understanding the subject properly now.

'Exactly. Also in *Macbeth*, and something crops up in *Julius Caesar*. Shakespeare trafficked a good deal in ghosts. Young Sinclair has a thick volume of research he is working on. I think the lad works too hard. I am worried about his eyes. He won't let me look at them, though he complains often enough.'

'Mr Sinclair has to wear green glasses,' Loo said. 'I don't think it is good for him to do so much close work as he does. It would be a pity to lose them – his eyes I mean. I am losing the sight of my eyes. I can no longer thread a needle to save my life. It makes me *furious*. And I am going deaf too, or else the whole world has taken to whispering. Except for Walter. He always shouts up good and loud for me.'

'I shall prescribe you a tonic, my dear Louise. What you suffer from is not blindness and deafness, but only a fit of pique that you are no longer young.'

'Prescribe me a new pair of legs and set of teeth while you are about it,' she begged. 'My body is worn out, plain falling apart. I wish I could get hold of a new one and start over again, with my brain intact. Do you think there is anything in this reincarnation, Walter?'

He smiled apologetically to me, but it was clearly his habit to humor Aunt Loo. He entered willingly into a discussion of this possibility, while I sat deciding how I would like to come back, if I got another whirl out of life. A man, I thought. Definitely as a man. Too many feminine qualities irked me; being coy and dainty, being backward in speaking to strangers, especially male strangers, having to wear skirts and ride sidesaddle. Yes, I would like to be a man, but with my present size and strength. When I tuned back into the conversation of the oldsters, the subject had changed.

'We shall have a session tomorrow night,' Aunt Loo was saying. 'Will you speak to the Franconis for me, Walter, or shall I write them a note?'

'I am going to the village. I'll arrange it. What hour would you like to have the sitting?'

'After dinner, ninish would suit me. If Pierre and Mr Sinclair are back, they will join us. Pierre is not very good at it, but Mr Sinclair shows a surprising flair. I am sure Valerie would like to try it as well.'

A 'sitting' conveyed to me having one's portrait taken, but this was obviously not the sort of sitting being spoken of here. I put the question to Dr Hill. 'A séance,' he confessed, not without a trace of shame. 'Your aunt has taken up an interest in spiritualism. There are a pair in the village who seem to have a knack for it. Franconi is their name – a man and his wife. She is the medium.'

'Medium what?' I asked, my confusion becoming deeper. Auntie had mentioned spiritualism at home, to explain her funny gowns, but had not expanded on it when she encountered Papa's scowl and Mama's dumbfounded frown. I thought she had her fortune read from time to time – something of the sort.

'Medium for contacting Edward,' she told me. 'Madam Franconi is trying to get in touch with Edward for me, my late husband, you remember, dear. Such a relief to know I can still talk to him. It is a wonderful thing. Do not judge it out of hand. Just think, if you could talk to your grandmother, or some dear departed one.'

'I don't remember Grandma Ford. I don't have any dear departed ones yet.'

'How very uninteresting the young are after all,' she said sadly to Walter.

'But I would like to be reincarnated,' I added, to placate her.

'Yes, that is an interesting alternative, but there is no saying you would come back as a human being, Valerie. You might very well come back as a mouse or a bird or anything. I wonder if Valerie was not a lion or tiger in her last incarnation, Walter! Doesn't she have the traces of it still? And Madame was saying just before I left that there will sometimes be a carry-over. She is quite sure Lady Morgan used to be a mouse, for besides looking quite like one, she is *petrified* of cats. Imagine!'

Walter smiled sheepishly, for a medical man to be countenancing such unscientific stuff. 'There is no harm in it,' he told me. 'It amuses us oldsters, who have little enough to keep us occupied.'

'Never apologize for your beliefs, Walter,' Loo commanded, her brindled head sitting back at a haughty angle, while her blue eyes snapped. 'Valerie is a child. *We* are older, and wiser. She is not required to believe, neither are we required to apologize for believing. Let her try a sitting. If nothing comes of it, she need not try again.'

'You need not try at all, if it does not interest you,' he told me.

'I'll try it. I'll try anything once,' I answered without hesitation. It was a custom I followed in my life to accept all new experiences that were offered. Whoever would have thought snails or oysters would taste so delicious, for instance, to look at them? Till I jumped into the lake, I never thought I would like swimming either, but I adore it. One would not have believed kissing Arthur Crombie would be at all satisfactory with that moustache, but it was very nice. I am all for trying new things. Except perhaps jumping over the tollbooth. I have still some reservations on that point.

Dr Hill prescribed a glass of wine and an early retirement for us after the exhaustion of our travels, then left to allow us to fill the prescription.

'He seems very nice,' I told her when we were alone.

'He is the oldest friend I have in Hampshire. He was Edward's good friend when we got married. He married some cousin of Edward's first wife. Edward was best man at the wedding, which was well before my time. Walter would have been our best man as well, except that we got married at Bath, where we met. I was there with Grandmother Ford, Valerie. I wonder if there is any chance of contacting her tomorrow night.'

'We shall see.'

It would be misleading to say I had grave doubts on that score. I hadn't a doubt in the world it was all a bag of moonshine, but the experience would be interesting. I would try it – once.

Chapter Three

In the morning, I tried another new experience: sleeping in till nine o'clock and having cocoa in bed. It was marvelous. I mean to try it every day while I am here at Troy Fenners. My aunt was locked up in her scriptorium when I came down for breakfast. I sat at the table alone, but before two eggs were consumed, I was joined by Pierre St Clair. He was a perfect little Napoleon of a man in so far as height goes, but not nearly so bellicose. In fact, he was charming, and not bad-looking either, barring his small stature. He was dark-haired, dark-eyed, swarthy-skinned, elegant in the extreme, stopping just a shadow short of being foppish. He advanced toward me at a leisurely waddle, caused by the outward turning of his toes.

'I hear you are the Miss Ford,' he said, performing a polite bow at the side of my chair.

'You must be the Pierre St Clair,' I replied, offering him my hand. I mean to be quite insistent in future on always shaking everyone's hand instead of curtseying. At twenty-one, I think I might take this privilege to myself without appearing brash.

The Pierre did not seem to know what to make of my gesture. He put his other hand over mine, and stood there, smiling and nodding for several seconds, while my eggs turned cold. 'Won't you have a chair, Mr St Clair?' I suggested.

'I have many chairs,' he smiled, looking around the table where he had, to be sure, a choice of eleven. Still, he was strangely reluctant to select one.

'Do sit down. Have you had breakfast?' I asked.

'I have had the coffee. I shall have more the coffee, to keep you companies.'

'How nice.'

'You will pour me the coffee,' he said, but in a polite, deferential tone.

After a brief consideration, I gave in and poured. 'Also of the cream and sugar,' was his next suggestion.

'Help yourself,' I said, nodding toward them. One can humor a foreigner only so far.

'Yes, very help yourself,' he agreed, sitting down beside me and adding an unconscionable quantity of cream and sugar to his cup. 'I am happied to make you welcome to *Trois Fenêtres*,' he went on.

'I am happy to be here.'

'I also. *Tante* Louise is the charming hostess, when she is here. Maybe I adopt her to me.'

'Plan to make a long stay of it, do you?'

'Only for the coffee. *Tante* Louise is not the true aunt, you understood. She is the cousin.'

'She is *my* aunt.'

'She is my cousin.'

'Quite.'

'Precisely. The Sinclair, you comprehend, is the St Clair, in bastardized English. Mr Sinclair, he tells me this. I meet many bastardized St Clairs at Wight. It is the island where I am gone with Mr Welland Sinclair.'

'Yes, so I understand.'

'It is not difficult to comprehend. They are all my cousins. I have many English cousins. I too am very English. In France, I am took always for an English.'

'I don't think you'll have that difficulty in England, Mr St Clair.'

'Call me Sinclair. It is better. When at Rome, do like the Italians do, as we say in English.'

'Yes, we say that all the time.'

'The coffee, he is too very much sweet,' was his next attempt at communication.

'He is darling, isn't he?'

'Too sweet darling,' he decided, shoving the cup away. 'I am to be the friend companion to show the *Trois Fenêtres* at you. *Tante* Louise, she tells me so. Yes?'

'Wasn't that sly of her? Shall I try to speak French, Mr St Clair? It might be easier for you.'

'But no absolutely! Speaking the French becomes very difficult to me. I speak the English best. I think to stay absolutely at England now on, with *Tante* Louise.'

'Lucky *Tante* Louise.'

'Lucky Pierre also too: I am very much at the home here. My chap friend, Welland Sinclair, who is my cousin you recall – he tells me every day I am more English. No one guesses but that for my name, so I call me Peter Sinclair in the future. You also will call me Peter Sinclair, please you.'

'I shall be very happy to, Peter Sinclair.'

'Good. Now stop eating, or you become too gross. We walk.'

'I haven't finished my breakfast.'

'*Tante* Louise, she wants that I show you the horse for jumping something. I don't know what it is. A very big she horse.'

'My tollbooth-jumping mount! Excellent, I'll go with you.' I hopped up, eager to see my mount, and wondering where Aunt Loo had got hold of it so early.

'*Mon Dieu!*' Pierre (sorry, Peter) exclaimed as I arose to tower above him. '*Comme c'est une grande fille!*'

'The English is best, Peter,' I reminded him.

'The most best English girl I ever see,' he smiled fatuously, offering his arm to accompany me to the stable. 'I think the horse, she is too big for a girl, but now. . . .' He gave a Gallic shrug that speaks so many words and hastened along to the stables, his elegant little shiny Hessians hopping to keep up with me. He tried to slow us down, for he was low-set, and not very agile in motion.

The mount was a cross between an Arabian and a Percheron, my favorite sort of jumper. She was a mare, called Nancy. 'Whose mount is she?' I asked Pierre.

'The Hill medicine man lent her. You can drive this animal?'

'No, but I can ride and jump her. I'm going to change into my habit now and try her paces. Want to come along?'

'I do not have a horse here. In France, I have many stables. My cousin, he is lending me a horse later soon. We English can't do without our horses,' he assured me.

He jabbered incessantly all the way back to the house. It was a relief to my poor ears to leave him at the door.

Pinny came running to my room when she saw me enter the house. She got out my riding habit and bonnet, brushed them meticulously, and took my gown to hang up as I pulled it off. It was lovely to have her there, picking up after me, and feeling honored to be allowed to do it. I suppose for her it was no worse than sweeping carpets and polishing furniture. 'That Mr St Clair is a wicked rattle jaw, Miss Ford,' she warned me, somewhat belatedly to be sure. 'Carries on with the girls when her ladyship's back is turned, and that isn't the worst of him either.'

'What could be worse, Pinny?' I asked her mischievously.

'He has a conning way about him. The mistress is so fond of him I don't doubt he'll become a tenant for life.'

'What, settle down at Troy Fenners you mean?' I asked, surprised that my aunt could tolerate his jabbering.

'We all think that's what he has in his mind. He certainly likes it here, especially since Mr Sinclair moved into the gatehouse. Close as winkle-weavers, the pair of them. If you want my opinion, miss, it's a case of the scavengers gathering to see what they can pick from her, and they pick plenty.'

'What on earth are you talking about, Pinny? You mean she

gives them things – money?'

'She's doing something with it since they came. We never were short of anything before, and *that's* a fact. She hasn't paid us our last quarter wages. Of course she was away visiting, but she'd never have let it go before, and she hasn't mentioned it since her return either. Cook says the grocer in the village was a knocking at the back door yesterday for payment of his bill, and her without a pence in her coffers to pay him off.'

'It must be an oversight. I'll speak to her if you like, remind her to pay the staff.'

'Oh, never in the world, miss!' she pleaded, her poor squinted eyes looking horrified. 'I wouldn't want her to know we've been gossiping, but it *is* odd, isn't it?'

'Yes, it is,' I agreed.

'Shall I give this muslin a washing, miss?'

'Good gracious no! I've only worn it for an hour. Hang it up.'

'I pressed the suit you wore for traveling. It's hanging in the clothespress. Is there anything else, miss? Any mending or polishing of shoes, gloves to be washed?'

'Do whatever you see needs doing, Pinny,' I answered, glowing with joy at shucking all my personal chores off on her willing shoulders. 'I must go now. I can't keep Nancy waiting.'

'That great whopper of a nag Dr Hill left off on his way to the village? I never thought a lady could ride it, but then you're not. . . .' She bumbled to a stop, too embarrassed to go on.

'No, I'm not, am I?' I asked unhelpfully, and left the room, smiling at her.

The smile faded as I considered her remarks about not getting paid. How was it possible my aunt was short of funds? She had, according to family gossip, ten thousand pounds per annum from Sir Edward, plus whatever small dowry she had brought to her marriage. Yet she had not given us girls a guinea on this last trip, as she customarily did. That is *all* she ever gave us. If her money was being used by buzzard-relatives, the Fords were not to blame.

I could not imagine Pierre being so sly, but then his particular brand of English tended to cloud his actual thinking. He might be a cunning rascal, made to appear a fool by his broken English. He spoke a good deal of his cousin, this Welland Sinclair who was staying at the gatehouse. Welland, according to what I had learned, was a pensioner of Lord St Regis. He might have thought to find easier pickings from a lone female relation. I would canter Nancy down toward the gatehouse and try for a look at Welland.

My brief stop at the stable decided me I must speak to my aunt. The head groom walked diffidently up to me, and requested me to 'just remind her ladyship that she forgot to pay the vet. He was here this morning to inspect a lame plough horse and happened to mention it.'

'How much is it?' I asked.

'Five pounds.'

'That is expensive for inspecting a lame horse!'

'It's for the whole year, like. She hasn't paid him all year.'

'Very well, I shall speak to her.'

It was early June. Pierre had been here for six months, since the beginning of he year. Her shortage of funds seemed to coincide with his coming, which might be coincidence, or might be something else. Its being June also made the weather intoxicatingly beautiful. In the morning, the sun was not yet high or hot. There was a refreshing breeze, an azure sky overhead, scudded with billowing white clouds, there were those spreading elms and oaks to give shade and variety to the park, and beyond there was the gatehouse, whose trellised wall was to be scaled by me in the near future. Best of all, there was a prime goer begging to be let out. I urged Nancy on, forgetting all else in the process. Instead of going to the gatehouse, I turned west to open ground, through all the park, the spinney, to a fence beyond that separated Troy Fenners from the neighbor. It was a nice high fence, over five feet. She took it without breaking stride, moving lightly, easily, fearlessly. I let her gallop on through the meadow, then turned her round and retraced her steps back to Aunt Loo's parkland.

The gatehouse was down at the road, of course. It was a small-ish gray stone building, with some pretentious gothic trim that did not suit its proportions. The trellis – it had to be mine, there was only the one – was on the back of the building. It went up to the second story windows but was not substantial enough, in my esti-mation, to carry me. A ladder seemed a likelier means of access for Gloria. I rode around the building twice, checking for other trellises, espaliered trees, or some illegal means of entrance, and also for a view of Welland Sinclair, without finding any of the things I looked for. I was not in a mood to curtail my ride by making a call on him, so cantered down the road to check out the scene of another of my coming feats; to wit, the tollgate booth.

It was very much like any other tollbooth you might see on the roads of England. The barrier itself could have been cleared on human foot, but I knew from Loo's conversation it was the actual keeper's booth I was to essay jumping. Just why Gloria should insist on this maneuver was not clear. A glance assured me Gloria must change her mind, and be satisfied with some other hazard. The hut was six feet high, and perhaps four feet on every side, a spot for the guard to sit down and wait for customers. He thought he had one in me. He came out and proceeded to make such a pest of himself by his ill-bred efforts at flirtation that I had to leave. I returned to Troy Fenners for lunch, and a private chat with my aunt about money.

Chapter Four

$\mathcal{M}$y aunt was just emerging from her study, which she called a scriptorium since she took up writing, when I came down the creaking stairs. She had on a pale blue cloud today, another floating, diaphanous affair with a muslin slip beneath to provide propriety. The creation defies naming; it was certainly not a gown, yet not quite a peignoir either. It was a huge circle of cloth, with a hole cut for her head, and some embroidered slits from which her arms stuck out.

'You met Pierre?' she asked.

'Yes, I did. I have also been riding Nancy. She is a superb mare. I must congratulate Dr Hill when next we meet.'

'That will be this evening. I have asked him to dinner. Pierre is inviting Mr Sinclair as well, to allow you to make his acquaintance. I breathe easier to tell you Pierre is taking his lunch with Mr Sinclair. He is a sweet boy, but his chatter is so distracting, and he *will* go on trying to be polite and talking all the time, without realizing what an awful infliction he is. I shall just wash up and meet you for lunch, Gloria. In the solarium today – nice and bright and warm.'

She was not totally out of her writing mood, since she called me Gloria. I wandered round till I found where the table was laid, in a smallish room with one wall windowed. It was the least gothicy room in the house, and the prettiest I had seen. By the time my aunt joined me, she was calling me Valerie. I mentioned that the groom had asked me to remind her to pay the veterinarian.

'Dear me,' she said, shaking her head, 'has *he* not been paid either? I don't know where the money goes. It just flutters away. I think I must owe the servants a little something as well, for they are wearing their Friday faces – you must have noticed it.'

A good bit of it had fluttered away during our stops at inns, but that still left several thousands to be accounted for. It was a difficult point to raise, being none of my business, but as she was not unapproachable, I asked, 'Don't tell me you are short of funds, Auntie'? How can it be possible?'

A look came over her face, or a lack of look – a strange blankness that was surely designed to conceal her feelings. 'No, not really. I daresay I haven't nearly so much money as your papa thinks I have. Edward left debts to be discharged, you must know. There are expenses to running a place like this. Always something to be repaired or replaced.'

I have occasionally been charged with being pushier than is acceptable in a young lady, but I was not bold enough to ask point-blank if she was giving money to St Clair and Welland Sinclair. I hinted at it indirectly instead. 'Company to be entertained too, like me. And of course there is Pierre, and Mr Sinclair. . . .'

'Don't mention it, Valerie. It is nothing – a bit of food. The house here is empty, the gatehouse the same. I am happy for the company,' was her uninformative reply.

She would reveal nothing, but the telltale signs of worry were quite evident on her face. Dr Hill was her confidant. His casual mention that the money from her writing was a help told me he knew something of her situation. I would question him when I got a chance – do it with the utmost discretion. If she were in a financial pickle, Papa was the one who could help her. He is a veritable wizard with money. You would laugh to hear how little income he gets from his estate, yet we keep up a very respectable appearance – a family of eight. I know he is putting some funds by for his daughters' dowries as well as educating his sons. Mama too has everything she wants, though she is careful not to want much.

Loo was chewing distractedly on an herb omelette. When she had swallowed, she said, 'I would prefer if you not give any indication to Mr Sinclair of this, Valerie. There is no need for him to know.'

'How should I say anything about it to him? I have not even met the man.'

'You will, and he has a strangely insinuating manner. I seem to find myself telling him things I had no notion of telling, and he will only. . . . Not that I *know* he would, but it is possible, and I would rather say nothing.'

'What is it you think he will do?'

'He is very close to St Regis – his secretary. It was St Regis who wrote asking me if he could stay at the gatehouse. How did he know it was vacant, I wonder? But he makes it his business to know everything about me, pest of a man. Just like his father before him. No, he isn't though. He's worse.'

'What business is it of St Regis if you have outrun the grocer?'

'He makes it his business. That is exactly the trouble. The estate, Troy Fenners, is entailed on St Regis. The Sinclairs always keep everything close in the family. If Edward had had any sons, Troy Fenners would have been theirs, but as he had not, it reverts to St Regis when I go. I have tenure of the place and the income during my life.'

'I know that, Auntie, but with such a large income you must have saved *thousands*.'

'Not at all, my dear. I do not live in your mama's nip-cheese way, making soup from bones and hankerchiefs from old shirts, and having my daughters act as house servants. Of course I do not have any daughters, but if I had, they would each have her own woman, as you have. But that is neither here nor there. St Regis has his finger stuck into everything. I am not at all sure he did not send Welland Sinclair down here to spy on me, and send him back word how I go on. He would have promised Sinclair he could have the use of Troy Fenners to live in after I am gone. Sinclair looks around the place with a very proprietary eye already.'

'I hope you aren't planning to go anywhere for a few decades yet. You are only fifty.'

'Fifty-four actually, my dear. Plus a few months. Twenty-six months, to be precise. I am getting on.'

'You are a spring chicken. Pray don't talk so foolishly. About St Regis, I don't see that he can do anything. You have control of the income to spend as you wish. He can't change that.'

'Yes, but he is the estate guardian, you see. He can recommend repairs and what not, recommend them very forcibly. Edward made the wretched mistake of appointing him to help me look after things, and he takes an overweaning interest in how I go on. Any mortgage or sale must go through him, for he would be responsible for the mortgage in a way if anything should happen to me. Not that it is likely to, but the odious man says ten thousand pounds a year should be enough, and he will never give me a *penny* more, besides making me spend a fortune to repair a *barn* – such a waste. And on top of it all, he is forever sending me the *snippiest* letters you ever saw.'

'Mortgages?' I asked, wondering that she should require more money than her income, even with the repairs to a barn deducted from it.

'Mortgages, selling pictures or jewelry or what not – he has his say about everything, making it impossible for me to raise . . . But it is only a nuisance. Not serious,' she added, without much conviction.

I took the impulsive decision it *was* possible to ask her point-blank after all, and did so. 'What in the world would you need more than ten thousand pounds a year for, Auntie?'

She looked around the room, hunching her shoulders, making poofing sounds with her mouth, undecided whether to tell me to mind my own business or to ignore the question. 'Occasionally, for an extraordinary expense. . . .' she said at last.

'What extraordinary expense?'

'The barn, as I mentioned. Helping people. Charity work. Things like that.'

'Helping Pierre?' I essayed.

'Pierre?' She laughed out loud at the thought. Laughed so hard I took the idea she was trying to hide something. I did not get anything else out of her. I knew she was in some financial trouble but would have to discover its cause in some other manner. I hoped for enlightenment from Dr Hill.

A few moments later I asked her where he lived. It was not more than a mile and a half down the road, in a pretty rose-covered Elizabethan cottage, which should not be difficult to find. He was coming to dinner that same day, but if no privacy was found, I could go to him.

Before long, our talk turned back to Gloria. I explained that I did not think it possible for Nancy to vault over a building, no matter what incentive she had. 'She is being pursued by the villain, and the tollgate keeper is his accomplice. She only realizes it as she approaches the booth, and hasn't time to stop.'

'She could go around it.'

'Oh, no, there is a river on one side, and an armed man on the other, prepared to capture her. It is over the top, or she is done for. I am convinced it can be done. Oh, and there is something else, Valerie. You must not tell Mr Sinclair why you are here. I would not want him running back to St Regis with the story I am writing books. He would dislike it very much.'

'It is none of their business, but if you want it kept mum, it is no difference to me. How about Pierre? He is on close terms with Sinclair. Will he not tell?'

'He doesn't know, my dear. I even told him once, but he does not understand a great deal of what he hears. He thinks I lock myself up mornings to write letters. So I would too, if the alternative were listening to him trying to talk to me. I like Pierre immensely, so charming and generous, but wearing. There is no denying he is hard on the nerves. Now, what would you like to do this afternoon, Valerie?'

'Go to see the oubliette, and explore the secret passage you spoke of.'

'I shall go down to the dungeon with you. There might be something in it for Gloria. . . .' Her voice trailed off, while she looked with unseeing eyes out the window, caught up once more in the tenebrous shadows.

The oubliette was a disappointment. There was clammy, cold stone, as promised, with a few puddles on the floor. There were three sets of clamps and chains hanging from the wall. There was no light whatsoever, save for the lamps we carried with us. A cloud of cobwebs stroked my cheek at one point, giving me a nice shiver down the spine, and I heard a dainty scuffle in a black corner that was very likely a mouse or a rat. With all this marvelous stuff, you will think I am hard to please. What was lacking was the element of danger. It was impossible to raise a goose bump when we had two footmen with us, and Aunt Louise would insist on talking in the most matter-of-fact way to them about cleaning the glass of their lamps, for it was smudged, and of having them come down to give the dungeon floor a good sweeping. She is peculiarly unimaginative for a lady who deals in gothic stories. Another slight disappointment in the exploration was that there was not a single sign of anyone ever actually having been confined in the oubliette. I did not hope to see whole skeletons hanging in the chains but had thought for at least a ragged bit of a jacket, a message scratched on the wall, even a dish or a spoon to activate the imagination. There was nothing of the sort.

'Was it never used?' I asked her.

'It was, hundreds of years ago, but Edward had it cleaned out. His first wife was fastidious. He did not want her to see the bones and all that, so he had men come down and shovel all the debris into boxes for throwing out.'

It was a great pity the first Lady Sinclair should have been such a ninnyhammer, but there is no arguing with facts. The next item to be seen was the secret passage. I am bound to say it was more satisfactory, though no more scary. I am not one of those who can scan the exterior of a building, compare it to the partitions within, and conclude that there are x feet of space unaccounted for. I had tried to figure out where the passage could be without any success. The walls were all about four times as thick as necessary; any of them might have been scooped out to make a passage.

In a playful mood, Aunt Loo had me 'guess' where it was. I had only common sense to guide me. It was obviously not entered via a window or door, nor was its access through undamaged sheets of wallpaper. Wood paneling struck me as a proper medium to hide an entrance way. The main saloon was paneled. It was done in sections, with a gothic arch design repeated at regular intervals. The thing was well concealed, stuck off in a corner where little light penetrated. There was no secret device to open it. What was there was a finger hold cut into the pattern of the design. Four notches, to fit your fingers into. I stuck my fingers in, pulled, and the panel, more or less the size of a small door, opened freely.

There was a narrow passageway painted an unpleasant bile green color. The most notable thing about the passage was that it was cold, unusually cold. The willows shaded the wall on that side from the sun. I followed the narrow passage to its end. It was not so narrow that I had to turn sideways to get through, and I am not a small person, remember. My arms nearly touched either side, not quite. At the end of the hallway was a staircase, nothing fancy, just the steps unpainted, of the sort that go into a cellar. There was no backing, what is called a 'riser,' I believe, and no hand railing. It was a steep and high staircase. At the top was a door without a handle. I pushed, rather hard, and it opened into a pitch-black little cubbyhole of a place, which one had to enter on hands and knees. I did so, holding my lamp aloft. Yet another door was before me, one about three feet high and two feet wide. I pushed, but it did not open. Someone was pushing against me on the other side.

I heard a sound of laughter. Within two seconds, the door was pulled wide to show me Aunt Loo, clapping her hands and laughing. She complimented me on having 'gone the course,' as she described it.

'Where am I?' I asked, glancing around at an elegant room, done up in oak and blue brocade.

'This is the master bedchamber. *My* room now. I sleep here. That little closet you crawled out of is a storage area for trunks or boxes of winter bedding. In the olden days, the lord of the manor had a means of escape from his bedchamber or the main saloon, you see, if someone should be after him. There seemed to be a deal of that sort of carry-on, according to Edward. It had to do with religion, which seems so unreligious, chasing people and killing them, or fighting them at least. I expect it was more commonly used to smuggle someone *into* the master's room,' she advised me, with a knowing lift of the brow and nod of the brindled head. 'A wench could come after mistress was tucked up in her own room, spend the night, and be gone in the morning, with no one any the wiser. They were rather wicked that way, the Sinclairs,' she admitted. 'The strain was diluted by the time it got down to Edward; not vanished, but less pronounced. They may say what they will about the world going to the dogs, but when you get looking into the past, Valerie, you will find things to have been much worse. I wonder if I should not put Gloria back into the sixteen hundreds,' she mused.

'She is finding plenty of mischief in the present century. I am going back down the secret passage, Auntie. I adore it.'

'It's rather sweet, ain't it? I used to use it sometimes to surprise Edward or the servants, but it is not as easy for me as it once was, because of having to get down on all fours to get at it. You think twice about that at my age.'

I was already on all fours, crawling into the cubbyhole, and making a shambles of my muslin gown in the process. Thank God for the Pinnys of the world. She was thrilled to have the job of laundering it for me.

'What will you be wearing for the dinner party tonight, miss?' she asked as she threw the soiled muslin over her arm. 'I'll get it out and see it's pressed up fresh.'

I sorted through my gowns, selecting a pale green lutestring with cream ribbons around the bottom. 'I was hoping you'd say that one!' Pinny grinned. 'It's my very favorite of all your lovely gowns.'

The six robes hanging in the closet, most of them a few seasons old, were not accustomed to such lavish praise. It was too early to dress for dinner yet. I put on a simple cotton gown for a long, rambling walk around the park on foot, to familiarize myself with the place. There was a terraced garden at the north face of Troy Fenners. It was elaborately and geometrically laid out, with clipped hedges in lines as straight as rulers, with assorted circles and parabolas of flower beds set at precise intervals. Though interesting, it was not my idea of true beauty. I prefer the more natural, even wild, side of nature, as is not surprising, I suppose, in one who fancies herself the queen of the jungle.

*C*hapter *F*ive

*G*reen glasses are associated in my mind with blindness, age, and decrepitude. Old Mr Pebbles from the Charity House at home, a cripple of eighty some years, is the only person I know who wears them. It was disconcerting to find an extremely robust young gentleman with these strange objects concealing his eyes when I went downstairs to dinner that evening. He sat in a dark corner with Dr Hill, while Aunt Loo sat with a pained face listening to Pierre be polite to her.

'The grand Miss Ford!' Pierre exclaimed, jumping up when I entered. I am sure he reverted to his French upbringing in his understanding of the word grand. I cannot think he intended to denote much of distinction or greatness, only largeness.

As I nodded and said good evening to him my eyes wandered toward that far corner where the newcomer sat. About six feet of well-formed manhood arose slowly from the sofa, as though it were a terrible imposition to have to do so. Dr Hill presumed on age's privilege to retain his seat, which I do not relate with any tone of pique. I kept waiting for Mr Sinclair to finish standing up, for while he was on his feet, his shoulders and head stooped forward. After half a minute, it was clear he had got as straight as he was going to. I went forward to say good evening to Dr Hill and to be presented to Sinclair.

Aunt Loo made the introduction. I waited impatiently to hear what manner of voice came out of the scholar. Though he wore the trappings of the afflicted, the glasses and stooping posture, there was actually no real sign of the invalid about him. His face was ruddy enough, his body by no means emaciated. His jacket was well cut, and his cravat well tied. I had an annoying feeling that if he would pull off his green glasses and straighten up, he might provide me a suitable flirt for the duration of the visit.

'Good evening, ma'am,' he said, in a weary, faint voice, the head drooping an inch lower to indicate a bow. He held his two hands together at his chest, like a demmed drapery clerk trying to con one into a purchase.

'Good evening, Mr Sinclair,' I replied in my loudest, firmest voice. I stuck to my resolution of shaking hands. When Mr Sinclair saw my fingers extended to him, he finally reached out and took them but was too spent with the effort of arising to exert the least pressure. I crushed his hand, as though it were a lemon to be squeezed, and still he did not respond but only drew his fingers away and shook them limply.

Pierre made a dart to his side. 'Do I not telling you the truth, Cousin?' he demanded in exultant tones of Mr Sinclair. 'Is it not the grand Miss Ford?'

'*Très grande*,' Mr Sinclair agreed, turning the green glasses to inspect me. There is nothing so disconcerting as being examined when you cannot even see the eyes of the examiner.

'The English please is best for us,' Pierre informed his cousin. 'Now we English have the sherries, yes? Frenchmens prefer a fine claret or burgundy, but in England everyone must drink his sherries.'

When we sat to drink our sherry, Aunt Loo joined Dr Hill in the dark corner. I fully expected the invalid would return with them to the shadows, but Pierre did not permit it. 'We gentlemans enjoy conversation now with the grand Miss Ford,' he told Sinclair. 'Here we shall be all sitting, on these sofa.'

Mr Sinclair, the unnatural man, displayed not the least sign of interest or amusement at his cousin. He stood, still drooping like a wilted rose, till I was seated, then took up a chair as far from me as possible, while Pierre cuddled up to my side like a puppy.

'My good cousin has give me the horse now to ride,' he began. 'Tomorrow I shall be riding with you. Where we shall want to go?'

'Perhaps your cousin has a suggestion. I am a newcomer. I don't know what is to be seen hereabouts,' I replied.

'I don't go out,' was the cousin's very uncivil reply. 'I am very busy. You must excuse me.'

'It is not necessary to go out to make a suggestion, is it, Mr Sinclair?' I asked, my voice so sweet that even this obtuse person must realize it was hiding my anger.

'I know all the hereabouts,' Pierre assured me at once. 'The good hard ridings, just as we English like.'

'Those of us who go out, that is,' I answered, never looking within a right angle of the recluse. 'Some are too busy, Pierre.'

'Please to call me Peter. Remembering? I must like to call you also by the premier name.'

'Call me Val, if you like.'

'Val?' he asked, his eyes widening. 'This is the English name?'

'Short for Valkyrie, Peter,' Mr Sinclair mentioned, in a bored drawl.

'How did you guess, Mr Sinclair? Most people think it short for Valerie,' I told him, refusing to recognize any slur on my size.

He adjusted his spectacles, declining to reply. After he had taken a little rest, he asked, 'Are you making a long visit, Miss Ford?'

'A month. It will be more than long enough,' I replied, with a chilly smile.

'A month?' Pierre howled. 'No, this is not long enough for nothing. Tell her, Cousin. The Valkyrie must stay more longer. Six months.'

Pierre, the perfect English host, soon hopped up to pour us more of the requisite sherries. I was determined to pierce Welland Sinclair's disguise, for I had taken the notion he was shamming it with his feeble airs. Truth to tell, I was angry as a hornet that he showed not the slightest bit of interest in me. 'Your – condition? – permitted a visit to Wight recently I understand?' I began.

'Condition?' he asked, his brows rising above his spectacle rims. 'I am not an invalid. I am a scholar. It is my work that keeps me in. The sunlight also is hard on my eyes. Yes, I took Peter to Wight to meet his cousins.'

'You are writing a paper on ghosts, I hear. Do you have a ghost at the gatehouse?' I knew this was belittling his literary project but was in a mood to belittle anything to do with the man.

'No, what I am engaged in actually is a retrospective look at the role played by the ghost in English literature over the centuries. What use the writers have made of ghosts and ghostly phenomena is what I mean. It will be interesting to compare the data, when I have it all assembled, and determine whether ghosts have been seen as benign beings, or malign, destructive.' The whole speech was delivered in a tone of offended imposition.

'Do you approach a conclusion yet?'

'Much remains to be done. They have been used most commonly to presage coming events, to warn the living of imminent disasters, and occasionally to badger the guilty, as in the case of Macbeth.'

He rattled on for some time, while Pierre became impatient, and I bored. To stem the flow, I asked, 'What is the point, exactly, of this work you are doing?'

'Why, it is a literary endeavor,' he answered, shocked at the question. 'St Regis feels it will add a little luster to the family. He does not want me to bury myself in the country as his secretary.'

'I understand it is a literary project, but if one's endeavors result in a new poem or play or novel – something to be enjoyed by humanity – then the reason for doing it is clear. I don't see just what you are trying to accomplish. Who will bother to read what writers of old thought about ghosts?'

The drooping shoulders began straightening, while the neck

stiffened as though for battle. 'This is not a matter of interest to the *common* man. It is research, for scholars. My don at Oxford thought it an *excellent*, original idea.'

'Did he indeed? Then you have *one* potential reader at least, Mr Sinclair. Two, if St Regis has time to glance at it.'

'I am not interested in writing trashy, silly romantic novels for bored ladies to fritter their time away on.'

Aunt Loo's head whirled toward us. Mr Sinclair's voice had been raised rather loud. I knew at once she thought I had let her cat out of the bag, and spoke up to assure her it was not the case. 'Mr Sinclair is just telling me about his ghost research, Auntie,' I said. Mr Sinclair's head twitched in annoyance, but before he could remind me again of the true nature of his work, dinner was called.

At the table, there were other things to speak of. The approaching séance and the Franconis were the subjects. 'The Franconis have been engaged in spiritualism for years,' Aunt Loo told me. 'All across Eurpoe – well, where they *could* go, with the war on. They traveled through Italy and Austria. They do not mean to stay long in England, only for a year or so. I was fortunate to discover them early on in their stay, about six months ago. It was Lady Morgan who put me on to them.'

'Is she a neighbor, Lady Morgan?' I asked.

'Yes, the Morgans have lived here forever. Madame Franconi was reading the tarot cards there for Lady Morgan and a few friends, including me. She sensed some emanations, some psychic vibrations from me. She is very sensitive to all such manifestations. She came along to Troy Fenners a week later to give me a private reading, and that is when I learned she and her husband also hold séances. I took the three-day reading of the tarot cards, for I was not interested in mere *amusement*.'

'A three-day reading!' I exclaimed, astonished at such a lengthy endeavor.

'One for the past, one for the present, and one for the future,' she explained, while a greater than usual liveliness illuminated her features. Her enthusiasm led her to expound at some length. I was sorry I had indicated the least interest in the subject.

'The first day, she cut right to the bone. It was incredible. She did not just read my past history, you know, for she could have got that from Lady Morgan or anyone. No, she went into a reading of my character, pinpointing with the greatest accuracy my misdeeds, and indicating in other sessions that it was not too late to make it up.'

'Misdeeds? What have you been hiding from us all these years?' I asked, in a playful way.

She became suddenly conscious of having said more than she intended, and shuffled me off with a vague, generalized answer. 'Selfishness, waywardness – those are my little flaws.'

'All revealed there in the cards, were they?' Mr Sinclair asked, displaying a polite interest.

'Nothing is hidden from the tarot cards. You will learn things about yourself you never suspected. Madame Franconi is greatly concerned with the highest triangle; the spiritual needs. Of course, she does not neglect the mid-most and lowest ones either. Well, after the reading, it occurred to me I must contact Edward, and naturally a séance was the only way to set about it.'

I considered this unlikely set of statements, trying to make sense of them. Her selfishness and waywardness made it necessary for her to speak to her deceased husband. To apologize for some unpleasant behavior, apparently. Foolish, quite absurd, but the whole thing was the height of folly, so there was no point in going into it in more detail.

What followed throughout the meal was equally ridiculous. Two fully grown and educated gentlemen, Dr Hill and Mr Sinclair, sat for half an hour discussing without a single smile or show of disbelief the theory behind tarot card reading. It is not worth repeating, for besides being a bag of moonshine, it is very complicated, having to do with assorted trees and pillars and sephirah, all involved, of course, with the cards. Between their chatter and Peter's comments on the food, the meal was enough to induce a migraine.

'Nice, dry, hard mutton, just as we English like,' Peter praised as he attacked his mutton with a noticeable lack of enthusiasm. 'In France they are serving many delightful sauces. Me, I do not caring for the wonderful French sauces,' he assured us, as his eyes scanned the table for a gravy boat.

I was interested to learn something about the séance. When Loo and I left the men to their port, I asked her about this. 'It is a sitting. That is all the word means, Valerie. We sit at a round table in a dark room, join hands, and wait. Madame Franconi goes into a trance eventually and tries to make contact with Edward for me. We shall ask her to have a go at your grandma as well, if you like. But it must be on another occasion. The trance leaves her quite fatigued, and besides it would not do to have Mama and Edward here together, for they never rubbed along well at all. She would be shocked. . . .'

'To find herself with him, do you mean?'

'Yes, yes, that is *exactly* what I meant!' she replied, too quickly to be telling the truth. It had rather the feeling of grasping at a straw.

'I believe you treated Edward badly when he was alive, Auntie. *That* is what all this selfishness and waywardness is about. You wish to apologize to him. I see through your trick.'

'*I* apologize! You have got the wrong end of the stick, I assure you, my dear. It is not an apology, but a good scold he will get if I reach him. Of course I must discover what he wants. . . . That is . . . . Well, well. I think it is time we haul the men out from the dining room. Walter will stay guzzling port all night long if I don't send for him. He can see that everything is ready in the feather room. He usually sets it up for me. That is where we meet. Madame feels the vibrations are best there. She thinks the feathers have something to do with it. She went through all my rooms to select the best and settled on the feather room. Feathers are organic matter, you see. God knows what spirits were embodied in the little creatures the feathers come from. They might be the mortal remains of some incarnation of Cleopatra or Caesar or even a Judas Iscariot for that matter, though I don't believe there are any vulture feathers, and I do not see him coming back as a pheasant.'

My memory of the strange little room told me the feathers were the remains of grouse with an occasional peacock to add a touch of color, but she referred, of course, to her theory of reincarnation. Of more interest than this diversion, and it was plainly a diversion, was her cryptic half-speech regarding Edward's wishes. 'What were you saying a moment ago – what will you scold Edward about?'

'It is not fit to discuss private matters between a husband and wife with an outsider, my dear. I like having you for a guest, but pray do not turn into a prying person. One is all I can tolerate at the moment. That Mr Sinclair. . . .'

'He shares your enthusiasm for taromancy and séances at least.'

'Yes, anything to do with the spirit world. It is his work on ghosts that makes him sensitive and interested. Madame Franconi even feels he might be a potential medium. I think she also feels him to be a potential lover,' she added more practically.

'Is she a *young* woman? I pictured her as being older.'

'She is not old, and she is rather attractive.'

'She has strange taste, then.'

'Oh, very. Her husband is next door to a simpleton. He is from Blaxhall, imagine! So unlikely a match. She is the brains behind their success.'

After ringing for the butler to summon the gentlemen, she turned back to me. 'How are you feeling tonight, Val?'

'Fine. Why do you ask?'

'Tonight would be a good night to scale the trellis. We must be getting on with the research. I am beginning to write that episode and want to get all the details from you. How it *feels*, you know. Take very particular notice of the texture of the vines and trellis against your fingers. Tell me what muscles pull and ache, and what sensations the excitement and fear, if there is any fear, cause. I want to know whether your throat is dry and all that sort of thing. I have never experienced any real physical danger. That is rather sad, is it not, that I must resort to a vicarious reporting of life's more exciting passions?'

'You have had an interesting life. But about scaling the trellis, should we not do it on some occasion when Mr Sinclair is not at home?'

'Oh, no, what would be the point of that? It makes it more exciting and fearful knowing he is there. Besides, he don't sleep in the room the trellis goes up to. He sleeps on the other side of the house. I asked him. You will not actually have to open the window and climb in. If you manage to get up the wall, I shall assume the rest of it to be possible as well.'

'I hope you are coming with me in case any explanations should be necessary to Mr Sinclair.'

'No explanations are to be made! I warned you Mr Sinclair is to know nothing of *Tenebrous Shadows*. I don't want St Regis to find out.'

'Oh, yes, I forgot.' I could not quite forget, however, that it would be embarrassing in the extreme if Mr Sinclair should catch me scaling his walls with a dagger between my teeth.

Chapter Six

Madame Franconi and her witless spouse were soon shown into the saloon. The female was a swarthy, black-eyed dame who resembled a gypsy. Her husband, as mentioned, was a farmer from Blaxhall in Suffolk. She was not only the brain of the duo, but the tongue as well. She was got up in a witchlike outfit, a dark blouse and full black skirt, with a black shawl over her shoulders. She wore fine golden hoops in her ears and had her blue-black hair pulled back in a knob. There was a certain foreign attractiveness in her appearance. She was by no means old, about thirty I would guess. Aunt Loo made me known to them, served wine, and it was time to begin the séance.

'The room is prepared?' Madame asked.

'Yes, the curtains drawn, the single taper lit – a round table, just as you like. Dr Hill attended to it. We are all ready to begin.'

'The young lady has an interesting aura,' Madame informed my aunt as her eyes stared at a point just above my head. I knew from my mirror that candlelight behind me causes an orangy halo effect, shining through my curls. I thought this was her meaning. 'Blue,' she went on, nodding her head in satisfaction. 'I hope the vibrations are not inimical. The rest of our little group has proved so compatible,' she added, with a sliding glance to Mr Sinclair. He grinned but did not open his mouth. It was a strange, cunning expression he wore.

'You will wait for us below, Robert?' Madame said, turning to her spouse, a man who wore a decent dark jacket but looked like a farmer despite it.

'I'll be in the kitchen,' he said, destroying any aura of gentility the jacket might have induced.

He darted off down the hallway while the rest of us went to the sitting. A feathered room, in the likely event that you have not seen one, is a very dark place, even in daylight. The feathers, dark browns and grays for the most part, soak up all light without giving any reflections. At night, with one lone taper burning in the middle of a table covered with a dark cloth, it strongly resembles a coal hole. Madame pulled her dark shawl up over her head for dramatic effect, sat down, and placed her hands palms-down on the table, fingers splayed. She had pretty hands, white, long-fingered, with highly arched and long fingernails, like a Chinese mandarin. She wore no jewelry, not even a wedding band. Familiar with her routine, the other members went without instructions to their preordained chairs. We were seated man-woman, like a polite dinner party. Mr Sinclair sat on Madame's left, Dr Hill on her right, with Aunt Loo beside him, Pierre beside her, leaving one vacant chair between Pierre and Sinclair. I sat down on it and put my hands on the table like the others.

Our spread fingers made a circular pattern on the dark cloth. By stretching them to the limit, we managed to touch fingers, the pinky of each sitter touching the pinky of his partner on either side. It was rather pretty, but I suppose the purpose of it was to prove no one was using his hands to manipulate things. Pity Madame had not insisted we put our feet on the table as well. Pierre, being so very 'English' you know, was no sooner in the dark than he began rubbing his leg against mine in the most insinuating way imaginable. Glaring did not the least good. He stared with fixed concentration at his fingers, while his feet stroked my leg.

If my good green gown was not covered with boot marks, I might count myself fortunate. I pulled my legs as far away as possible, only to come up against Mr Sinclair's limbs on the other side. His head jerked toward me. He was surprised out of his wits by what he imagined I was up to. His brows rose right up above his spectacles, which he did not remove, even in this dark chamber. After his initial shock wore off, he began trying Pierre's pedal maneuvers, but with some Anglo refinements. There was a gentle pressure first, then a sliding movement. I pulled away, and spent the remainder of the séance shifting my poor legs from left to right to escape molesting.

These efforts interfered with observing what was going forth above the cloth. It appeared to be the fashion to let your head hang down and close your eyes. At least the others all did so. We sat thus for an interminable length of time, while the candle flickered, Pierre massaged my lower limb, and Sinclair tapped playfully on my toes, with an occasional start up my shin bone. I eventually got my foot on top of his, exerting every ounce of pressure I was capable of to keep it pinned to the floor. With Pierre, who was the more adept at the art of playing footsie, I had less success. He kept sliding out from under my toes.

Suddenly Madame's head fell back. Some crooning, gargling sounds issued from her throat, while her fingers convulsed on the cloth. None of the others paid the least heed, but I gave over any intention of hanging my head and closing my eyes at this point. If I was going to see a séance, I was going to *see* it. She went into a chant in some language I did not recognize, a sing-song bit of stuff repeated four or five times. The word 'Ahmad' was said more than once. Then she came to rigid attention in her chair, began snorting most theatrically, like a mare about to bolt. I could swear that beneath that shawl her ears were pulled back. Perhaps she was rehearsing to be a race horse in her next incarnation. She took a deep breath and said, 'Edward . . . Edward . . . lady . . . justice . . . Louise. . . .' Then she shivered, opened her eyes, and the visitation was over. Her black eyes stared accusingly at me. The others recognized this for the end of the session.

'The spirits are not communicating tonight,' she announced sadly. 'I was afraid that blue aura might interfere. Ahmad could not complete the passage to us. A pity. He had Edward with him tonight. The sensation was very pronounced.'

'Who is Ahmad?' I asked.

'Our guide to the other side,' she replied, rather unhelpfully.

'Other side of what?'

'The beyond.'

'Is it not possible to get an English guide?'

'One has not the privilege of choosing. Ahmad is the one who came when I called,' she told me. 'He will return another time. I fear we accomplished nothing tonight. Did he say anything?' she asked of the table at large.

'No, but *you* mentioned Edward, and a lady, and justice,' I told her, thinking to be helpful. 'You also said Louise.'

'Ahmad said that?' she asked, quite surprised.

'The guide speaks through Madame,' Mr Sinclair informed me, easing his toes out from under mine and giving my ankle a sharp rap for punishment.

My aunt began puffing in her chair. I noticed Dr Hill's fingers had closed over hers protectively, or perhaps restrainingly.

'What can it mean?' I demanded.

'The cards will tell us,' Loo said. I had long since come to realize any mention of cards referred to tarot cards. I hoped it would not require another three-day session.

'Is that all there is to it?' I asked, disappointed at such a poor showing. No ghosts, no rapping or jumping table, no candle blowing out. It was pretty dull entertainment.

'Try Anastasia for me,' Mr Sinclair requested, 'if you are not too fatigued, Madame.'

She sighed wearily but nodded her head in acquiescence. We resumed our original hand-touching. Madame lowered her head on to her chest, closed her eyes, and the others followed suit. After the usual interval, she began snorting again. Anastasia did not come. I looked around the table with interest and noticed that Mr Sinclair's green glasses, which looked perfectly black in the gloom, were turned toward me. The table gave a wild leap, knocking over the candle. The grease that spilled over on to the cloth was the last thing I saw before the flame was extinguished, and we were plunged into total darkness. Pierre attacked like a tiger, coming at me with his hands instead of his feet. I gave him a sharp pinch on the underside of the arm, the *upper* arm, where it really hurts. It would likely leave a bruise. He muttered a soft French curse and laughed. The table went on jumping up and down for a few seconds, but any one of the sitters could have been doing it with his knees, or his hands for that matter, since we were in total darkness.

The séance ended in this foolish manner. Everyone was jumping up, exclaiming, running to open the door and get more lights. When the lamps were brought in, Madame was seen to be just coming out of her trance. We waited politely for her to return to normal. When she had done so, she arose and told us we would retire now. From the room I assume she meant, since it was by no means late enough to retire to bed. I, for one, had a trellis to climb before I could close my eyes.

Pierre, his passions aroused by the under-the-cover games, put an arm around my waist to lead me from the room. Mr Sinclair was behind talking to Madame, and finding it eligible to hold both her hands while he did so. She must have been curt with him. Before Pierre and I reached the saloon, he had joined us. He kept his hands to himself.

'How did you enjoy it?' he asked me.

'Not much. Remind me never to enter a dark room with you two lechers again. My shins are black and blue.'

'Shame on you, Peter,' Mr Sinclair said very sternly.

'Ha, she squeeze very hard,' Pierre replied, with a little twinge of pain as he massaged his arm.

'You haven't felt anything yet,' I warned him.

'It is very hard to get feeling you,' he replied, unoffended and unchastized. What can you do with a person like that?

It was time for sherries again. I had hoped for tea, but Aunt Loo, Dr Hill, and Madame stayed behind discussing the séance, so our host poured us about six ounces of sherry and told us to drunk it up.

'Is Anastasia another guide to the great beyond?' I asked Mr Sinclair.

'Yes, she puts me in touch with my mother. Madame Franconi is very gifted. One's first instinct is to take it all for a hoax, but she has told me things no one but my mother, who is departed, and I could possibly know. There is more to this spirit business than we like to acknowledge.'

'Providing the spirit is willing. What things did she tell you?' I asked.

'The best example I can give you has to do with a golden locket my mama used to wear. It could not be found after her death. I wanted it as a keepsake, for she wore it a great deal. It contained a lock of my father's hair. I thought it must have been buried on her, but no one remembered. Anastasia told me I would find it under an apple tree in the garden, where it had been dropped by my mother some time before her death. I wrote St Regis asking him if he would have someone look in the spot, and within a week he sent it to me. It was exactly where she told me. Anastasia is a Slavic countess. She is only ten years old. It is quite fascinating, the whole business.'

'That is certainly impressive,' I was forced to admit. 'Have you had any experiences with contacting anyone, Pierre?'

'None. I have not the good chance. I am atheist in this affair. I partake only to please *Tante* Louise. Now I please me. Tomorrow we shall be riding on the good horse my cousin supplies, Valkyrie?'

'That is *Valerie*, Pierre.'

'*Peter*, Valerie,' Mr Sinclair corrected. 'My cousin wishes us to use his English name, you recall. That was a joke, Peter, calling Miss Ford a Valkyrie.'

'Ha ha, we like the good jokes,' he laughed heartily. 'That is very good funny joke, Valkyrie. What it means?'

'It means Mr Sinclair has noticed I am taller than most ladies, Peter. So observant of him,' I answered, for I did not know precisely what a Valkyrie might be, but took it for a northern Amazon.

The scholar insisted on a more detailed explanation, which totally confused Pierre, and did little to enlighten me. It had to do with Norse mythology, in which Valkyrie get to choose people to be slain, which struck me as a marvelous privilege at that moment.

'Very excellent,' Pierre said, halfway through the speech. 'So we shall be riding tomorrow, Valerie?'

'Yes, why not? We shall go in the morning, while my aunt is writing.' I stopped short as I realized I had spoken the great secret.

Pierre came hastening to the rescue, though he did not realize it. 'She writes much letters. Every morning *Tante* Louise is writing her letters. She has much friends.'

'She is a marvelous correspondent. She writes to Papa twice a week,' I added hastily.

'Strange, she never writes to St Regis unless she wants something,' was Mr Sinclair's acidic comment.

There was a commotion in the hallway as the Franconis prepared to depart. The husband came up from the kitchen to join the company and say his farewells. Mr Sinclair hopped to his feet to have some private, smiling talk with the lady. What I overheard led me to believe he was arranging a private reading of the tarot cards. A three-day session no doubt, probably three nights as well. When it was settled, Madame turned to me.

'The others think it best if you not join us another time, Miss Ford. Your presence was not acceptable to Ahmad. It is nothing personal. Not all souls advance in harmony. If you should wish for a private reading of the cards or teacup, I would be very happy to oblige you. Your aunt will give you my direction in the village. You have a very interesting aura,' was her final shot. It was a lure to con me into a reading, but I did not bite. If I were bored some day, I might visit her for fun. You are familiar with my philosophy of trying anything once.

'I shall go straight home now,' Madame said, turning back to Aunt Loo. 'I am always exhausted after a sitting. The trance state is debilitating. I am sorry we accomplished so little tonight. We shall try again soon.'

'I look forward to it,' Loo replied.

Mr 'Franconi – how did he get such a name, coming from Blaxhall? – bowed, muttered his good-nights and led his wife to the door, where my aunt's carriage was awaiting them.

'Did you get your money's worth, Auntie?' I asked her, when they had left.

'Oh, yes!' she said, very seriously. 'I know what I must do now. Justice – she is quite right.' Then she noticed the gentlemen all sitting waiting for their tea, and ordered it.

I sought to escape Pierre by taking a chair beside Dr Hill, whom I had some private questions for. My little French friend was not so easily discouraged. He trotted over to join us, jiggling from side to side in his haste, with his toes pointed straight out. 'I am very exciting,' he told me. I blinked at this presumptuous remark.

'Peter is excited about riding with you tomorrow,' Mr Sinclair explained. He had not dashed quite so quickly as Pierre to my side, but I noticed with some amusement that he was not so indifferent to my presence as he let on.

'I also am exciting, Peter,' I assured him.

'We would do Peter a better service if we corrected his mistakes, rather than repeat them for our own amusement,' Mr Sinclair said, in an odiously pompous way. He was right, of course, which did nothing to sweeten my temper.

'I am excited too,' I corrected.

'I don't miss it for all the trees in China,' Peter went on. 'A very excellent horse my cousin got me.'

'Lord St Regis was kind enough to have one forwarded for Peter's use when he heard he did not have one with him,' Mr Sinclair explained. 'He has an excellent stable.'

'I must compliment you on Nancy, Dr Hill,' I said, to include the doctor in our talk. 'She is a beautiful bit of blood. Arab and Percheron I think?'

'That's right. She was given to me in payment for a patient's debt. We country doctors receive many of our fees in barter. She is too large for some folks, but she suits me, and I am happy to hear you can handle her, Miss Ford. Your aunt tells me you ride like a lancer, straight and hard. Nancy is gentle-mouthed for all her size.

'That is a prime goer you have, Mr Sinclair. Out of St Regis's stable I fancy?'

'Yes, a pure-bred Arabian.'

I stared to think of this invalid on such a dashing mount. 'Is Peter's mount also an Arabian?' I asked.

'A bay mare. Mine is a gelding. I've clocked him at forty miles an hour.' Then as soon as he had made this dashing speech, he sighed and drooped his head. 'I hope this tea doesn't keep me awake,' was his next utterance as he accepted a cup. I hoped so too. I preferred that he be sleeping soundly when I climbed up his wall.

'I don't sleep worth a brass farthing,' my aunt commented. 'The past year I have not had a single good night's rest, except when I take a sleeping draught. I need more laudanum, Walter. Will you tend to it?' He nodded. 'Is it my age, do you think?'

'You are young. When you get to *my* age is time enough to hint you are old.'

'Oh, I am old all right. You get old at forty-six. That's when it hits you. Everything goes on you. The eyes, the ears, the teeth. I used to be tall and thin; now I'm short and fat. I could understand being tall and fat, but I do *not* understand how I got *short* and fat.'

'I expect that is my fault,' I said. 'Did you feel short before I came?'

'Not such an utter squab as I do now, but the past few years I cannot reach the top bookshelf, and I used to be able to.'

'The arms may be shrunk,' Peter suggested, trying to follow our conversation.

Mr Sinclair took advantage of it to pour himself another cup of tea, having apparently forgotten his fears of insomnia. In a short while, Hill and Sinclair took their leave. Peter suggested we two take a romantical stroll in the moonlight. I would as soon have gone for a walk with an hyena, and told him so. He was flattered.

I wished to change out of my good gown before climbing, and excused myself, intimating to Pierre it was a final good-night. 'Now we shall discuss our business, *Tante* Louise,' he said, after kissing my hands a couple of times.

My aunt directed a cautionary glance at him. I was curious enough what private business they had to discuss that I lingered a moment outside the doorway, pretending to have dropped something on the floor, lest a servant wander by and catch me eavesdropping.

'Please not to frown, dear *Tante* Louise,' I heard Peter say. 'You are thinking always too much about the monies. What sum shall I be getting this time? A thousand pounds, same like the last, yes?'

'It is a great deal of money.'

'Very much great. The silence is of gold, as we say. You are a naughty lady. But me, I get the monies, and I say no words to no one. Mum is the words. My cousin teached me these idioms.'

'I don't know where I shall ever find the money. But Justice must be done. You are correct,. Peter. I *am* a naughty girl. I am willing to pay, however. A thousand pounds it is, and you must tell no one.'

I was hardly able to get up from my crouching position on the floor, so great was my shock. Pierre was blackmailing his aunt at the rate of a thousand pounds a shot! Good God, no wonder she was purse-pinched. He was bleeding her white. I would not have thought him so devious. His way of talking gave one the notion he was frank and open, almost to a fault, but that was his trouble with the language leading him astray. I went upstairs, my head pounding with anger, and my heart pulsing with a determination for revenge.

Chapter Seven

*I*t was a fine night for murder. A white fingernail of moon floated in an ink-black sky, with a sprinkling of stars discernible after our eyes became accustomed to the darkness. There was a translucent rag of cloud chasing the moon, which followed us as we hastened through the park, down to the gatehouse. The only sound was the whisper of those towering oaks and elms. An hour had elapsed since the departure of the guests, time enough for Aunt Louise, who accompanied me, and myself to have donned dark gowns, and, we hoped, time for Mr Sinclair to have retired. The signs were propitious. The gatehouse windows were dark.

Night had the inexplicable effect of making the house much taller than usual, the walls more sheer, the trellis much more rickety and unstable. 'You'll not have a bit of trouble,' Loo said bracingly as she reached out to shake the trellis. A piece of thoroughly rotted wood, soft as a bread crumb, came off in her fingers. Undismayed, she went on, 'The thing to do is to grab on to the vine. The vine is as sturdy as may be.'

I do not know in what manner Gloria intended scrambling up the wall, but I had taken the precaution of wearing gloves, an old pair of white kid ones that my aunt did not detect in the shadows. The vine proved more solid than the trellis. Its main trunk was a couple of inches thick. I stuck with the main branch. The major difficulty, and it was no small one, was in discovering footholds. These were available at those points where a hefty minor branch left the mother trunk, but unfortunately they were not so closely or evenly spaced as a climber could wish. I took mental note of all the physical discomforts Gloria was being subjected to: the fingers turning numb as they clutched at spiky knobs of hardened wood, the cheek grazed by assorted protrusions, the skirt destroyed beyond repair as it caught on every stray twig and was nearly pulled from my body, the back aching from the peculiar gyrations it was being subjected to, most of all, the stomach in a state of violent agitation from fear of detection and falling. Aunt Loo's part in the whole was to hold the vine steady for me, as though it were a ladder.

The thick trunk petered out as I rose up the sheer face of the wall. It was only stubbornness that kept me going through the several eternities till the window ledge was within my grasp. I knew I had never been a fly in any previous life. The climb was quite terrifying. Finally I placed my rigid fingers on the ledge and heaved myself up till my cheek leaned against the pane of glass. The room beyond was in total darkness; it was scanty reward for my arduous climb. I intended doing no more than catching my breath before climbing, or possibly falling, back down. While I leaned against the ledge, gasping, a light bobbed into view beyond, in the depths of the building. It was not in the room whose window I was at, but in the hallway. I came to sharp attention, watching it, and trying to discover who was the bearer of the light.

It was the absence of green glasses that misled me. Within seconds, Welland Sinclair loomed into the doorway of the room, then entered, not at his customary lagging invalid's amble, but with a long, steady stride. He set the lamp on a dresser and turned to talk to someone over his shoulder. A man followed him into the room, a footman in dark green livery, or possibly a valet, as Mr Sinclair was in the process of undressing. He had already removed his jacket and was unbuttoning his flowered waistcoat as he spoke. Also while Sinclair spoke, the valet went down on his knees and began rooting under the canopied bed in the corner. While the master pulled off his waistcoat and threw it on a chair, the valet staggered under the weight of a metal box, roughly a foot square, which he hefted up to the bed. Sinclair said something else over his shoulder, and the valet left, soon returning with a set of keys dangling from his fingers. Then, while Sinclair proceeded to undress, untying his cravat and pulling it off, the man unlocked the box. I was on pins for Sinclair to go forward and open the box, but instead he removed his shirt and walked to a pier glass to do a bit of posturing in front of the mirror, in the style of Gentleman Jim Jackson. When he stopped this nonsense, he struck a pose of a Bartholomew Fair strong man, flexing his muscles and throwing out his chest, all the while admiring himself in the mirror. He bent his arms up in front of him in right angles, inviting the valet to come and admire his biceps.

It was rather an amusing show. After squeezing the biceps, the valet stepped back. Next he advanced with his fists curled and landed Sinclair a blow in the diaphragm. Sinclair pretended not to feel it, though he did in fact wince noticeably. The master then retaliated, 'feinting' a few punches, as my brothers would say, at the valet's face and shoulders. After a bout of boyish boxing, Sinclair *at last* walked to the bed and lifted the lid of the box. I strained forward so hard I was afraid I would bend the glass. It did not occur to me to worry they would see me. They were top well involved in their own business. What was drawn out of the box was a pile of bills about two inches high. Even if the denominations were small, there was a considerable bit of blunt there for a poor relation. Possibly even a thousand pounds. I remembered that Pierre and Welland were very close, and while it had been difficult to see Pierre as a blackmailer, it was not difficult to see him as a dupe for his rogue of an English cousin.

Loo was beginning to make inquiries from below as to my reason for staying so long at the window. She would have seen the light and be worried. I risked removing one hand from the windowsill to wave her to silence. It was very nearly my undoing. I pitched back precariously, but my one hand held firm, and soon I was back safely at my perch. The short space of time was long enough for Sinclair to have extracted more goodies from his traveling vault. It was a jeweled necklace that hung from his fingers. He made some facetious remark to the valet, holding the jewel up by its two ends against the man's throat. He next tossed it carelessly on the bed and took out a large ring, whose solitary stone caught the lamplight to reflect a blinding prism of light. All the while the two men chatted amiably, jokingly. The various items were returned to the box. Then, as if on impulse, Sinclair reached in and took the money out again. When he left the room, he carried it in his hand, weighing it, as though it were a brick. The footman or valet, whatever he was, relocked the box and pushed it back under the bed. He walked out behind Sinclair, his lamp highlighting the smooth ripple of muscles on his master's naked back. It was a handsome back.

There was nothing more to do but descend the vine, one painful step at a time, repeating all my agonies of the ascent. 'How did it go?' Aunt Loo asked eagerly.

'I'll tell you when we get home,' I replied, gasping too hard to enter into lengthy explanations as we nipped quickly up through the park.

We had cocoa served in my aunt's room as a reward for our job. She had her pen out, wanting to get down my observations while they were fresh in my head. This had to be done first, before she would listen to the important news.

'Impossible,' was her firm declaration when I told her Sinclair had a wad of bills big enough to choke an elephant. 'He has not a sou to his name. He is St Regis's pensioner. If he makes two hundred a year, I would be very much surprised.'

'He had it, and he had valuable looking jewelry too.'

'Stage money and paste jewels. St Regis holds little amateur theatricals at Tanglewood, you must know.'

'Why would Sinclair have brought them with him? He is not holding any amateur theatricals here, but doing research for his treatise.'

'It is odd, but there must be some explanation for it. *Red* stones in the necklace, did you say?'

'Yes, rubies or at least garnets, and a ring with a diamond as big as my eyeball.'

'Very strange indeed,' she allowed, frowning. 'It sounds very like the *Huit Rubis* necklace, but it cannot be that.'

'It was not wee; it was very large.'

'It is the French again, dear. There are eight rubies in it, you see – *huit rubis*, like our *trois fenêtres*. It would be so much more pleasant if they would give things English names, but the jewel is old, like the house. It is quite ugly. I never wear it.'

'You mean it is *your* necklace?'

'The *Huit Rubis* necklace is mine. In a manner of speaking, I mean. I have the use of it during my lifetime, but it is entailed on St Regis on my death, of course, like everything else. Pest of a man. What does he want with a ruby necklace and another diamond ring? He has a vault full of heirlooms already.'

'Is the diamond ring yours as well?'

'I have one that sounds like it, the St Clair diamond.'

'Where are they? I mean, where do you usually keep them? For they are at this moment under Mr Sinclair's bed in a black box, and we must call a constable at once to get them back.'

'That is not at all necessary. Mine are in my own safe.'

'Have you checked recently?'

'Not since I left, but. . . .'

'Auntie, you must see Sinclair stole them during your trip! Let us look at once.'

She began her chest expanding and poohing again, but I would not let her off with it. She led me to a vault that was hidden behind a double pedestal desk, right there in the room we sat in. It was necessary to get down on the hands and knees to reach the door, then necessary also to bring a lamp for her to see to work the combination of the safe. After these necessities had been taken care of, she lifted out a green leather case and opened it to show me not only the *Huit Rubis* necklace and big diamond solitaire, but several other *gorgeous* bibelots as well. There were earrings and brooches, other rings and bracelets, mostly in diamond and rubies.

'The Sinclairs had some business dealings in the east. The rubies are from Burma, and the diamonds from India. Try them on, if you like.'

I lifted a glittering tiara of diamonds from the box and went to the mirror to regard myself. I looked like a queen, if I do say so myself. I also felt an uncharacteristic urge to grab the thing and run like the devil. I don't know what it is about diamonds; they turn a law-abiding citizen into a coveter of her neighbor's goods. Slowly, I removed the tiara and put it back in its box, declining the offer to submit myself to more temptation.

'So it is plain as a pikestaff Sinclair did not get them from here,' she concluded.

That point had to be admitted, but it explained nothing. It was not till my cocoa cup was empty that the explanation descended on me. 'He means to steal them! He has got descriptions of them somehow from St Regis and had paste copies made to substitute so you won't notice the theft.'

There was more poo-poohing, but in my mind, the mystery was solved. It remained only to convince my aunt and get her to put them in some safer place, such as a bank vault. She was not about to be convinced in one night, however, and I was quite exhausted from my endeavors, so did not belabor my point.

'It still doesn't explain the money either,' I remembered as I walked toward the door.

'No, indeed it does not,' she agreed.

'Unless he got it from Pierre.'

'That is entirely possible. Pierre is very generous.'

'He can afford to be!' I pointed out, in an ironic vein, hoping to give her a hint I knew something of the source of St Clair's wealth, but she was being obtuse.

'Yes, he's rich as a nabob. You have done a good night's work, Gloria. Tomorrow I shall clean up these notes I have got, put them into the story. Then you will have to carry a man across the meadow and jump the tollbooth, and your work will be over.'

I felt my real work in rescuing Auntie would be only beginning, but there was something about the image of that enormous tollbooth advancing at me that tended to dry up any words except, 'Good night, Auntie.'

Chapter Eight

We settled for a sack of oats in lieu of a man to be carried across the meadow. It was clear from the outset our hero would have to be very emaciated indeed, not more than a hundred pounds, if Gloria were actually to carry him. Rather than have the poor fellow worn to a thread, a donkey was introduced into the story. We decided Gloria could get a man of a hundred and fifty pounds on to the back of a donkey, if he were able to give a *little* help himself. This interfered with the poignancy of Gloria's fearing he was dead, till I pointed out his body could become as lifeless as she liked once he was on the donkey. A groom was ordered to get across a mule's back with his head hanging down one side, his feet the other, while Aunt Loo looked to see which was more pathetic, a hand dragging in the dust, or a head thumping against the donkey's flank. This was done first thing in the morning, before Auntie went to her scriptorium.

After she had gone, I prepared myself for my ride with Pierre. It was my intention to pick his brain, in a subtle way, to see what I could find out about the mysterious business of the thousand pounds blackmail. First I had to admire the 'most excellent animal' Sinclair had provided him. She was excellent too, a bay – well muscled, deep-chested, long-legged. All this excellence was quite wasted on Pierre. He was an indifferent rider, who chose a walk as the best pace for carrying on the dalliance that was his main purpose of riding at all. As it suited my true purpose, I gave him no trouble.

Due to his strange way with words, I could not make heads or tails of what he said. He either misunderstood or pretended to misunderstand my every word. 'I expect you lost your inheritance in France as a result of the revolution, Peter,' I began, in a commiserating manner.

'The title I do lost at this present moment. I am the Comte d'Ambérieu, from the province of Ain. We English like our titles.'

'I referred to your estates, your money. You are without funds is what I mean.'

'Ha, I do not liking the funds. Five percent is the too small interest sum. Welland, he agrees with me on this. I do not put into the funds my monies. The Consols, I do not engage in the Consols funds, me.'

'What I mean is, you do not have any money.'

'The cash, he is always short. Realizing the funds is my small difficulty. But I am not poor, you comprehend. When I realize my funds, I will be not cash shortage.'

'How do you set about realizing these funds? How do you get your money?'

'It is necessary to selling things.'

'Yes, but as your estates were confiscated, what is there to sell?'

'Very much true. The real estates is confiscated. The movables are not so confiscating.'

'You brought things with you from France?'

'I am looking after these subjects. My cousin Welland, he helps me. Now we are admiring the sceneries.'

'Your cousin is also without funds, I believe.'

'He is have the rich patron, St Regis. St Regis also is my cousin. He too helps me with realizing my funds.'

'Does *Tante* Louise help you too?'

'Yes, very much helps me. The rack and manger she is giving. What it is, the English rack?'

'It means bed, in this case. Does she also give you money?'

'Ah,' he said, tilting back his head. 'Welland, he tells me this is of worry at you. No, I do not steal your monies from *Tante* Louise. She can be giving it all to you, Valerie. I do not want her monies.'

'I beg your pardon?' I asked, wondering if I had understood him correctly.

'Certainly, you are welcome to all my pardons.'

'Did Welland tell you. . . .'

'Absolutely. That Miss Valkyrie is wanting the aunt's money. Is it not so?'

'She never gives me a penny!'

'She is very much not realizing the funds at this precise moment, you comprehend.'

I was so incensed at Welland Sinclair's telling Pierre I was a gold digger that I lost track of my real project in the ride. 'He's a fine one to talk! Living off his cousin, St Regis. *I* don't batten myself on anyone. I don't think you should have anything to do with him, Pierre. He is *using* you. Be very careful of that man. You'll end up in jail, the way you are carrying on. Blackmail is a crime. It is also extremely contemptible.'

He sat smiling and nodding throughout my lecture, then prodded his mount closer to mine and tried to grab my hand. 'Valerie is most very beautiful, but I don't know why she is angry with me. We do not doing any crimes, my cousin and me.'

'I am wasting my time.'

He smiled in anticipation and began to dismount, thinking, I believe, to get down to some serious flirtation. 'We shall be having much better time not riding on horses' backs,' he said.

'Get back up there, Peter. I shall take it up with Sinclair himself.'

'*Comment*? Take it up? What that means?'

'It means. . . . Oh, never mind. I am not angry with you, but with Sinclair.'

'Good. He also is angry with you too. For my own self, I think cousins should help each one other. Kissing cousins, as we say in

English. What one has realized monies, he should helping the others one. I always help all poor cousins. Do you require funds, *chérie*? I have very much funds soon. We shall pretend at being kissing cousins.'

'We are scarcely even connections, let alone cousins.'

'Kissing connections?' he asked hopefully.

'It is not English, Peter.'

'If you were not so grand quite, I would be marrying you. Welland is thinking you would not dislike to marry me, since I am being so rich. This is true?'

'Please do not tell me any more of Welland's theories. When *I* marry, money will have nothing to do with it.'

'This is very foolish talk, Valerie. Poor girls must marrying the money. The same thing very much so in France. The French look much at the dowry, same like we English.'

'We are going to gallop very fast now, Peter, before we lose our tempers.'

'Ah, good. A nice galloping,' he agreed, but proceeded on at the pace of a constipated crab, while I galloped away some part of my anger. The latter part of our ride, when I rejoined him, was no more enlightening than the first, so I shall omit it, except to mention I will not be helped down from a mount by Pierre St Clair again – ever. That man could turn a handshake into an obscene encounter. He is so *small* too, but very strong.

My aunt possessed a charming little whisky, a light two-wheeled gig painted a spruce green color. I had been looking forward to a drive in it and got her permission to try it that same afternoon after luncheon. I turned left at the main road, toward Dr Hill's place, to see what I could learn from him about my aunt's situation. He lived in a pretty half-timbered cottage, with pink rose gardens in front. It would make an ideal subject for an artist's sketch, but unfortunately I have no talent in that direction.

The doctor was at home, working in his study, where the butler took me. Hill's Harley Street practice had been profitable, to judge

Valerie

from the elegance of his home. I am not one who can pinpoint furnishings and artworks as to exact periods or even schools, but I have eyes enough to distinguish fine things from inferior. There was nothing inferior in the doctor's cottage. I had come expecting to see a provincial, mediocre establishment, for his own plain appearance suggested such a background. Instead I found a scholar in a book-lined study, with tomes open before him, a pair of pince-nez perched on the end of his nose, and a piece of paper half filled with small writing before him.

'I'm sorry to disturb your work, Doctor. It is a social call only. Shall I leave and come back later?'

'Not at all, Miss Ford. I am delighted you should take time to pay me a visit. An unlooked-for pleasure,' he said, arising and removing his glasses to show me a seat.

'My, such a lot of books. I did not take you for a scholarly sort. I expect I am interrupting some vital piece of medical research.'

'Far from it. I am involved in my true love. I pretend to be a doctor, but I am really a detective.' I stared blankly at this statement, causing him to go on and explain. 'I am a delver into the past, to discover its mysteries. To be exact, my field is archaeology, Miss Ford. What you see me scribbling out here is my views on Stonehenge. A strange affair it is, a real mystery. Nothing serious has been done on it since the work of Aubrey in the sixteen hundreds. England is not without its remnants from antiquity. My love, archaeology, is not a well-paying mistress, however, and I was obliged to eke out a living with the practice of medicine.'

'Eke out a living is the wrong phrase. I could not help admiring your home as I was shown through.'

'You refer to the few things my late wife left. Anything fine in the house was hers. She was a ring above me, socially speaking. A cousin to Sir Edward's first wife. I met her when she was visiting Alice at Troy Fenners. I was no more than the family physician then, but she took me up to London and made me fashionable. I did not stay long.'

'Actually it is my aunt I wanted to speak about, Doctor. I am worried about her.'

'Worried? You must not give it a thought. It is the change of life – a little insomnia, depression. She is better since coming back from her visit. What is it that disturbs you?'

'I was not referring to her physical health.'

'Is it this séance business? It is a passing hobby. Last year it was orchids. Next year it will be something else. Bird watching, or collecting dried flowers, or playing the pianoforte. It is good for her to keep occupied.'

'No, it is not that either. It is something more serious. She is being blackmailed.'

The poor doctor nearly fell from his chair in fright. 'What in the world are you talking about, Miss Ford?' he demanded, angry at being frightened.

I told him everything. He was an old and trusted friend, and I had to confide my fears in someone, had to receive advice from an elderly person. 'Young Sinclair, you think, is at the bottom of it?' he asked, his interest mounting to worry.

'He had copies of her jewels. Why would he, if not to substitute them and take the originals? *I* cannot think of any other explanation, can you?'

'You're sure he hasn't done the switch already? Were they the originals you saw? Could you swear to it?'

'Good gracious, no! I am not a connoisseur. Do you think he might already have. . . ?'

'It's possible. You mentioned he had stacks of money. Where else would he have gotten it, if not by selling off others of her pieces?'

'No, I told you Pierre gave it to him, or is working with him – I don't know exactly how it works, but I know Aunt Loo gives Pierre large sums, and it is Mr Sinclair who ends up with the money hidden under his bed. He has some business involvement with Pierre – gets money for him somehow, and *from* him I am convinced.'

'Hard to believe St Clair is involved in anything crooked. The thing is, Miss Ford, he is as rich as may be. His estates in France are uncertain at the moment, of course, but when we beat Boney, they will go back to him, and in the meanwhile my understanding is that he brought a king's ransom with him in gold coin and jewelry. His family contrived to hide it somehow, and with the help of friends he got a good part of it to that monastery or what-ever the deuce it was where he was raised. He is selling part of it as he requires funds. I wonder if *that* is not the jewelry you saw in Welland Sinclair's room. His cousin helps him with transactions, as you mentioned. They make no secret of it. I don't suppose you got a very close look, through a window in the dark of night.'

'I could not *swear* the design was identical, but certainly it was remarkably similar. Pity I could not get a closer look.'

'Yes, one dislikes to put it to the chap in so many words. Mean to say, if we are wrong, you'll look no how, an interfering busy-body.'

'The matter is too important to let that stand in the way.'

'I wonder if your aunt is not purchasing some of St Clair's pieces. She would be happy to have them – sentimental, family meaning, you know. It would give the lad some cash. Just like her. She is generous, and would not bruit it about. I know she is short of cash lately, but she did not confide the reason in me.'

'There would be no reason to hide a sensible business transac-tion. There is no shame in it for Pierre. No, she told me not to interfere, so she has something to hide. Besides, I *heard* Pierre demand money.'

'In payment for his jewelry, possibly. The way he speaks will often cloud his meaning, poor fellow. Then too your aunt has a few devious twists in her, Miss Ford. I don't mean to say she is paying him less than the stuff is worth, but she *likes* to have secrets. Those books she writes, for example. No harm in it, but she has taken the notion St Regis won't like it, and runs around hiding her papers when Pierre or Sinclair are in the house.

Women like playing at secrets. I have often observed an intelligent mind with insufficient to keep it busy will invent intrigues. I think we have found our explanation. She is buying Pierre's jewels and has taken the notion she will keep it a secret. Welland must be in on it, of course – good friend of St Clair. That explains the demand for money, the cash you saw in Sinclair's room, and it explains the jewelry. It also explains her shortage of funds. Ties it all up right and tight.'

'I suppose it could be that. I wager Sinclair has told St Regis the whole thing too.'

'For a certainty. I'll do a gentle quizzing of your aunt, if you like, to confirm our suspicions. I hope you have set your mind at rest. Let me know if you come across anything puzzling. You came here for a holiday, not a month of worrying. How are you making out with Nancy?'

'She's marvelous. Are you sure you don't need her for your own use?'

'No, she's a spare. Got her in payment for a debt.'

'Do you think she is capable of jumping over the toll-booth?'

'She could jump over the moon, but I hope you will convince your aunt the testing of her theory is not necessary.'

'You really think she could do it?' I asked, feeling an unsettling stir of interest deep within myself.

'I'll let you in on a secret, Miss Ford. She *has* done it. Or so the fellow who gave her to me told me. I made the grave error of telling your aunt the story, and that is where she got the idea of having her heroine do it. She wants to know if a female can repeat the performance. I doubt Nancy could make it with *my* weight, but yours. . . .'

'I wonder.'

'Don't try it. Nancy is capable of it, and let that be enough for your aunt. Well it has been done before, so no one can claim she is being inaccurate. It is a fact, or a legend at least, that Pitt the younger did a similar thing. It *can* be done, and there is an end to it.'

We chatted for a while. Dr Hill offered me tea, but instead I asked him to show me his roses, which he was happy to do, since he was rather proud of them. I thought, as I drove home, that he was probably correct about the mystery of Aunt Loo's missing money. She *did* love a secret, an air of intrigue. In any case, there was a way to find out. If I could get Auntie to show me her jewels again, examine them carefully to try to discover if they were genuine, and if I could then get into Sinclair's strongbox, I could see if his pieces were identical, or only similar. Perhaps I could tell too which set was genuine, if the design proved identical. The doctor was certainly correct about one thing. Women *did* love secrets and intrigue. My heart was walloping with happy excitement as I stabled the whisky and went back into Troy Fenners.

Chapter Nine

While I went for my visit to Dr Hill, Aunt Loo was in hands with the tarot cards and Madame Franconi. The feathered room was always used for any occult session. Madame wore the same loose, black outfit. Over the next few days, there was a heavy rash of these readings. Something big was in the air, but with the door of the room firmly closed, and with my aunt puffing up like a pigeon and poohing the moment I hinted for information, I discovered little. I *did* wheedle her into opening her safe once more to allow me a close examination of her various heirlooms. I memorized as best I could their design. My aim was to get into the gatehouse and complete the comparison while the memory was fresh.

I do not mean to give the impression my visit at Troy Fenners was one long ordeal of investigation and worrying. I was enjoying myself hugely. I had Pinny to tend to all my personal chores, so that my time was absolutely my own, to fritter away on pleasure. I had Nancy for pleasure riding, the green whisky for a change of pace, a new village to be visited, a new friend in Dr Hill, who came so often to the house that I soon tumbled to it he was a suitor to my aunt. I had as well two gentlemen to court and to be courted by. I rather enjoyed Pierre's foolishness. He was half-lecher to be sure, but such a small lecher that I had no fears for my safety. The larger lecher, Welland Sinclair, was not nearly so forthcoming, though he was by no means the recluse he first implied he was. We met by accident a few times when he was out for exercise.

This exercise was taken by him on an Arab gelding that reminded me forcefully of pictures I have seen of some old Greek or Roman horse with a pair of wings growing out of its sides. You would think Diablo had wings, the way he flew over fences, streams and hedges. A *magnificent* animal.

It smacks of vanity for me to say Mr Sinclair made a point of being in the meadow on Diablo each afternoon, after finding me there once. It smacks of man-chasing for me to have returned each day myself at the appropriate hour. I accept the vanity, but the only reason I was chasing him was to get into his gatehouse, and eventually into his strongbox. The very sight of his green glasses got my back up. One feels she is being spied upon, to be on display without getting a fair chance of reading her companion's thoughts, through his eyes. I tried to damp down my frustration, for I saw no good to be gained from antagonizing him. Considering the many insults I had got indirectly from him through Pierre, I think I did not do too badly.

The first time we met at the meadow, my admiration of Diablo was expressed spontaneously.

'He's a goer,' Sinclair admitted modestly. 'From St Regis's stable. He breeds horses.'

'I wonder he would have had this one gelded. He would have been a fine stud.'

'Too rambunctious to ride before he was fixed. Gelding tames them down a little. You are managing to control Nancy, are you?'

'*Control* her? She is not at all unmanageable. My only complaint is that she is a little lacking in liveliness.' When you pride yourself on your horsemanship, a hint that you might have difficulty controlling a tame mare is not welcome.

'She's big though. Not a lady's mount. Of course you are not. . . .'

It was at such moments I revolted against the green glasses. Impossible to read his expression. Was he making fun of me, or merely run into an awkward pause? 'Oh, but I *am* a lady, Mr Sinclair.'

'Not small, I was going to say.'

'How observant of you. How does your work go on? Found any new ghosts lately?'

'The problem is not the lack of them in literature, I assure you. From the ancients – Odysseus trying to embrace his mother's ghost – to the gigantic Alfonso in Walpole's *Castle of Otranto*, they have been an integral part of literature, but no serious study of them has been undertaken. I begin to reach the conclusion they are most commonly viewed as benign presences, except when they come to harrass wrongdoers. Even then, they could be viewed as benign to mankind in general. Don't you agree?'

'I really never had the least interest in ghosts.'

'Madame Franconi feels my interest in the beyond has sensitized me to the spirit world. She is going to hold a séance for me at the gatehouse. The usual group will meet, and try if the new location is better for my mother. I think, at times, I feel her presence there.'

I was fully awake to the opportunity to get inside his gatehouse. 'How exciting! When do we meet?'

'Tomorrow evening, but I am afraid she specifically requested that you not be present. You impeded Edward's coming the other night at Troy Fenners. I hope you will join us afterward for some refreshment. Madame is always hungry after a sitting. It is fatiguing for her, the trance state.'

'I will be happy to join you.' Here was my chance. I would be there early, to scout through the house while they had their séance.

'Good.'

There was more stupid talk of ghosts, which I shall not bore you with. The next afternoon we met again and spent the better part of an hour trying to outride each other. There were no barriers high or wide enough that Nancy could not take them, but it was clear as glass Diablo left more clearance. That gelding could jump over a church steeple. Pierre, who usually trailed after me like a puppy, came straggling down to the meadow on his borrowed mare at about the time we were both tired. Neither of us could admit it, of course, so we used Pierre as an excuse to stop and rest.

'You ride like clowns,' Pierre complimented us.

'Now there is a plain case of the pot calling the kettle black!' I charged, glancing at his haphazard manner of sitting his mount.

My idiom stymied him. 'Not black. White face, like the clown riders in London,' he explained.

'Astley's Circus,' Welland translated for me. 'High praise indeed.'

'I too ride like the clowns,' Pierre added. With those green glasses turned on me, I did not say a word.

'We are having another séance this evening *chez Tante* Louise,' he said next. 'The Madame Franconi has just left.'

'Has she?' Welland asked, springing to sharp attention. 'I shall canter over to the road and see if I can catch her on her way home.' He darted off on the instant, without even saying goodbye.

'You comprehend what it is?' Pierre asked, with a knowing look.

'Yes, I am not quite blind. I comprehend he is throwing his handkerchief at her.'

Until a speech was out, I often neglected to notice how confusing it was to poor Pierre. 'I do not think Madame has the rheum,' he said.

'It means he likes her. A flirtation, you know.'

'Ah, throwing his hat at her, you are meaning, Valerie. I know all this things very well. No, Welland is throwing his hat at Mary Milne. He is betrothed with her. His patron, St Regis, makes this match for him. Miss Mary is the grand heiress.'

'What?'

'But yes. Absolutely he is betrothed with Mary. He is much enamored of her.'

'Odd he never mentioned her.'

'Very much odd, but he enjoys the flirtations with all the ladies. The bird in the finger is more better than the bird in the little tree. Mary, she is the bird in the finger.'

'A well-plumed bird, I think you mentioned?'

'Precisely. Me, I am the bird in the tree. Also well-plumed too. Fine feathers. I am the peacock. You are admiring my jacket?'

'Very nice, Pierre.'

'Jackets make the men, as my cousin says. Bosoms make the lady. This is not indiscreet?'

'No more so than usual. How long has he been betrothed to her?'

'During six months. When he is returned, they will be making the marriage. St Regis is very happy for this.'

'When does he plan to return? He never speaks of it.'

'To me also he does not speak of the when. I shall make the inquiries, if you wish.'

'Don't bother. I couldn't care less.'

'I think you should be caring less, Valérie,' he said, with a wounded face. 'I am eligible, me. Very rich, very not betrothed with anyone. The bird in the tree. Welland is in the fingers of Mary. We return now to *Trois Fenetres* and have the sherries.'

'An excellent idea.'

'Absolutely.'

Mr Sinclair was just finishing his chat with Madame Franconi when we reached the gravel walk to the house. He joined us to issue his invitation for the séance at the gate-house to Aunt Louise. She was spread out on the sofa, espaliered like a tree against a sunny wall.

'I have done it!' she gasped, fanning herself with a newspaper. 'Today for the first time I went into a mild trance. It occurred just as Madame laid down the Magician – the power of the will, freedom of choice, you see. Very significant. That is what the reading was all about – the choice of being a deceiver, or devoting myself to the spiritual life. Saint Joan too was hazy for me. She represents silence, discretion. I cannot *begin* to describe the sensation. A sort of numbness and tingling invaded my limbs. My mind floated out of, my body. Afterward, I was consumed with a strange lethargy, and a great thirst. This is my third glass of sherry.'

I could not but wonder how many she had had before the reading of the cards, but it would not do to say so. Welland hung on her every silly syllable, asking eagerly how it had happened. She was only too happy to tell him. Incense was a part of it. Madame had burned incense that afternoon for the first time. He had to get a piece to take back to the gatehouse with him.

My aunt was not hard to convince to try a new site for a séance the next evening. She leapt at the chance, even when it was made clear it was to be Welland's séance, with Anastasia and his mother being the likely guests, rather than Ahmad and Edward. 'But first we shall have one here this evening, in our feather room. So congenial to the spirits. The room must not be disturbed. The vibrations are excellent just now. She will come tonight. I do hope you will join us, Mr Sinclair?'

'If you had not asked me, I would have invited myself,' he replied, pink with enthusiasm. 'I wouldn't miss it for the world.'

Pierre, not to be outdone in enthusiasm, would not miss it for the absolute universal. I was the only one who was to miss it, it seemed.

'I wonder if the season has anything to do with your entering the trance state,' was Welland's next piece of non-sense. 'It is not the equinox, and it is not the ides of anything. It approaches the summer solstice. We must arrange a sitting for June twenty-first.'

After a good deal of such chatter, Welland left, and Peter went abovestairs to pester a certain upstairs maid who was not averse to his attentions. I went off to have a look at the feather room. The fact of Madame's insisting it not be disturbed made me suspicious. A few further chats with Dr Hill had half convinced me Pierre and Welland were innocent. St Regis, it seemed, was a man of good character, and as he placed implicit faith in Sinclair, had written an enthusiastic letter of character for him, it was hard to go on imagining him a criminal. As he was engaged to a good fortune, he would not be apt to risk it all by skulduggery. Certain hints dropped by Hill intimated to me that it might be the Franconis who were relieving my aunt of her excess spending money. If she were already buying Pierre's jewels, and if she had just enough left to live on, and if then the Franconis began raising their prices. . . .

It was a possibility at least, and if they were taking money for pulling the wool over her eyes, it might be stopped by exposing them. I noticed the curtains had been closed, and that the exotic aroma of incense was still heavy on the air. Other than that, nothing had changed, including the dark table cover that still held its spilled grease stain. It was difficult to see how they could manage anything very elaborate in this room; anything like an actual appearance of Edward, for example. The space was small, with no large furnishings to hide an accomplice's body. Edward had not actually materialized, but that must be the lure they were holding out. They could not keep her interest indefinitely with promises. Sooner or later, they must provide her a ghost, or a reasonable facsimile thereof.

Whatever Dr Hill may say or think, I knew Aunt Loo was concerned about Edward, and this business of justice that she occasionally mentioned. Right today, after her trance, she had spoken of it again. The power of will, and something about being a deceiver. Yes, of course the Franconis were up to something. And Welland Sinclair was on the very best of terms with at least half the couple. As he was engaged, romance was probably not the Madame's attraction at all. Business was more like it. I was inordinately disappointed to find not a single clue to indicate wrongdoing when I examined the room. If only I could hide tonight and watch the performance, but there was nothing to hide behind. The room had been cleared of all furniture, save the table and chairs. Behind the curtains possibly. . . . But how could I get away without being detected, and conceal myself there?

Then I remembered Gloria's wall-scaling ability. This one would be very simple to scale; it was on the first floor. If I left the curtains open an inch or so, I did not think it would be noticed in the gloomy atmosphere Madame favored. I opened them an inch and a half, which should give me a good view of the table. It remained only to have a ladder from the potting shed moved close to the window, and I was ready for the séance.

Chapter Ten

I was careful to wear a dark gown that evening. Dr Hill dined with us, but Mr Sinclair did not arrive till eight o'clock. Country hours were kept by our whole little circle. I felt a strong urge to compliment Welland on his engagement, but as it was by no means a new occurrence, I took the idea he would think it showed too much interest on my part, and behaved just as usual. Aunt Loo spoke at length on her trance during the meal, and while we awaited the arrival of the Franconis. Any mention of the Magician or St Joan, or in other words freedom of choice and deceit, had been expunged from her comments. Mr Sinclair expressed rampant interest in the trance, often expressing the desire that he could be entranced himself.

'Perhaps you will tonight, Mr Sinclair,' my aunt told him. 'I feel some peculiar stirring in the air. Can you not feel it?'

He imagined he could, but Pierre outspoke him. 'I close the door. I too am feeling the cold drafts.' Loo smiled commiseratingly at Sinclair, her major listener.

'You are wearing the novel robe,' Pierre congratulated me, his wandering eyes taking in every seam and tuck of it. 'Very much elegant.'

'Thank you. I do not mean to be outshone by your new jacket, you see.'

'The jacket is not shining yet. All the naps are on it still. The old jacket had the shining elbows. Ha, but you mean my shining buttons, yes? I comprehend your joke.' He admired first his brass buttons, then my crystal ones, which paraded down the front of my gown. He soon became lost in admiring other parts of me, so obviously that I felt compelled to pull a shawl about my shoulders.

'You mentioned closing the door, Peter,' Sinclair said, turning his glasses toward us. 'Pray do so. Miss Ford is feeling chilly. She has covered her – shoulders.' There was a grin hovering about his lips. How I *longed* to rip those lenses from his eyes! I could not restrain myself much longer.

E'er long, the Franconis arrived. I thought Mr Franconi would join the others at the table tonight, since six had been mentioned as a good number for a séance, and my not sitting would make the party five. He felt more at home in the kitchen, I expect. He did not even enter the saloon, but vanished belowstairs as soon as they arrived. When the group arose to adjoin to the feather room, Pierre sat behind, to bear me company.

'I shall not be joining with the ghosters,' he announced. 'I am atheist in this matter. Valerie and I shall be staying here.'

I wanted to crown him with a candlestick. 'No, no! Go along with them, Peter,' I begged.

'We will be having more enjoyments here alone together with each other.'

'No, please. It is not at all necessary to stay. I don't mind being alone. I shall read the newspaper. I haven't a notion what is passing in the world. I haven't seen a paper since leaving home.'

'We shall reading the newspaper together,' he decided, arising to get only the one paper. He drew his chair up till it touched mine, opened the paper, and then leaned over to read my half.

'We insist you join us, Cousin,' Mr Sinclair said, removing the paper from his fingers and handing it to me. 'Miss Ford will have to do without your company for one evening. You are indispensable to the séance.'

Pierre rather liked the unusual idea of being indispensable to anything, I think. He arose with a laugh. 'Very well. I go, then. You will tell me all the passings in the world when I return, Valerie.'

'That will be the obituary column you must read,' Mr Sinclair mentioned over his shoulder as he turned to leave. 'Lively entertainment for you.'

I kept the paper up before my eyes for a few moments after they left, in case anyone should return. It was not my plan to go to the window till they had had a few minutes to settle down. I did not peruse the obituary notices, but the social page. It was a London paper. The carryings on at St James's were not of much interest to me. I read with some trace of interest the gala parties going forth in the city, then turned my attention to the engagements. The words jumped off the page and hit me in the eye. Mr and Mrs Edward J. Milne were pleased to announce the engagement of their daughter Mary to Mr Welland Sinclair, of Hereford, cousin to and second in line to the title of Lord St Regis, of Tanglewood, also in Hereford.

I folded the paper carefully, found a pencil to circle the announcement, and laid it aside. Now I had an unexceptionable excuse to mention to Mr Sinclair my great joy at his match. It did not say a single thing about Mary, other than the name of her parents. I was curious to hear the girl described.

When a suitable length of time had elapsed, I tiptoed down the hallway to ensure the door to the feather room was closed, indicating the séance was safely underway. I went out the side door, round to the window, and the ladder. I was careful to make a minimum of noise as I jiggled it into place, then climbed carefully up. A narrow band of light showed me my trick of leaving the curtains slightly open had not been detected. The séance had reached that stage where the heads were bent, the fingers splayed round the table's edge, but they did not quite touch. This would be due to the smaller number of sitters.

After a moment, Madame's head rose, then fell back. Her snorts and grunts were not audible through the windowpane. She opened her mouth to say some quiet words, then all the heads at the table suddenly rose from their respective chests, as though on ropes. They turned and looked toward a corner of the room. I could see only an edge of the apparition, but certainly the half of a face I saw looked remarkably like Uncle Edward, as I remembered him, and more particularly as I remembered seeing his portrait in the gallery. It was a pale, insubstantial, floating thing, not quite white, but slightly pink, like one of my aunt's chiffon robes. If it was not a ghost, it was a very good imitation of one. It was floating, bobbing along quite merrily across the room. I pulled my eyes away from the apparition, with the greatest difficulty, to observe those at the table. Aunt Loo had gone into a complete trance, slumped forward on the table, her brindled hair catching the candlelight. Pierre was smiling in happy surprise, Dr Hill looked astonished, Madame Franconi sat with glazed eyes, not even seeing the ghost, and Mr Sinclair wore his green glasses as usual, robbing me of any reading of his expression. His head was stiffly erect, at attention.

My aunt's collapse brought the séance to an abrupt end. As soon as Dr Hill noticed her, he jumped up. Madame finally roused herself to attention, and simultaneously the others came to an awareness of Loo's faint. There was a general hubbub of jumping up. The apparition, when I glanced back, was gone. There was chaos in the room, with arms raised, mouths open wide in exclamations of shock, but of course I witnessed only the visual aspects of the scene. I scooted down the ladder, tossed it into the bushes, and darted back into the house. Fearing movement in the hallway from the sitters, I entered by the kitchen door, causing some little alarm to the servants. I did not stop to make any explanations to them. I had to get myself reinstalled in the saloon before my absence was noticed.

I made it, but just barely. 'What happened?' I asked, jumping up from the chair I had just jumped into a split second before.

'The ghost of the *oncle* Edward is appear,' Pierre told me, smiling brightly. 'The most nice ghost. Very friendly. He do not hurt no ones, like my cousin says so.'

His simple explanation was soon overridden by the more vocif-
erous exclamations of Aunt Loo and Mr Sinclair, the former not
much more substantial looking than the last-seen image of
Edward. She was pale as a sheet. Madame Franconi too looked
peaky. She went to the darkest corner of the room and sat down,
her head leaning against the back of a wing chair. Welland hopped
to pour her a glass of sherry, and held it to her lips. A touching
scene. I took the cue and poured Auntie a glass, only to find when
I got to her side that Dr Hill had already handed her a glass of
wine, so I drank up the other glass myself.

When the ghost chasers were restored by a couple of sherries,
Madame allowed modestly that it had been a successful sitting. 'I
wonder if we are wise to move to the gatehouse tomorrow
evening, Mr Sinclair,' she said. 'When the present location is so
conducive to results, it is not wise to move.'

'I receive very strong emanations in the study at the gatehouse,'
he insisted. 'It is not Sir Edward, but my mama we wish to reach
tomorrow evening. I hope we will be half so successful.'

'There is no saying. It took a while to get Sir Edward to come
through. We cannot look for success with your mama so soon, I
fear. If I had some token, some talisman of hers to draw her forth,
it would be of help. Do you have a picture, something belonging
to her? That locket you mentioned, for instance, with her likeness. . . .'

'I always carry it with me, next my heart, but it has not got her
likeness in it. It is a lock of my father's hair.' He reached into some
inner pocket and drew the trinket out.

Madame opened it and peered inside. 'Is this lady not your
mama – a likeness taken in her youth?'

'No, it is a friend,' he said, rather quickly, and closed the thing
with a snap. 'I shall give you the locket tomorrow before the
séance. I would not want to be without it for a whole day.'

'Sweetheart?' Madame asked, a coy smile sitting uneasily on

her swarthy, foreign face.

'You are a mind reader,' he answered, his white teeth flashing.

'Very pretty,' she complimented. Before many moments, she asked for her husband to be called, for she was tired and wanted to leave.

'I'll offer you a lift, to save Lady Sinclair's having her horses put to,' Dr Hill offered. He reached into his pocket to look for his snuffbox and found it missing. 'Must have dropped it in the feather room,' he mumbled, and went to look for it.

I paid little heed to their leave-taking, for I was most curious to get a look at the picture in Welland's locket. He still held it in his hand, shaking it back and forth. When the party was diminished to Loo, Pierre, Welland and me, I picked up the newspaper.

'Read any interesting obituaries?' Mr Sinclair asked.

'No, but one engagement announcement that might be of interest to *you*.'

'If it is another royal duke about to take the plunge, I am not at all interested.'

'It is not a royal anything. It is a plain Mr Sinclair and plain Miss Mary Milne I am speaking about.'

'Is it in the paper?' he asked, startled out of his usual complacency. His hands reached for the paper. As I handed it to him, I relieved him of the locket, without his even noticing what I was about.

I opened it to see a bland, pretty, but slightly bovine countenance smiling at me. The girl had black curls, blue eyes, and an insipid smile. Distinction was the last word that would occur to anyone looking at it. Strangely, it was the word that came to mind in connection with Mr Sinclair, especially on those occasions when he forgot his pose, straightened up his drooping shoulders, and ceased behaving like an invalid. After he had read the notice, he handed the paper back to me, and I returned his locket to him, and still he did not appear to realize that I had opened it. 'Surprised?' I asked him.

'No, not particularly. Mary did not mention to me her parents were having it put in the papers, but it is the custom, of course.'

'When is the wedding to be? I did not notice a date. Does it say?'

I knew very well it did not but was careful not to display too vivid an interest in it. 'July the tenth,' he answered, so automatically that it was obviously a familiar response, indicating the match was of long standing and long planning.

'Your days are numbered, sir,' I said lightly.

'I can hardly wait. I am looking forward to my marriage with the greatest eagerness.'

'It is strange you should leave your home at such a time. I wager Mary – was not that the girl's name? – is not well pleased with you.'

'She proved so much distraction I could not get my work completed with her in the neighborhood. St Regis suggested I finish it off before the wedding. I must confess I now spend all my spare moments writing her letters.'

I doubt his chasing of Madame, and occasionally me, left him much free time. 'Why do you not try if Madame can conjure up a vision of her?' I suggested.

Pierre was not happy at being left out of the conversation. 'What a sorceress the Madame is!' he said, inserting himself between Mr Sinclair and me. 'Making the ghost pop out from us.'

'You pop out pretty well yourself,' Sinclair said, in his ironic mood, as he glanced down at his cousin.

'Like the corks of the wine bottle, popping out,' Pierre laughed, sliding an arm about my waist.

I lifted his fingers away and pushed him aside. 'Little boys must watch their hands,' I told him.

'Otherwise big girls might slap them,' Sinclair added in a didactic way to Pierre.

Lady Sinclair arose with a weary sigh, gathering her chiffon skirts around her. She was still pale, distraught. 'I am going to retire now, Valerie. This has been a most fatiguing experience. It is not at all late, however. Don't let me break up your meeting. Please don't feel you have to leave, Mr Sinclair. My niece will be happy to entertain you and Pierre. Ask the servants for something to eat if you are hungry later on.'

'Best offer I've had all day,' Mr Sinclair said, sitting down after having arisen to bow my aunt out of the room, and throwing one leg over the other. 'What entertainment have you in mind, Valerie. Dancing, singing, wrestling match?'

'Strolling in the moonlight is fine entertainments,' Pierre suggested with a hopeful look.

'Strolling in the moonlight with you two would be my second choice of entertainment, after sticking my head in a guillotine. I too shall go to bed.'

'We're not likely to get a better offer than that, Peter. I for one think we must take her up on it,' Welland said.

As he was being so playful, I did not hesitate a moment to reach out and remove his green glasses from his nose. I wished I had not. He had a pair of dancing brown eyes that could have seduced a statue. Long and thick lashes too, that any lady might envy. After one bold, startled stare, the eyes fell to my feet. I took the misguided idea he was embarrassed. Ninnyhammer that I am! It was nothing of the sort. He was examining me in a leisurely fashion, not from head to toe, which I am accustomed to, but from toe to head, which is more insulting somehow. I felt remarkably like a prize milcher on display at the county fair.

'What do you know? Peter was right,' was his bland comment, when he had had his fill of staring.

'Would it be too much to ask what Pierre said?' I asked, turning to deliver a glare on Pierre, who had wandered off to pour more sherries, and was unaware that he was in bad odor with me.

'*Très vive*, as we English say,' Sinclair said. Then he set his head on one side and laughed, while those chocolate eyes continued to dart hither and'thither all over my body.

I took a deep breath preparatory to delivering a setdown. He smiled musingly, his eyes resting on my swollen bosom. 'And *très grande*,' he added with a lecherous twinkle.

'Come now, Mr Sinclair, we must speak English, for Peter's benefit. You always insist upon it.'

'I find myself thinking in French when I am with you. A strange phenomenon too, for I hardly speak the bong-jaw fluently at all. But I see by your maidenly blushes I am embarrassing you, poor helpless flower that you are. I promise to behave like a dull old clod of an Englishman.'

'You are hard on Englishmen. *I* have not found them to behave with any particular dullness.'

'The English are very much naughty,' Pierre told us from his stand at the sherry table.

'Some of them are,' I agreed, 'but one expects decent behavior from them when they are engaged at least.'

'It is wiser to wait till one is safely married,' Sinclair decided, after a little consideration, 'but for me, that will not be till July, you know, and you are here *now*. I have never made a fetish of resisting temptation.'

'I would not have guessed it if you hadn't told me!'

'Sherries,' Pierre announced, balancing three glasses rather precariously in one hand. 'What good talks am I missing here?'

'You haven't missed a thing, Peter,' I assured him, with studied ennui. 'Mr Sinclair was just telling me what a dull clod of an Englishman he is.'

'I too am dull English, like Jean Taureau. This is the new idiom.'

'That's John Bull, Peter,' Sinclair explained aside.

'Absolutely. When I am fatigued, sometimes I am speaking French. It comes very hard for me, the French. You are not wearing your spectacles, I see.'

'No, he is making a spectacle of himself tonight without his glasses,' I pointed out.

'This is a joke, yes?' Peter checked, before going off into peals of laughter.

'Yes, an hilarious joke,' Sinclair agreed, without any slight trace of a smile, as he put his spectacles back on.

'Is it really necessary to wear them at night? The sun, surely, does not blind you in a dark room,' I said.

'No, but your radiance, Miss Ford, does,' he replied, bowing deeply.

It was a weasel answer. His naked eyes showed no sign of strain, no bloodshot quality, no squinting, nothing but a healthy luster. The only other reason for wearing dark glasses was concealment, but from whom? For anyone who knew him, the spectacles were hardly enough disguise, and there was no need for any concealment from those of us who did not know him before. Surely he was Welland Sinclair. He had gone to Wight to visit with cousins; St Regis had written verifying his credentials.

I was careful to get upstairs before Sinclair left, for I had no desire to be alone at night with Pierre. Aunt Loo's lights still burned, so I stopped a moment to chat. During our brief coze, I asked her if she had ever met Welland Sinclair before his coming here.

'Once, some years ago. The Sinclairs were not infatuated with Edward's marriage to me, and never came to see us. We visited St Regis one summer at Tanglewood – the old St Regis, not the present one. We stayed a month, met them all. Welland was around, but only a boy. He was thirteen or fourteen, home from school with his cousin Hadrian, who is the present St Regis. I could not positively say I recognize him, for he only wore clear spectacles then, you know, but there is a familiar look to the fellow. St Regis mentioned in his letter that Welland would be wearing dark glasses. The boy is Welland, Valerie, whatever you may think. Pure Sinclair. There is no faking that Roman nose. They all have it, including my Edward. I'm sure St Regis sent him to spy on me.'

I let her exhort a while on this old familiar theme before taking my leave.

Chapter Eleven

*I*t rained the next day. I spent the morning writing, like Aunt Loo. My writing did not take place in her scriptorium, but in my own room. Its purpose was to inform my parents and sisters how I was going on at Troy Fenners. As so often happens with our family letters, I went in detail into all the irrelevancies, and said nothing of the matters that really interested me. A stark announcement that Loo spent her time trying to communicate with the spirit of Edward would have Papa sending for a straitjacket, or a minister of the church, while any reference to her being poor would probably have brought Papa pelting down upon us in person. I told them about Nancy and the whisky and Dr Hill, and to tease my sisters a little, told them all about Pierre except that he was a midget. I also mentioned St Regis's cousin being nearby, and that he was engaged.

Pierre was prowling the halls, waiting for me to finish my letters that he might go for a walk in the rain. He assured me this would be very romantic. He was too impatient to wait the necessary hour and in the end went to visit some local businessman whom I assume had a pretty daughter. With free access to the rest of the house, I did a bit of exploring. One viewing of a secret passage was not enough; I went through it again, then to the feather room, next to the gallery to check Uncle Edward's picture out against the ghost who had danced across the air the night before. My memories of Sir Edward were hazy, for I had not seen him in several years, at which time I was a mere child. The picture was very like the ghost. Even the pose was suspiciously similar. Uncle Edward was painted from the waist up, wearing a red hunting jacket, and looking rather stern. I remembered him as a happy, laughing man, much older than the gentleman in the picture. While I was there, I had a look at his first wife. She was a haughty-looking lady, with yellow hair and a sulky mouth. Petulant, I believe, is the proper word to describe her expression.

By noon the rain had let up. Aunt Loo had company coming to call, some neighborhood ladies who had been invited to make my acquaintance. One of them thought she had been to school with my mother, and another claimed to be some kin through her husband. The former asked me if I spoke French, and if I thought I would be happy living in France. She was under the delusion that I had come to make a match with St Clair, you see. I wondered that she made so many broad hints regarding our relative sizes, till I learned she had a small daughter to be disposed of herself. Once I let her know Pierre was nothing more than a distant connection to me, nothing romantic in the air, she became much friendlier. She invited me to call on Sharon, and bring my cousin with me if I liked. They would be happy to see us. I think all the same they would not have been nearly so happy to see me, unattended by Pierre, land at their door. No definite date was set for the visit, which I had no intention of making. Let Sharon do her own running.

Night finally came, with the visit to the gatehouse to be made. As I was wearing my second-best bronze crepe gown, I declined to walk across the park with Pierre. We all went in Auntie's carriage. Pierre, deprived of the walk, sat beside me and made do with a furious mauling of my fingers along the way.

Our host awaited us in the parlor of the gatehouse. While he made us welcome and showed us to our seats, I was busy to locate in my head the room I meant to visit while the others séanced. I was happy to see there was no surfeit of servants about.

'Who takes care of you here, Mr Sinclair?' I asked, to see if I could count up menial heads, and try to discover where they might be. I was worried about his valet.

'I have only the one woman who cooks and cleans, and of course my valet, who also acts as groom.' The cook was no problem. I trusted that even a bachelor would present us with some token tray of food after inviting us down for the evening. 'I am sorry I did not bring a real groom with me. My Diablo has developed a touch of colic. Napier is with him now, but he is not so good with horses as St Regis's stablehands.'

This was sweet music to my ears. Much as I admired Diablo, I hoped he would not make a speedy recovery.

'I hope you will not be bored here alone during the sitting,' he went on politely.

'I will sit with Valerie,' Pierre offered at once.

'Nonsense. I enjoy to sit quietly and read. Mr Sinclair will provide me some literature.'

'What a wretched host I am!' Sinclair exclaimed. 'I should have got you some ladies' magazines in the village. I thought you might like to play the pianoforte while we are out, or perhaps you would bring your embroidery with you.'

I never could decide which of those two pastimes was the more irksome. I rather think it is the embroidery. Once a wretched execution at the piano is finished, there is no embarrassing evidence save the memory, whereas needlework lingers for years, being trotted out for admiration by a proud mama, or a spiteful sister. 'The newspapers will be fine,' I said.

'I shall leave a decanter of wine and a plate of biscuits,' he offered.

'I don't spend every spare moment eating. It just looks that way.'

'Ladies always like a sweet to nibble on. I know Mary does.'

'My taste differs from Mary's,' I answered.

He was bright enough to read the intended disparagement of

her taste in gentlemen into my words, and good-natured enough to smile over it. 'Touché, Valerie. An excellent hit. I am cut to the quick.'

'Would it disturb the séance if I did a little looking about the house while I am alone? Auntie tells me she believes there is a secret passage in it, as there is at her own place.'

'What – a secret passage at Troy Fenners?' he asked, excitement lending a sharp tone to his words. 'I didn't know that. How interesting. You must show it to me.'

'Oh, yes, a marvelous long one, but it is not very scary. It is painted green.'

'Where is it? What room is it in – the feather room?'

'No, it connects the main saloon with Auntie's bedroom. The master bedroom it is that she uses.'

'Just the one passage?'

'I believe so. There is also an oubliette in the cellar. She is thinking of having it shored up. Imagine!'

'She mustn't! This is monstrous good news. St Regis will be delighted. He dotes on secret passages and oubliettes. He is a bit of a romantic, you know.'

'That was not my impression of him. Auntie does nothing but scold of his interfering.'

'Does she indeed!' he exclaimed, indignant on his employer's behalf. I recollected that the nephew was a spy for his lordship, and changed the subject back to the one I wished to pursue.

'Certainly, look around if you like, but there are no secret passages here. I'll have Mrs Harper show you about, if you like.'

'I would not dream of disturbing her. I made sure she would be busy preparing something for us to eat after the séance.'

'I am happy to see you do occasionally take a bite,' he reminded me. 'It would be a pity for that fine figure to melt away.'

Before I could think of a sharp retort, the door knocker banged, announcing the arrival of Madame Franconi and her husband. I really don't know why the man bothered to come with her. She made the trip in her client's carriage and was taken home in it. He did not participate in the sittings but just disappeared to the kitchen, where he would feel most at home.

My charms did not rate a single glance from the host once Madame arrived. Before long, the group went to the room chosen for the show, while I dashed to the staircase, grabbing up a brace of candles from the hall table, for the upstairs was in complete darkness. I had not the least difficulty in locating either the room or the black metal box under the bed. Getting it open was something else. I had to make a rapid scramble through three chambers before finding a ring of keys sitting on top of a dresser in Sinclair's room. I was curious enough about the man that I took a close look at the place while I was there. There was no manuscript of his treatise, nor any reference books on the subject of ghosts. There was no framed picture of Mary either, as I expected to see in an adoring fiancé's chamber. No letters to or from her. The golden locket, mentioned as being always carried next his heart, was tossed into a leather jewelry case, on top of a welter of watch fobs and tiepins. There was a handsome set of brushes bearing a crest that was probably that of St Regis. The cousin was kind, indeed generous. They looked like gold-backed brushes, but might have been vermeil or even brass.

I snatched up the keys and returned to the black box. The smallest key opened it. The others were quite obviously door keys. I ought not to have been surprised at the box's contents, for I had a good notion what would be there. There was the stack of bills, and of no small denomination either. There was the diamond ring and the ruby necklace, a replica of the *Huit Rubis* my aunt possessed. Or was this the original? I examined it closely. It felt heavier than my aunt's. Though I was no expert, I felt quite sure I held the original, and my aunt's was a somewhat inferior imitation. This one looked richer, the stones more deeply colored, the workmanship finer. He had already made the switch, then. The man *was* a thief, and possibly a blackmailer to boot. What else could account for the extraordinary appearance of the items mentioned?

There were other extravagant bibelots as well. Not the tiara, and not *all* of my aunt's pieces by any means, but enough to indicate what was going on. He had got paste copies of the heirlooms made, substituted them for the originals, and was in all probability selling them off to someone, and piling up the money in this box. Was he doing this for St Regis, or at least with the man's approval? It was difficult to believe so. He was more likely a conning, cunning criminal who imposed on his cousin's gullibility to find a soft berth, while awaiting marriage to an heiress. By checking the denomination of the bills I tried to calculate the amount of money he had amassed. As I thumbed quickly through them, I noticed a tiny green mark had been made on the top left corner of each. Marked bills.

This was a curious enough detail that I sat pondering it for a moment. Had *he* marked them? Or – beautiful thought! – was some higher authority already suspicious of him, and paying him in marked currency in order to entrap him?

His keen interest in the secret passage took on a new meaning now. How much easier his job would be with that piece of information I had handed him on a platter! Or was the job done? Why would he not make all the substitutions at one time? It was possible some jeweler was making up one piece at a time for him, but my own way of proceeding in such a case would be to wait till I had all of them, then make one comprehensive substitution. Once this was done, I would depart rather quickly too, and not stay around pretending to be writing a treatise. It was a very curious affair indeed. No sensible explanation came to me. I must tell Loo about this and let her decide what action was to be taken. In the back of my mind lurked the suspicion that the odious St Regis was mixed up in it somewhere. He took a keen interest in the estate that was not yet his. Dr Hill too might have a sensible suggestion to offer. I would convince my aunt to seek his advice.

I locked the box back up, stuffed it under the bed, but was not wise enough to let well enough alone. When I took the keys back to his room, I decided to do a spot more of spying, hoping for some written proof of the jewelry transactions, a name, a draft design of some of my aunt's pieces, something that could be followed up. What I found, stuffed on to the floor of Sinclair's clothespress, was the ghost of Uncle Edward. A very thin piece of white calico was what he had used. It looked like a very well worn bed sheet. It was white, the flesh tint lent to it by the play of light from behind. It was rigged with strings on four corners, while the face and body were sketched on with black ink. That's all. Danced across a dark room in some manner on the strings, and with a light carefully played behind it, it gave a lifelike, or ghostlike enough appearance to deceive the gullible. Sinclair must have taken a sketch from Uncle Edward's portrait in the gallery, redrawn it carefully on to the calico, and. . . . And what? How had he manipulated it, while sitting at the table, with his two hands spread out on top? There were more of them in on it, then. The Franconis of course, that went without saying. The great friendship between Madame and Welland was clear now. The husband must be the other party. I could not be certain, but did not think he had been in the kitchen the night before, when I had made my wild dash from window to saloon. It was said he went there, but really I could not remember seeing him. He was in that feather room all the time. I cannot imagine how he concealed himself. Maybe he had a grouse suit, but he was most certainly there, dancing this sheet of calico across the room on strings. What a take-in! My poor aunt being fooled by these unscrupulous scoundrels. It was surprising indeed that Sinclair would bother with them, when he had such a profitable rig running on the side in stealing jewelry.

Thinking I had still a quarter of an hour before the séance would be over, and highly curious to prove that it was Uncle Edward's ghost I held in my hands, I tried tying the strings to the posts of Sinclair's bed and the other to his dresser handle, then placing my candles behind it to view the results. At this close range, the effect was not so good as it seemed the night before. The light did not penetrate so well, the drawing of the features too was blacker than I remembered, but my dim view through a dust-laden window might account for the difference.

It was while I stood observing the calico sheet that I got caught by my host. He came sneaking up the stairs on silent toes and was at the doorway before I realized he approached. I hadn't time to do a thing but stand and look guilty as sin, and wait for his vengeance. He was not wearing his glasses, which surprised me, till I saw them dangling from his fingers. 'Clever stunt, don't you think?' he asked, in a pleasant, conversational tone, as he observed the ghost-calico.

'Clever enough to fool a gullible old lady. One can only wonder you would have bothered. . . .' I stopped dead. There was no point in revealing that I knew his other, more heinous secret. The keys were safely back on his dresser, the box put away under the bed. *All* was not lost.

'I was curious to discover how it was done. That's all. You were not present when Edward materialized, but to me it seemed this was how it was managed. His likeness sketched on some thin, nearly transparent material. It was not calico they used, I think, but chiffon.'

'They?'

'The Franconis. The Phonies would be more accurate. They are obviously a pair of con artists, who make their livelihood preying on lonesome and credulous people like Lady Sinclair.'

This about-face in his whole attitude toward the couple threw me for a loss. If it was a way of wiggling out of my discovery, it was a good one. 'You have nothing but praise for them! What of your mother's locket? How about Anastasia?'

'They are not likely to welcome me to the sittings if I profess to doubt their talents, are they? You notice how quickly your aura was found to interfere when you began making sane comments?

I have played the role of an enthusiast to win their confidence, to try to learn more about how they operate. Madame's asking me a couple of times if I had a picture of my mama confirmed my feeling the ghosts were done up from portraits. As to the locket, Madame made some vague reference to an apple tree when I was trying to contact Mama, and I invented the bit about finding the locket. I had it with me all the time, for it holds Mary's miniature. It was a parting gift from her. Anastasia is Madame's invention, like Ahmad.'

'How did you get away from the sitting so soon?' was my next question.

'Well, you know, it's a strange thing, Valerie,' he said, lounging against the dresser, crossing his arms, and assuming an amused face, 'it just struck me as a little peculiar, your sudden interest in looking over this house. There is nothing of the least interest in it real interest, I mean. A simple question to Loo told me she had not mentioned any secret passage existing here to you. You wanted an excuse to snoop. Once I realized that, I fell smack into a trance, and the séance broke up. I am at this moment lying down to recuperate my strength before joining the others below. Very fatiguing, these trances. Of more interest to me is to discover what you were looking for.'

'This,' I answered boldly, pointing to the sheet. 'I did see Uncle Edward the other night, through the window. I was outside, perched on a ladder. When you were so eager to move the sitting down here, I began to wonder whether you were not working with the Franconis. I was looking for evidence; I am not sure I haven't found it.'

He nodded his head, considering this explanation. 'Flimsy evidence on which to suspect me, but I suppose it could have happened that way. Wait here. I'll be right back.' With this arrogant command, he turned and left the room. I was about to follow him out, when the door closed in my face, and the key turned in the lock. Glancing to his dresser, I noticed he had picked up the ring of keys without my having noticed it. I knew instinctively where he was going. He was going to see if his black box had been disturbed. Surely I had left no telltale sign! He could not *know*.

He knew. When he returned about forty-five seconds later – he must have run all the way – he knew I had been into his box. 'Nice try, Valerie. You think fast, and under stress too. That is unusual in a lady. They usually fly to pieces at the first sign of pressure. So, what is to be done about it?' he asked, rubbing his hands together with the greatest relish, while he stared at me, a bold smile decorating his lips.

'What is to be done, Mr Sinclair, or Mr Whoever you are, is that I am going to report you to a constable as a jewel thief, and you are not going to do a thing to stop me. Within hollering distance are my aunt, Dr Hill, who is bound to recognize a bullet wound or marks of strangulation on my neck and wonder how they got there, the Franconis, and Pierre. If you are half as cunning a rogue as I take you for, you will jump out the window this instant, hop on your colicky horse, and get out of here, before you are clamped into irons. You had best leave my aunt's jewelry and the money obtained from the sale of same behind, or it will be necessary to give chase.'

He unfolded his arms, which had been crossed against his chest during my speech, clapped his hands lightly and bowed. 'An excellent rant. So *that* is what your muddled efforts at thinking have led you to conclude. I was premature to compliment you on your un-ladylike powers of thought. If a constable is called in, it is dear little old Aunt Loo who will be in shackles, where she belongs,'

'What is that supposed to mean?' I demanded, becoming frightened at his threat, for he seemed very sure of himself.

'This will take a deal of explaining. I can't recuperate from my trance forever. We'll talk tomorrow.'

'No, Mr Sinclair, we will talk tonight. I don't trust you as far as I could throw a cathedral. You're not going to disappear while we all sleep, with the jewelry and money stuffed into your carriage. I am not that big a fool.'

'What a suspicious little mind the lady has! One might be forgiven for wondering who is a rogue in the affair. I know you have a vested interest in your aunt's fortune, but you won't get your grasping hands on *that* pile.'

'Fine talking, sir. You can try to redistribute blame as much as you like, the facts are, *you* have got money and jewelry that don't belong to you. That will take some fancy explaining to a constable, and I am not at all sure St Regis would approve of your getting caught either, whatever about his views on the theft.'

'I begin to think hauling in the law is not a bad idea. Shall we go arm-in-arm to an officer, watching and abusing each other all the way?'

'*I* don't intend to leave this room till I have an explanation.'

'You are more than welcome to remain the night, dear Amazon. In that case, we must have our wine and food brought up, and served here on my bed. There is Lady Sinclair calling you now.'

Her voice came wafting up the stairway. My decision had to be taken in a split second. 'We'll talk tonight.'

'I'll drive you home.'

'No, it will look too odd, and Pierre would be sure to tag along. I'll sneak back after Auntie goes to bed. No – I won't though,' I added, as the various and totally obvious ineligibilities to that scheme rolled over me.

'I'll go up to Troy Fenners. Let me in at the library door about an hour after you get home, after the others are in bed.'

'How do I know you'll come? You could run away in the meanwhile.'

With a worried, startled look, he handed me his key ring. I was so hurried and alarmed at my aunt's approaching steps that I took that as a safeguard, a sort of hostage. Of course I realized even before the three of us reached the bottom of the stairs that it was no safeguard at all. He could hammer the box open with a rock or hammer or anything.

The others were already having their sherries, and some cold meat and bread were awaiting us on a table, with a quite delicious-looking cake about a foot high. It was a pale yellow cake, flavored with lemon, which tasted as good as it looked. My recollections of that party are not at all clear. I expect Pierre acted as badly as usual. I have a memory of Madame sighing and expressing fatigue, and of Dr Hill lifting his eyebrows as I came downstairs, finding my having been above with Welland a strange business. I know the party lasted much too long. No one was in a hurry to get away that night except me. My only desire to get away was that I wished to run back very fast to the gatehouse to make sure Welland did not bolt with the box. How should I stop him if he did? Nancy – I'd ride Nancy down, and I could at least give chase.

At one point during the remainder of the evening, Welland found an opportunity for a private word with me. 'You think it safe to meet at Troy Fenners? Would it not be wiser to meet outdoors, well away from Peter?'

'I would prefer to meet you in the safety of my aunt's home, thank you.'

'It's up to you. I can strangle or shoot as well indoors as out.'

'I shall bring a gun.'

'Do you carry one?' he asked, with a surprised laugh.

Actually I did not possess such a thing, nor did I recall having seen one about my aunt's house. 'No, I see you don't,' he went on. 'Never mind. I'll bring one. For *you*, I mean.'

I could hardly believe it when he actually slipped a little pistol into my reticule five minutes later, after making an excuse to leave the room. 'It's loaded,' he cautioned. 'Handle with care.'

I was nervous as a kitten with the thing in my reticule.

Chapter Twelve

I went up to my room the instant we got home and slipped out again as soon as my aunt's door closed, to dart to the stables for Nancy. Pinny did not know what to make of it. 'Your night dress is all ready, miss,' she pointed out.

'Keep it warm for me. I shall be back soon.'

'But miss, where are you going at such an hour?'

'Out.'

My trip to the gatehouse on Nancy, while still in my second best bronze crepe, created some extra work for Pinny. How happy she would be. She loved washing and airing my gowns. It was well soiled from the ride. The scent of horse is not an easy one to dispel. The ride was all in vain too. About forty-five minutes after the party broke up, Welland came out of the house and walked up to Troy Fenners on foot. It was necessary for him to wait a few minutes at the library door while I stabled Nancy and entered the house by the kitchen door.

'What the devil kept you?' he asked impatiently. 'I've been waiting an age.'

'I had to make sure Auntie was settled in for the night.'

The library was in total darkness. There was a diffused lightening of the darkness at the window, where a scrap of moon struggled to get out from under a cloud. Mr Sinclair wore his green glasses, if you can imagine the absurdity. 'I had better light a taper,' I decided.

'Why?'

'Why not?' I countered.

After this brilliant exchange, I lit the taper, just one, to allow me an inkling of what my guest's expression was as he prepared to fabricate his Banbury tale.

'I see what it is. You want to be able to shoot me, and fear to miss your target in the dark. Where is the gun?'

'In my pocket, Mr Sinclair,' I lied, for I had forgotten the thing in my reticule. 'Pray be seated. Have you had time to arrange your story? I am on thorns to hear it.'

'I believe I have the details all worked out. I have had a month in which to do it. It goes as follows: Lady Sinclair, as you know, enjoys the use of a large income while she lives, along with Troy Fenners and the Sinclair heirlooms. Being a foolishly generous lady, she has always managed to spend every cent of the income. It is in her sole discretion, however, and St Regis had nothing to say against it. When she began trying to mortgage the estate, he became worried, for he is the one who would eventually have to settle the mortgages, for Troy Fenners is entailed on him. He quite sensibly refused to approve the mortgages. He was in a position to do so, since he is the trustee of the estate. Your aunt's next clever ploy was to sell family heirlooms – jewelry – which are also entailed on St Regis. Reputable agents would not touch the stuff with a pair of tongs. They know their business, know what pieces of national importance are entailed, and which are free to be sold. When Hamlet, in London, was offered the *Huit Rubis* necklace, he was kind enough to notify St Regis of it. Hamlet did not buy it, but he knew the fellow who was trying to peddle it.'

'Who was this man?'

'A dealer in stolen and misappropriated gems, whose name would mean nothing to you. He uses the name Farber, which may or may not be his real name. In any case, that is where I came in. St Regis was too busy to handle the matter personally. He appointed me to track down Farber, buy up the jewels at the lowest price possible, and try if I could discover in the meanwhile what is going forth here at Troy Fenners that Lady Sinclair should require such colossal sums of money.'

'Those are genuine pieces you have then?'

'Yes, does your aunt have copies tucked away in her vault? I expect she would take the precaution of having ones made up and occasionally wear them, to deflect suspicion that they have vanished.'

'Yes, she has.'

'So – now *you* understand the presence of the jewels and the money in my black box. The money is to buy back any more she might have outstanding. I am not sure I have got them all. Time for me to understand how you went so unerringly to the spare room and ferreted out the goodies. How the devil did you know where to look?'

'A lucky guess. I don't understand why you don't just ask my aunt why she is doing this.'

'Do you take St Regis for a fool?'

'No, an interfering busybody, but probably not a fool.'

'He wrote her several times when first she began trying to raise mortgages. She explained to him the necessity of lending or giving large sums to your father to help him raise his family. It was regrettable it should be necessary, but. . . .'

'I beg your pardon!' I exclaimed.

'For what?'

'She never gave Papa a single sou! She didn't even give Marie and Elleri and me the usual guinea last trip. She has *never* helped to support us. Oh, how *dare* you say such a thing!'

He blinked in surprise. The green glasses had come off when the taper was lit. 'It is what she told us. She mentioned several thousand pounds annually.'

'It's a *lie*! She didn't, *ever*.'

'How do you know? It is possible your father did not see fit to mention his private financial doings to his children, especially doings of such a nature.'

'I am privy to *all* financial doings in our family. I know to a penny how much we spend on everything. We discuss it all the time. That is – well, we are not *rich*, and have to make some economies, but we do not borrow or just plain take money from relatives, I assure you.'

'What the devil has she been doing with it, then?'

'She's being blackmailed by that little buzzard of a Pierre, *that* is what.'

'Don't be ridiculous. He could buy and sell her.'

'How could he? He lost all his estates in the revolution.'

'Only the French estates. The St Clairs were far-seeing, and had bundled oodles of money out of the country long before the revolution broke. St Regis himself, the old earl, arranged it all for them. He personally brought back a trunkful of beautiful, priceless art objects when he was visiting, and brought a good deal of gold coin as well.'

'Why doesn't Pierre stay with this marvelous St Regis clan, then, instead of sponging off Aunt Loo?'

'She is a member of the St Regis clan. Pierre chanced to call on her first when he came to England, and he feels sorry for her, living all alone, so he decided to remain here. As to sponges, I don't believe you have got that quite accurate.'

'Neither do I. Sponge was not the proper word for him. He is a blackmailer. I overheard him demanding a thousand pounds – same as the last time, he said.'

'Yes, she is cutting pretty deep into him. You cannot have heard aright. It is Loo who is 'borrowing' from Peter. Whether she will ever be able to repay him is a moot point. I have arranged a few sales of articles for Peter, some jewelry and a few paintings he wished to be rid of, to get ready cash. I don't mean to let him beggar himself for the lady, however.'

I sat silent, trying to remember the precise words spoken by Pierre and my aunt. I could not do it but did remember his saying

families had to stick together, help each other, and had more than
once heard my aunt call him extremely generous.

'Convinced?' he asked.

'I'll ask my aunt.'

'You do that. While you are about it see if you can find out what
the hell she is doing with all the cash that passes through her
fingers.'

'She won't tell me. She only says she does not like prying
youngsters. Welland, if this is true, what you are saying. . . . It's
even worse than I thought.'

'It is true,' he said simply.

'How could anyone spend such sums? She has nothing to show
for it. All that money gone. She is being swindled by someone.'

'It looks that way.'

'What are we going to do about it?'

I have not mentioned it, but it must be clear to you that I
believed his story. It made sense to me. Aunt Loo, Dr Hill, Pierre,
and now Welland had told me Pierre was astronomically rich. He
did not seem like a blackmailer, and it was logical that St Regis
would have sent someone to investigate matters here, considering
the mess they were in. All details were accounted for, so far as I
could tell. I would face Auntie, brave up, and ask about the loans
from Pierre and the paste jewels, but in my heart, I had already
accepted that it was true.

'St Regis will handle it,' was Sinclair's highly unsatisfactory
reply.

'I'd like to give that gentleman a piece of my mind. Thinking
Papa was the one bilking her.'

'Lady Sinclair told him so,' he replied patiently.

'I'll give her a blast as well. She didn't even give us our guinea
last trip.'

'That sits as ill as all the rest, I see. I shall personally filch a guniea
for you from St Regis's stacks of blunt, Valerie, but Elleri and Marie
must shift for themselves. Even St Regis is not made of money.'

'It is not a joking matter. Who can be doing it? *I* think it is the Franconis, with their painted sheets and tarot cards. She keeps muttering about justice and deceit, and there was something about a lady too, at that one séance I attended. She mentioned Edward as well. You don't suppose. . . .'

'What, that Edward had a ladybird on the side who is now demanding justice? A bit late for that. He's been dead over a decade. Of course ladybirds have been known to lay eggs. A byblow, a child born on the wrong side of the blanket. . . . But a Sinclair would not behave so badly,' he decided, after a moment's haughty reflection.

'Would he not? Odd they had that secret passage built on to the master bedroom, then. My aunt intimated it was used to smuggle a girl in and out during the night, without the wife's knowledge.'

'What an intriguing idea,' he said, with a whimsical smile. 'St Regis will be excited when I tell him about the secret passage. I made sure, when you mentioned it, that it would lead to the feather room. There must be one there too, to have allowed the manipulation of the shade of dear old Sir Edward.'

'I wonder if the Franconis are not working with someone else, they softening Auntie up with these dancing sheets and tales of justice and a lady and discretion, while the mysterious lady bilks her dry, leaning on her guilty feelings and good nature to cadge huge sums of money from her.'

'Guilty feelings about what? It is Sir Edward who is guilty in this imaginary synopsis you have been expounding. The silly old lady herself is more victim than guilty.'

'The silly old lady, as you so kindly describe my aunt, is not the one who did it, but naturally any person with proper feelings would want to atone for her husband's victims as well as her own. She said she would like to crown Sir Edward, and I come to realize *exactly* how she must feel,' I said, with a measuring glare at my companion.

'Very likely,' was his appeasing answer. 'My association (I

snorted at the word) with Madame has revealed that she and the insignificant husband are from Blaxhall, in Suffolk. There is a strain of dark people there, like Madame, believed to be descended from gypsies. Those tales of traveling through Europe are apocryphal. She doesn't know a word of any language save English, and was not even aware, in fact, that Italy is a peninsula. She has the notion it lies between England and France. You see the nature of our 'association.' It is all talk of a cultural nature. If, and it is a big if, they are connected with the business, it is possible she was brought forth from Blaxhall to play her part. I wonder if Edward or Lady Sinclair were ever in Blaxhall, or thereabouts.'

'What has that got to do with anything?'

'If the Franconis were lifted up out of Suffolk, someone from around there must be associated with them, and with Edward or Loo. They would not have heard of the Sinclairs by themselves. Someone put them on to this rig. Someone who knew them, and knew the Sinclairs. Know anyone from Suffolk?'

'I have never been there in my life.'

'Neither have I. I think it is time that situation was rectified. You can help from this end. Get into Auntie's scriptorium, where she scribbles up those great secret volumes of gothic stories, and go through the family records. See if you can find any reference to Suffolk, specifically the Blaxhall area.'

'How did you know about the books?'

'Her brain is twisted, like the plot of a bad novel. Besides, I peeked when she was not looking. I rather liked the *Search for the Unknown*, but I prefer Gloria to Debora. I wonder Loo did not give her those Titian curls, in lieu of the insipid ones. I thought the lady too large for beauty, till. . . .'

I clamped my lips shut and stared him into silence. 'I should have thought you would prefer raven tresses and insipid – *shy* smiles.'

'No, why should I?'

'Because you are engaged to a reasonable facsimile of them, to judge by the picture in your locket.'

He looked thoroughly chastened, and thoroughly sly. 'We are not all in a position to marry for love. St Regis arranged the match for me. Mary is a family connection, a well-bred, well-dowered lady.'

'Whom you can hardly wait to marry, according to your own account.'

'Mary is a nice girl, and she *does* have all that lovely money.'

'You *parasite*! You should be ashamed of admitting it.'

'I am dependent on my uncle. I must do as he wishes.'

'Why must a strong, educated young man be dependent on anyone but himself? If you would get a position instead of wasting your time on that stupid treatise about ghosts. . . . Oh, never mind. It is nothing to me what you do with your life.'

'Your opinion of me could hardly be lower, could it?'

'No, it couldn't,' I answered, without hesitation.

'Nothing to lose, then,' he said in a businesslike way, and arose up suddenly. I thought he was leaving. I also arose, to be snatched into his arms for a quick, hard, impatient kiss.

I was going to slap him but decided to be dignified instead. 'I was wrong. I *could* have a lower opinion of you. You are not even man enough to know how to kiss properly,' I said airily.

He was not man enough to take offense either. He smiled a heart-destroying smile, while those chocolate eyes laughed in amusement. 'Shall we see if I can do better?' he asked. Without waiting for an answer, he went straight ahead to do *much* better. He folded me tightly in his arms, smiled softly, then lowered his lips to mine for the best kiss I have *ever* enjoyed. I am not the missish sort who has felt no lips but Arthur Crombie's moustached ones, at my advanced years. I was tingling from my scalp to my fingertips, while a herd of butterflies rampaged in my bowels. As we eased from passion back to rationality, I prepared my setdown.

'I am vastly relieved to learn the Sinclairs never behave badly,' I said, destroying the thing by my breathless voice.

'I didn't think it was too bad for a start,' he replied, with no loss of breath at all, but only a devastating smile.

Oh, lord, he was too good for Mary Milne, whoever she might be! He had to be *mine*. Some things you want to try more than once. Being kissed by this man was one of them. 'I have experienced worse efforts. And better,' I added, as he took a possessive grip on my fingers.

'I cannot cavil with that. You could not have become so expert without *some* practice. Good God!' he exclaimed suddenly. 'You don't mean, Pierre!'

'I am seed!' Pierre said, jumping out from behind the door. 'What very excellent good watching I am having.' He was apparelled in a silk gown of bright blue, with gold piping and fringed sash.

'Pierre!' I exclaimed, starting up a foot from the floor in my astonishment. 'How long have you been there?'

'Since many seconds now. I hear everythings. You do not pulling the woolens over my eyes. I am come downstairs for the sherries, for I am not sleeping. You will have with me the sherries?'

'An excellent good notion,' Welland said, walking nonchalantly toward him, while I experienced a burst of outraged anger with the intruder. 'Coming, Val?' he asked over his shoulder as a mere afterthought.

We took up the taper and went to the saloon, where a decanter and glasses usually rested on a side table. The host poured wine, then took up a stand before the sherry table. 'I am thinking this is not correct, what I am seeing,' he announced in lofty accents, while the pair of us miscreants were subjected to a stern scowl. 'Welland has already the fiancées.'

'Just the one, Peter,' Welland corrected.

'Me, I am having the none,' Pierre pointed out. His excitement that night made him even more difficult to understand than usual.

'Shame on you,' Welland answered. 'I should think nuns of all ladies were safe from such as we.'

'I too am liking very much the girls,' Pierre continued undaunted, and uncomprehending. 'You have got the Mary fiancée. Me, I shall be having the Valerie. This is understood.' The last speech had no tone of a question at all. It was all settled unanimously by Pierre. He glared hard first at his cousin, then at me, the beloved.

'Don't make such a cake of yourself, Peter,' I suggested.

'You are kissing of Welland. I see this. Now you must be kissing me.'

'I am going to my room while you restrain this Bedlamite,' I told Welland. 'I have no intention of being wrestled to the ground by him after you leave.'

'There's just one thing I wanted to ask you, before you leave.'

I looked hopefully, though my happiest imagining could hardly read any hint of a proposal into the 'one thing,' since he already had one fiancée.

'I too shall be hearing this question,' Pierre warned us.

'No, you will wait for me here,' he was told, and accepted it. sulkily, like a child.

I said good-night to Peter, and received a pouting, 'Very much not a good night,' in reply. Welland did not even bother stepping outside of the door with me, but stopped a foot from it.

'What was it you wanted?' I asked, feeling the flush stain my cheeks at the closeness of him, and his eyes lingering on my face.

'How did you know where to look for the black box?' he asked.

'I flew up past the window and peeked in,' I answered angrily. I assure you that was not the question I hoped for.

'Part bird, or part witch? You are looking part cat, ready to spit, at the moment. I think I have figured it out all by my lonesome. Part Gloria. Take care, or she'll have you toting Dr Hill across the park. I read the outline. But *when* did Gloria make the ascent?'

'The night you took off all your clothes, Mr Sinclair. What shocking things the ladies of England will be reading soon, if Loo decides to use all my observations. Good night, sir.' I made a curtsy and let myself out.

'Very much not a good night to you, Miss Ford,' he called out after me, laughing. 'Better lock your door,' he added as I set my foot on the stairs.

I did just that, and was soon sleeping like a baby. I have no idea how long the gentlemen remained below drinking, nor what plans were made for the disposition of my body. I knew pretty well which one of the cousins I meant to have though.

Chapter Thirteen

$\mathcal{I}$ was anxious to escape my French suitor in the morning. To this end, I asked Pinny to bring me breakfast to my room, and tell Pierre, if he inquired, that I was sleeping in late. When she brought the tray up, there was a very satisfying note on it from Welland. 'Dear Heart: A thousand apologies for last night. I must see you as soon as possible, *alone*. Meet me in the feather room when you can evade our French cousin. I prefer to search for secret passages in English, and while Loo is composing. May I please have my gun and keys back? I promise to behave, if you don't tempt me past resisting.' It was signed, 'the Parasite.' I was happy to see my jibe had not run off his back, as I feared. Any self-respecting man must be ashamed of laying himself open to such a charge. I had high hopes he would discover some other career than marrying Mary Milne. Half a dozen had already occurred to me on his behalf.

When I glanced up from reading, Pinny was squinting in horror at the pistol that had been left overnight on the dresser. 'Oh, miss, what in the world are you doing with this wicked thing?' she gasped.

'Shooting birds, Pinny. Give it to me, please, and those keys.'

'You got to bed awful late last night, miss,' she admonished gently, handing me the things. 'You should have woke me up. I just dozed off, but I meant to do for you, as usual.'

'That is all right. You got my bronze gown?'

'I did, miss, and it smells of the stables. Washing crepe is next to impossible, but I'll hang it in the sun.'

'Wash it. You have to press it with a flannel cloth on top.'

'I know *that*, miss,' she said, offended. 'It hasn't got no marks, just the smell.'

'Is Welland – Mr Sinclair downstairs now?'

'Yes, talking to Mr St Clair. He's trying to convince him that nag he lent him needs exercise. I fancy he don't know it got exercise last night.' This was a hint to discover if I had been out with Pierre the night before. I failed to recognize it, or at least to acknowledge it.

'Let me know at once if St Clair leaves, will you?'

'Yes, miss. Will there be an answer to the note?'

'That won't be necessary. Come back in ten minutes and help me with my hair, Pinny. I want to look especially well today.'

'You always look grand, miss. Like a queen. I don't mean poor old Queen Charlotte either, the quiz. Isn't it a wonder how the likes of her ever got her body on to a throne?'

'Yes, and our next promises to be even worse, but we must remember we have a farmer for a king, and he would not want too stylish a lady.'

I sipped my chocolate, devoured two eggs and gammon, demolished the couple of bits of toast and was satisfied. Pinny came in just as I finished. 'He's gone, Mr St Clair, muttering off a string of French that was oaths, or I ain't a Christian. I was looking at the pictures in her ladyship's magazines last night while I was trying to keep awake, and know just the rig for you. Ringlets, miss.'

'Do be serious, Pinny. Ringlets on *me*! Leave them for the dainty girls. I shall have it brushed back today, with my tortoise-shell hair band. I hadn't time to put it in papers last night.'

When she finished, I asked, 'Does it look all right?'

'Perfect, miss. Why are you at pains to look better than usual today? There's no one belowstairs but Mr Sinclair, and he won't see a thing of all your style for them green glasses he wears.'

'Is he wearing *them* again?'

'He can't see a thing without them. I heard him tell Lady Sinclair so, when first he came.'

He was not wearing them when I joined him in the feather room a few moments later. 'Very elegant. I approve,' he complimented me, looking at the new hairdo. 'I got rid of Peter, but he is suspicious, to say the least, that I planned to be kissing his Valerie during his absence. He may come leaping out from behind the door at any moment. We better get busy.'

'It's in the main saloon.'

'No, I meant we better steal our kiss while we have the privacy.'

'You must be a good boy, Welland, or I'll take my secret passage and go away,' I cautioned, wagging a finger at him.

He grabbed it and placed a loud smacking kiss on it. 'I waited till three at my window for you to come flying in. Gloria was not working last night, I take it?'

'We heroines require our rest, like everyone else.'

'You don't deserve it. You robbed me of mine.'

'Shall we go and see the panel, or do you have a few more of these ill-considered bits of nonsense to relieve yourself of?'

'Gather ye rosebuds while ye may.'

We went to the saloon. The passage, its entrance, length, and eventual debouchement in Auntie's closet I have already described to you. It had not changed. 'This is not it,' was Welland's opinion, when we stood back in the saloon. 'It's got to be the feather room. There must be another passage there. I have been measuring the outer walls against the inner, by eye only, and believe there is room for one behind the east wall.'

He was one of those impossible people who resort to reason and science to make discoveries. 'I have checked that room rather carefully, wondering where Mr Franconi hid, but found nothing.'

'We shall see. We know where to look now, and if not behind the wall, then he was up above the ceiling. That ghost did not dance across the room without human help.'

'It was dark. I was wondering if he was not dressed up in feathers, like a rooster.'

He did not dignify this suggestion with a denial, but only shook his head sadly to see so little sign of wits in me. We went to the feather room again.

'What a gross of grouse have given their all to create this monstrosity,' he declared, looking about at the bizarre wall covering.

'It is rather sweet. So original.' Actually it was hideous.

'I sincerely hope it may be unique. *I* have never seen another like it, and I have been in a good many of the finer homes in the land. We have one wall done in alligator hide at Tanglewood that is usually considered the ugliest room in England. This gives it stiff competition.'

'You live right in the same house with St Regis, do you?'

While I had been rearranging his future, it occurred to me he might have a separate establishment, something in the nature of a dower house.

'Yes, a part of the family. A favorite relative of his lordship.'

'So you mention, frequently. Well, there is obviously nothing here. No fireplace, no wood paneling, no door, except the one into the hallway.'

'That one section there is bedizened with a few peacock feathers. I wonder why.'

'For ornamentation. Pictures would look strange, hung on feathers, unless they were pictures of birds.'

'Shall I pluck you a bonnet?' he offered, walking forward to examine the peacock feathers. 'This is where the ghost popped out, remember?'

'It must have been about there. My ladder was against the window, so I could not see the wall actually, but he came from that direction.'

'There has got to be something here,' he said with total conviction. He began feeling the feathers, his two hands flat up against them, pushing lightly up and down. A feather became dislodged and fluttered to the floor.

'Not so hard. You are destroying the decor.'

'You could *help*, you know, instead of standing there smirking.'

'I was taking the opportunity of admiring your shoulders, Welland.'

'Oh, well in that case, don't bother helping me. Go ahead and admire. Eat your heart out.'

I went to help. 'It is perfectly obvious there is no panel here. No break in the feathers at all. Smooth as a swallow's back.

'When a swallow has folded his wings, it is hard to see just where the body stops and the wings begin. Feathers are a *perfect* means of concealment. I cannot think of any other reason to disfigure the room so. I'll have them removed when I take over.'

'Auntie mentioned Troy Fenners might be your reward for catering to St Regis. I daresay he is sick to death of having you underfoot, pulling your forelock and saying, "Yessir," but I think in deference to Aunt Loo, you might refrain from mentioning your plans for the place. She is not quite at death's door yet.'

'I am always at pains to conceal our rapacity from her. And about your use of the word *parasite*, Miss Ford, I might just remind you I *work* for St Regis. I am not quite a barnacle growing on the man.'

'Did I hit a nerve, Welland? What position is it you fill that he chooses your whole life for you? – home, bride, occupation. The lot.'

'Private secretary.'

'Puppet is more like it.'

I am delighted to be able to relate it was I, and not Welland, who found the secret passageway. At least I was swift to grab the success for my own, though I am not positive whether he did not notice his wall coming out before I noticed mine was going in. The way it worked was on a sort of ball-bearing thing stuck into the frame around a wide door that had no knob, no hinges, but pivoted in the central part, one side swinging out, while the other went into the secret panel. I hope I am making this understandable. I am sure there is a technical term for it, but I don't know what it may be. There was a large frame built into the wall, and the door set into it, pivoting on ball bearings, one at the top, one at the bottom allowing the panel to revolve. It doesn't really matter. The pertinent point is we had found the panel, and behind it we found a lantern, and length of fine rope. The ghost of Uncle Edward had been removed, but I was as sure he had been here as I was sure Mr Franconi had been pulling the strings.

'What did I tell you?' Sinclair crowed, as though *he* were the one who had found it. 'There must be some hooks in the wall on the other side of the room. Those strings were hooked through metal eyes, like a pulley clothesline, you know. Black rope, you will notice, to be invisible during our' candle-lit séance. Very neat. I wonder how he held the lantern up. Must have been hooked on to the top rope somehow. Does this passage go anywhere, I wonder?'

It was the length of the room, and about a yard wide. That was it. It was not painted green, not painted at all. 'Priest's hole maybe,' Sinclair thought. 'I wonder how the Franconis discovered it. They may have got a look at Sir Edward's portrait in the gallery easily enough. Mr Franconi roams freely during the séances, but your aunt did not even know this was here. She never mentioned it, did she?'

'No, she doesn't know about it.'

'Funny. *Somebody* in the place does. An old family retainer might know. Did you get around to looking at the family records yet?'

'I haven't had time. Aunt Loo works in the scriptorium all morning.'

'Do it this afternoon, as early as you can.'

'I am not your servant. Don't order me around as though I were.'

'Are you not interested in cleaning up this mess?'

'Of course I am, but I'm not taking orders from *you*. One would hardly guess you are accustomed to taking commands yourself, you give them so freely.'

'Pretty please and thank you, my dear Miss Ford, if it is convenient for you at some future time, and completely at your leisure, will you be so kind as to cast an eye over the family records, and see if you can find anyone from Blaxhall, or thereabouts, in Suffolk.'

'Possibly, if I find time.' I was tired with his pretending to be in charge of everything when I was the one who found the passage.

'Do you know, I think there's a trapdoor in the ceiling of this passage?' he said suddenly. During his playful request for help, you see, he had not even bothered to look at me, in my new hairdo, but was craning his neck back to look above him. 'Get a candle. It's too dark to see.'

'Get it yourself, at your leisure, when and if you feel like it, my dear Mr Sinclair,' I suggested. Then I nipped smartly out of the passage and pushed the panel closed on him. I leaned against the wall, which had quite the opposite result from what I intended. It sent me sailing inward, while the other side opened up, instead of barring Sinclair within.

'Thank you. You are extremely helpful,' he said, with a curt bow, before he turned to go out the door in search of a light.

'There is one on the table, stupid,' I was happy to remind him.

His nostrils were beginning to dilate by the time he got back with the candle and tinderbox, both from the séance table. He lit the taper and held it up above his head to try to decide whether it was a trapdoor he looked at. 'Can't tell. It looks like it. I'll lift you up.'

'I'll lift *you* up. I'm bigger.'

'You are not bigger than I am.'

'I'm taller.'

'We are the same height when you are wearing high heels. I

don't see why ladies wear such uncomfortable things.'

'Come, hop on my shoulders, Welland. I can bear the weight.' I certainly had no intention of letting him bear mine. The occasional time does crop up when I could wish I were a trifle smaller. This was one of them.

'I'll get a chair,' he said, after mentally weighing me, and deciding he was not eager to embarrass himself by failing to get me off the floor, or worse, dropping me.

Even with a chair, he could scarcely reach the area suspected of being a door. He poked at it, and decided it was only a crack in the wooden planks. He was careful to take the chair back to the table himself, instead of asking me to do it.

'So we know the Franconis are a pair of frauds; we know how they do it, but we really still do not know that they are the ones getting large sums from Lady Sinclair. It may be only the guinea a sitting they are making. That's all I pay them. They have not even hinted for more. They don't live in a high style either – no carriage, nothing of that sort. This may be a total irrelevance to the major mystery going forth here.'

'Will you be going to Suffolk to see what you can discover anyway?'

'Not till my reluctant assistant gets her nose into the scriptorium.'

'You don't have an *assistant*, Welland. You have an equal partner.'

'It is time for the sherries,' he decreed, brushing the dust from his hands and jacket.

'I'll try to examine the records this afternoon, if I can find a chance.'

'My sweet idiot partner, I shall *make* a chance for you this afternoon. I shall beguile your aunt to come out for a drive, to allow you the opportunity.'

'I don't expect she'll go with you. She does not care much for you.'

'We shall see. I can *usually* persuade a lady to do as I wish. Not all of them are so headstrong as some parties, who shall be nameless.'

'Hill is coming for lunch. She may go out with him,' I mentioned, for I really had grave doubts that Auntie would prove biddable to his persuasions.

'Excellent. I too shall accept an invitation to lunch, if it is offered. Thank you, Miss Ford. I would be delighted to take my mutton with you. I *do* hope it is not actually mutton. Better tell someone I am staying. At your leisure of course,' he added quickly.

'I believe I hear Pierre lumbering toward us,' I cautioned, as slow footfalls were heard in the hallway beyond.

'No exit. We're caught.'

'I don't mind. He is coming to seem less annoying lately. I wonder what can account for it.'

'Simple bad taste on your part,' he opined as he strolled from the room, leaving me standing alone, trying to think of a setdown.

Chapter Fourteen

We were all – Aunt Loo, Dr Hill, Pierre and I – subjected to a disgusting display of servility over luncheon. My aunt was the butt of it. I expect it is the manner in which Mr Sinclair butters up his patron when he is at Tanglewood. Aunt Loo was praised for everything from her latest wisp of a chiffon tent to her mutton. At least it was mutton, which gave me some satisfaction. Initially, Aunt Loo's brows rose in astonishment at the compliments, but as we progressed to the dessert, astonishment ascended to pleasure, and eventually to girlish titters, tinged with coyness. Before coffee was poured, she had accepted to drive out with Welland. He cocked a triumphant brow at me and relayed a tacit command to get to the scriptorium.

'I ought not to take you away from your work,' Loo mentioned, but in no resolute manner.

'My work nears completion. In such weather as this, no man with blood in his veins can stay cooped up all day.'

'I also have got bloods in the veins,' Pierre said, with an adoring smile in my direction.

'Hot blood,' Welland warned.

'I must wash my hair this afternoon,' I said quickly, grasping at the first excuse that offered.

After a few glowers and as many comments that the hairs did not look soiled, Pierre eventually decided he would drive into the village, where he would doubtlessly annoy every chaperone on the streets with his marked ogling of their charges.

'Would you mind dropping in at the bank for me, Peter?' Welland asked. 'I have got a draft from St Regis that I am eager to cash.'

'I do not go to the bank,' was Pierre's sulky reply. There were not likely to be any young ladies in that establishment of course.

'Pity I had not known. I was there this morning,' Dr Hill said. 'How much is your draft for, Mr Sinclair? Perhaps I can oblige you.'

'Only five pounds. It would save Lady Sinclair and me the bother of trotting into the village before our drive, if you could.'

'I can manage five,' Hill said.

When Loo went to prepare herself for the outing, I followed her upstairs. 'Rather sweet of Mr Sinclair to offer to drive me out,' she said, still smiling. 'I never cared for the young fellow above half, but I know he is reporting to St Regis, and I must be nice to him. He could be a helpful friend.'

I had not come to twit her about her change of heart. I got right down to it. 'Are you worried he will tell St Regis about your selling off the family heirlooms, Auntie? You have known all along what I saw in his room that night was the jewels you sold.'

I half hoped she would deny it. 'I felt it must be the case,' she admitted. 'He will have told St Regis. No question of that. What I hope to do is explain to him *why* I did it.'

'I trust you will think of some other explanation than giving the money to Papa.'

'Oh, dear, he told you! I was hoping he would not.'

'He told me. What I am curious to discover is what you *did* do with it.'

'Money just dribbles away, Valerie. If you ever had any real quantity of it, you would realize how it happens. Edward left debts to be paid off. There are the servants' salaries, food, the house to maintain, the barn St Regis made me repair.'

'There is ten thousand from which to cover those ordinary

expenses. Papa manages a larger family on a tenth of that sum.'

'To be sure, he was always a clever manager, but the tenants don't always pay their rents, you must know. I don't *always* get ten thousand. Do you think this blue bonnet, Valerie, or the black?'

'I think you are evading the issue.'

'Yes, my dear, I am, for it is really not your business, is it?'

There was obviously no decent reply to her question. I hoped Welland would have better luck than I. He had sweet-talked her into the drive; anything was possible.

Welland was just stuffing the money into his wallet when we came downstairs. Dr Hill took his leave, Pierre tried one more time to discourage me from washing my hair, then he too left, and I finally got into the scriptorium. It took several minutes to find that portion of the cupboards where old accounts were kept. I flipped through them quickly, my eyes alert for the single word 'Suffolk.' It was a thoroughly dull afternoon's work I can tell you. How had I let him stick *me* with this job, while he jauntered down the pretty country lanes behind a pair of high steppers? My aunt had no recognizable manner of keeping accounts. There was a bootbox ful of loose bills, none of them bearing the address looked for. I dug deeper, drawing out hard-covered account books from the days of Sir Edward, but still the magical word did not occur. It was in a metal box at the back of the cupboard that I made the discovery, and really I did not see it as being particularly helpful.

What I refer to is the fact that Sir Edward's first wife, Alice Sedgely, came from Suffolk, not far from Blaxhall. Little Glemham was the name of the village. The last box held personal papers, letters from her father and her father's solicitors arranging the marriage settlement, even the marriage certificate, but nothing seemed of particular significance. His wife had been dead for two decades. I read the letters without any feeling of guilt or shame. The two main characters were dead, which made their story seem more like history or fiction than prying on my part. The first Lady

Sinclair had brought a few servants with her, providing some hope for a contemporary representative of Suffolk in the house, but the names were not familiar. I knew the servants' names from Pinny, an incurable chatterer. Alice had brought her own woman, a dresser cum companion, and a maid to help in the kitchen, but this had been nearly thirty years ago. The names were no longer heard at Troy Fenners.

I could make nothing of it, but decided to let Welland peruse the contents, to which end I would smuggle them out of Auntie's scriptorium. In passing, I took a look at her story, spread in an awful jumble on her desk. Gloria was just saddling up her mount at the end of chapter seventeen. The first sentence of chapter eighteen revealed that she was off on her mad gallop down the turnpike road. Before the sun set, or at least before Loo took up pen again, she would want details about how it felt to fly over a six-foot house, mounted on horseback. I could tell her the very anticipation of it sent my heart to wild beating, but this would not be enough to satisfy her. Maybe I could *pretend* I had done it.

As I did not have time to wash my hair, I was amused at Pierre's heavy complimenting on how brightly it shone 'with all the soils gone from it.' Of course he did not really have a very good view of my hair from his low height. I sat with him in the saloon, passing the time and busying his hands by playing piquet, till Welland and Loo returned. She was still smiling when they entered, but the wearing pastime was beginning to show on her companion, who looked hagged from the necessary show of good spirits.

It was while we were having our sherries that Mr Sinclair surprised us all by inviting us to dinner at the gatehouse. He wished to have us that same evening, with a man's simple ignorance of the fact that cook had been at work already for a few hours making her preparations here.

'It would be more than my life is worth to give cook such a message at four-thirty in the afternoon,' Loo told him.

'Tomorrow, then. Make it lunch tomorrow,' he pressed on. 'We shall ask Dr Hill to join us as well, and have a little party.'

'Walter mentioned he is going to visit his friend at Southampton tomorrow,' Lady Sinclair told him. 'He will not be back till evening. He has a medical friend from London who retired at the same time as he, and opened a nursing home near Southampton. They usually get together once a month or so to talk over old times. Walter goes there, since Dr Bentz has trouble getting away from his sanatorium.'

'That is only twenty miles away. He can be back in time for dinner. We'll eat late to accommodate him,' Welland insisted, with some curious excitement indicated by his manner of speech.

'You had best let him know today, then,' Loo advised. 'He leaves early in the morning, to be there for luncheon with his friend, and have time for a chat.'

'I'll take a run down to his cottage now in my curricle and invite him,' he answered. 'Come with me, Valerie. You have not been out today. The fresh air will do you good.'

'Yes, I'll tag along.' I was eager to impart my meager findings to him.

'I also like to be going,' Pierre said at once.

'What a pity my curricle only holds two comfortably,' Welland said, with every show of regret.

'We shall be squeezing in,' Pierre suggested.

'No, thank you. I have had enough of your squeezing, Peter,' I said, and arose up to get my bonnet.

'I'll talk to you later, Peter. I have something I want to ask you,' Sinclair said, as a palliative for robbing him of the excellent squeeze.

'What I must be purchasing is the curricle for driving my own ladies my own self,' Pierre decided. 'Very fine yellow curricle, with only two seats. This will be most excellent for ladies.'

By the time I had brushed out my curls and tied up my bonnet, which I did in my room, the delighted squeals of an upstairs maid, cornered by Pierre, were issuing down the hall.

'That wench ought to be turned off,' Pinny adjured. 'When she ain't winking at the footmen, she's hotfooting it after Mr St Clair. Disgraceful I call it.'

'You're just jealous, Pinny,' I teased her. 'Why don't you roll your eyes at him and see if you can steal him from her?'

'My eyes don't roll, miss. They only squint up like a mole caught in the sun,' she answered simply.

'Maybe you should wear green glasses.'

'Mr Sinclair beat me to them. He took up the old pair belonging to Sir Edward's father as soon as ever he came across them.'

'You mean he only started wearing them after he got here?' I remembered Auntie saying St Regis told her in his letter that Welland required them.

'It's only what his valet told me,' she replied, blushing red as a beet.

'Pinny, are you seeing Mr Sinclair's valet?' I asked. 'Once in a while I do,' she admitted. 'Napier is ever so nice, miss. Not a forward sort of a lad at all.'

'Good for you! See what you can pry out of him about a certain Mary Milne, will you?'

'Oh, miss,' she tittered, thinking I was joking, till I advised her otherwise.

'I'll ask him tonight,' she volunteered, when she understood me to be serious. 'It's strange he never said a word about her, for he's always singing his master's praises.'

'Will you just check in a subtle way too whether Mr Sinclair was wearing green glasses before he came here. St Regis said he needed them. It is odd he didn't bring any with him, if that is the case.'

'Napier mentioned how they found them at the gatehouse, and Mr Sinclair hadn't had them off his nose since. Isn't that odd, then, miss?'

'There are many odd things go on with that pair,' I said.

'If you're talking about Napier giving Diablo the wrong feed and causing the colic, miss, it ain't his fault. He never had to do stable work before. He's Mr Sinclair's valet. He looks after all his jackets and linen and boots.'

Not the least odd thing about Sinclair was that he had such a handsome wardrobe, and a full-time valet apparently, when at Tanglewood. Not many secretaries were so well looked after.

'All set?' Welland asked when I descended the stairs.

'Yes. I have earned this outing, since I spent my afternoon in a stuffy office, rooting through old papers while you had the pleasure of a drive.'

'Why did you not open a window if it was stuffy?' was his unsympathetic question.

'Because it would have blown the papers all over.'

'Did you find anything?'

I outlined my scanty find, while he listened silently. 'I had no idea Alice Sedgely was from Suffolk,' was his only comment. 'I assumed she was a local girl.'

'There is no reason you should know.'

'St Regis takes a keen interest in all the family, even the French branch.'

'Pity his interest did not include where the wives came from, and I might have been saved a boring afternoon's work. I don't see what it can possibly have to do with Auntie's missing funds either.'

'There was talk of a mysterious lady at the first séance, remember?'

'How could it refer to Alice Sedgely? How do you do justice to a corpse?'

'I have no idea. Can you smuggle the carton of papers out to me?'

'I'll have Pinny take it to the kitchen as though it were waste paper, and you can pick it up at the back door. Or better, have your valet do it, Welland,' I asked, smiling at the opportunity this would throw in Pinny's path.

'Do you think we ought to encourage the servants to carry on so wantonly?' he asked, aware of the attachment.

'Pinny is not a wanton. If your man is not serious, pray do not encourage him to see her. She is such a sweet little thing.'

'Barring the squint.'

'Pity you beat her to the family's green glasses.'

He turned and directed a stare at me, then reached up and removed the offending lenses. 'I accidentally left mine at home. I was fortunate to find this replacement at the gatehouse.'

'A strange accident, to forget them when you were about to make a long journey in the daylight. I should think you would have remembered before you got ten feet. Who are you hiding from? No one here would recognize you if you are some desperate criminal in disguise.'

'St Regis mentioned in his letter of introduction to your aunt that I wear green glasses. There is no mystery to it.'

'I find it mysterious you know the contents of that letter, sir. It was written by St Regis, and delivered to my aunt.'

'It was written by *me*, *for* St Regis. I am his secretary. A secretary writes letters, among other things. Did you ask Lady Sinclair about the heirlooms?'

'Yes, she confirmed your story. Did she convince you to put in a good word for her with your patron? That's why she agreed to drive out with you, you know. Don't think your shop-worn charms had anything to do with it.'

'Are you always such a delightful conversationalist, or has the stuffy room got you in a bad mood? Take deep breaths, and I shall tell you about the drive. She knew I was acting for St Regis in buying back the jewelry. She asked me if he was very angry, and tried to convince *me* to convince *him* not to press charges.'

'She has a high opinion of your influence over St Regis.'

'Not unduly high. He listens to me. Unfortunately, she gave me no reason for having sold the stuff, other than that she needed cash. It is not a good enough reason.'

'She wouldn't tell me a thing either. *I* still think it's the

Franconis. They'd be sly enough not to flaunt the money if they had it. They'll move away and set up in the next county with her cash. It's not fair.'

'I'm not sure they are sly enough to be doing it.'

Dr Hill was happy to accept the invitation to dinner the next evening. He served us wine in his rose garden, talking of his hobby, archaeology. Welland was a better partner in this subject than I. He had some little interest in it. They discussed the Rosetta Stone, some tablet from the banks of the Nile, which seemed to be of wonderful importance, if only someone could decipher its hieroglyphics.

'Lenoir's work was pure rubbish,' Hill said. 'Botched up scholarship, eked out with pure invention. I have got a copy of it translated from the French. Are you familiar with it, Mr Sinclair?'

'St Regis has the French version. He agrees with you that it is nonsense, and speaks often of a young French fellow, Champollion, who is expected to do better, though he is very young. Quite a genius, I believe.'

'Yes, I am familiar with his work. His *Egypt Under the Pharaohs* is remarkable, and done by a mere stripling. The French have the jump on us in Egyptian matters, due to Bonaparte's campaign there.'

'I expect you have heard the deSancy archaeological library from Paris is up for sale?' Welland asked, while I picked a rose and began pulling off its petals to put in my pocket, for the scent.

'I did not hear it! When did this happen? How was it got out of Paris at this time?'

'Smuggled out by an escaped aristo, I believe. Peter mentioned it to me. I wrote St Regis at once and told him.'

'Who has it? What price is being asked?'

'Millar, from Lombard Street in London, the fellow who deals in rare books and expensive collections has it. The asking price is two thousand pounds. A bit steep for an individual.'

'That is a great deal of money.'

'It will likely end up in a university library, where it belongs.'

'The proper place for it. Or the British Museum, where scholars can get a chance to look at it.'

'Exactly. Well, Doctor, we must be going now. Thank you very much for the wine. We shall expect to see you tomorrow evening at seven.'

'I look forward to it. Nice to have the young people visit.'

After we had taken our leave and were in the curricle returning to Troy Fenners, I said, 'I'm glad Aunt Loo has a good friend living close by. He's nice, isn't he?'

'He's interesting. A very elegant little house, is it not?' We had been inside before moving out to the rose garden. 'An extensive library, and some quite excellent paintings.'

'The bibelots are his wife's dowry. He told me so on my first visit. About the books, he is a scholar. I hope you are not thinking *he* has anything to do with this blackmailing business. He dotes on Aunt Loo. I should not be at all surprised to see a match between them.'

'Marrying money is one way of getting one's hands on it.'

'Very true, but I doubt *Dr Hill* would be so low as to marry for money,' I said innocently.

My hit was rewarded by no more than a slight stiffening of the jaw muscles. 'I wonder if he ever actually proposed to her,' he said a little later.

'Shall I ask her, and be accused of prying again?'

'Please do, discreetly. You might also assume your innocent look and hint whether the good doctor has ever had any dealings in Suffolk, if a likely opportunity should arise. Lest there be any misunderstanding, that means you create the opportunity.'

'I shall raise the subject of Mr Franconi being from there, my own regret at never having seen the place, and throw in at the end, quite as a postscript, a question as to whether Hill has been.'

'Why not just announce we are trying to tie him to the blackmail? Don't mention Franconi in the same discussion. Say some friend or relation is going there on a visit. It will sound more by chance.'

'Why would anyone go to Suffolk? Flat terrain and marshes. . . .'

'It is a prime agricultural district. Your papa is a farmer. A spot of imagination might find him an excuse to visit. Must I do *all* the thinking for us?'

'Don't whine, dear boy. It is so terribly unattractive. So far as I can tell, St Regis does your thinking for you, so you can spare your brain to do mine for me.'

'I am more than a scribe and errand boy for St Regis. He's not really such a bad fellow as your aunt thinks. I think you might like him. He is neither a nipfarthing, nor does he take a consuming interest in matters that do not concern him. Troy Fenners *does* concern him, since it will be his one day, and there is no reason he should inherit a load of debt with it.'

'I know very well he is no nipcheese, Welland. Did he not send you a whole five pounds today? Is it your quarter allowance, or a bonus for buying back the heirlooms?'

'My annual salary,' he answered humbly. 'But he also houses and feeds me, you know, and occasionally tosses me a few pennies when I am ripe for a spree – a night on the town.'

'How nice for you. I wish I had a rich patron.'

'I suppose you are hinting for that guinea I promised you when Aunt Loo failed to come across. I have not forgotten it. I have one of my precious five pounds earmarked just for you.'

'It was a guinea we spoke of.'

'I can swing the extra shilling too. Will you take payment in coin or paper currency?'

'In hair ribbons, Mr Sinclair. That's all it is good for.'

'Any preference as to shade?'

'You decide what will suit me.'

'Then it will be emeralds, not ribbons.'

'A nice one-guinea emerald, the paste sort that Auntie has in her vault it will be.'

'You would prefer a gentleman who could supply you with real ones, I expect?'

'Not necessarily, but I would insist on a gentleman who supplied me with whatever he supplied me with himself, not through the courtesy of his patron. I am very demanding in that respect. A little idiosyncrasy of mine, liking a man who stands on his own feet.'

Mr Sinclair suddenly developed a keen interest in the back of his team's heads. After a few moments' sulking, he said, 'Can I pick up the carton of papers now, while I am at the house, instead of waiting for you to set up a tryst with Pinny and my valet?'

'If the coast is clear, I shall throw them out the window.' As it turned out, the coast was so clear I was able to carry the carton down the front stairs and hand it to him at the foot of the stairs. 'A little light reading for you, when you become tired with ghosts.'

He grimaced at the weight. My own arms felt as though they would like to rise up in the air when I unloaded them, so heavy was the box. 'This will keep me busy tonight,' was his highly unsatisfactory remark.

'I shall be busy fighting off Pierre's advances.'

'A well-inlaid gent, Valerie. I am surprised you don't let him win occasionally.'

'*You* would be. Not everyone is on the catch for a fortune. Happy reading,' I said, and ran upstairs, feeling I had belabored my point as much as I could without becoming a bore on the subject.

Chapter Fifteen

I had to fight off not only the advances of a determined Pierre, but an even more determined Aunt Louise that evening. Her advances had to do with my putting Nancy over the tollbooth. 'For I have reached chapter eighteen, and must get on with describing the jump,' she explained patiently.

'Nancy seems to be developing a sprain.'

'I'll have the groom tend to it. It must be done tomorrow at the latest. You have been down and checked out the booth, I hope.'

'Several times.' It grew a foot every time I went down.

'Ah, good, then you will have figured out your approach, and all that. We'll go down about ten-thirty tomorrow morning, while you and Nancy are fresh, and the crowds on the road are not dense. I have worked out that the traffic is lightest at that time. Those going to the village go earlier, for market and work and so on, and between ten-thirty and noon there is very little traffic. Just a few ladies making calls, and even they do not go out in volume before eleven. Ten-thirty is our time.'

'Could you not just describe it from your imagination, Auntie? You have such a wonderfully vivid imagination.'

'Yes, I have, but I like to get my facts all straight too. That is what sets me a little apart from the other writers, you know, the accuracy. When I had Debora's uncle dope her for the second last chapter of *Search for the Unknown*, I had Walter make up a black drop and took it myself. I was gibbering for ten days afterward, but it was worth every gibber. My account of Debora under the influence of opium was much praised, Valerie. Such horrors as went through my poor head. I thought Alice was accusing . . . all sorts of horrid things. Goblins and ghosts and green giraffes. I don't know where the green giraffes came from, unless it was my having read an extract about them the day before, out in the garden with the green grass and trees all around me. The giraffes' necks reached right up past the trees. And they were singing, which is so very strange, for they don't, you know. Talk I mean, or make any noise at all. They are quite mute.'

'Alice was accusing whom, of what?' I asked, when she had run to a stop.

'The green giraffes of singing when they should have been silent,' she replied with a conning smile. She might as well have been a giraffe herself for any information I could ever wring out of her.

It was not anticipated that Welland Sinclair would visit us that evening, but at about nine-thirty he came up, complaining of tired eyes from all his reading. This conveyed to me something quite different from what it conveyed to my aunt. 'You work too hard on your treatise, Welland,' she scolded, quite like a fond aunt, which was not her customary manner of dealing with him.

'I am eager to finish up and return home,' he answered.

'You must be, with your wedding getting closer all the time. July the tenth I think you mentioned as the date?'

'That's right.'

'Will you and Mary live at Tanglewood, or does she have a place of her own?' my aunt asked.

Sinclair twitched in his chair, disliking this line of talk before my disapproving presence. 'That has all been arranged long ago. We have the dower house at Tanglewood,' he replied stiffly.

'St Regis is very generous to you. Do you find him usually a generous, understanding man?' was her next hopeful question.

'Extremely generous, yes.'

'He must have changed a great deal. I find he never gives an inch on anything.'

'He has been kind to *me*. Is Peter here? I came to see him actually.'

'He is having a cold tub. Valerie recommended it, he tells me. Why did you do that, Valerie? A cold tub is more uncomfortable than anything, even in summer,' my aunt chided.

'He was overheated,' I answered briefly. 'I shall have him called, if Mr Sinclair only came to see him.' There was a bellcord in the room, but I was so incensed at the conversation that I went myself to call him. He was still following my instructions abovestairs, so we had to wait a few minutes for him.

'I hope it will be a nice day tomorrow,' Aunt Loo was saying when I returned.

'Yes, with your friend, Dr Hill, making his trip, it would be a pity if it rained,' Welland answered, with a noticeable lack of enthusiasm.

'Dr Hill? Oh, no, I referred to Valerie's plan.'

'What plan is that? You spoke of no plan to me,' he said, turning his head quickly in my direction. 'Are you going somewhere too?'

'No, I plan to ride. That is all my aunt meant.'

'It is the jump I referred to,' Auntie said, fearing I was trying to shab off on her again.

'What jump is this?' he asked.

'The tollbooth,' Loo blurted out, before it occurred to her that our visitor was supposedly unaware of her novel writing, and the purpose for my feat of daring.

'What!' he shouted, rising up on his feet.

Then, when the damage was done, she collected her wits and dumped the whole idea in my dish. 'Dr Hill has told us the previous owner jumped Nancy over the tollbooth, and Valerie is eager to try it,' she explained, with never a mention of her own involvement.

'Don't be ridiculous! It's impossible. You'll fall and kill yourself.'

'I am not quite set on doing it,' I capitulated, looking to see if Loo was deterred by this objective opinion.

'There is no danger in it. It has been done once already,' Aunt Loo assured him.

'Not by a *woman*,' was his immediate, instinctive response.

I had been long wavering between mortal terror and a creeping urge to give it a go. The creeping urge leapt forward at this slur on womanhood. 'I can jump as well as any man,' I said calmly.

'No sane man would try it,' he pointed out. 'It is the greatest foolishness I ever heard of. I *forbid* it.'

Aunt Loo began poohing in her ineffectual way, while I, like our caller, jumped to my feet to glare at his spectacles. 'Forbid it? *Forbid it*?!!' I demanded, my voice rising alarmingly at his impertinence. 'I'll have you know, sir, my own father has not *forbidden* me to do anything in three years.'

'It is patently clear you have been allowed to get out of hand. You *must* forbid this folly, Lady Sinclair,' he said, turning his attack to her.

There was more poohing, but no mention of an injunction against the act by Lady Sinclair. 'Valerie is strong as an ox. A great walloping monster of a girl. She can do it if any woman can.'

It is one thing to be called Junoesque; even Amazonian I can tolerate, but to be called an ox, and in front of a young gentleman too, was coming it a bit strong for me. I opened my mouth to object to these descriptions.

Welland opened his faster and beat me to it. 'No woman *can* do it!' he declared.

I knew at that moment that one strapping monster of a girl was going to try. 'Would you care to place a wager, Mr Sinclair?' I asked, my spirit kindling. 'The five pounds your patron sent you for being a good, docile puppet, perhaps?'

'You are not making the attempt,' he stated flatly.

Pierre came waddling in at his customary, leisurely gait. His hair was slicked down from his recent dunking. 'I have had the cold bath,' he reported to me with a bow. 'It do not moisten down the ardors like you are suggesting, Valerie.'

'Dampen, Peter. Dampen the ardor,' I said, happy for the interruption. There was a sound remarkably like a snort from Sinclair's direction. 'I think Mr Sinclair could benefit from one as well.'

'But no, absolutely,' Pierre warned his cousin. 'It is very much unpleasant. I am taking the rheum, I think. You shall be nurse for me if I am becoming ill, Valerie.'

'It is Valerie who will require nursing if she tackles the jump she plans,' Welland retorted. 'It is her intention to jump Nancy over the tollbooth,' he informed Pierre.

'Very excellent,' Peter replied. 'I have heard before these story of jumping Nancy high. I wish you *bonne chance*. That means the good luck, as we English say,' he explained, rectifying his lapse into his mother tongue.

'Are you all out of your *minds*?' Welland demanded of the room at large. There was no actual oral reply, but only looks and stares of various sorts.

'Why you are wanting to see me for, Cousin?' Peter asked into the silence.

Sinclair shook himself to attention, straightened his shoulders and said, 'I wanted you to accompany me on a ride tomorrow. I am going to Winchester, and thought you might enjoy to see the cathedral.'

'Ah, the famous old church,' Pierre said, in a bored tone. 'I know much of its histories, how the old Saxon kings were put in the ground there.'

'Many other famous persons as well,' Welland added. 'The son of William the Conqueror. The place is well worth seeing. The choir is the longest in England, and the windows too quite fine. Will you come?'

'Absolutely. I like always to be looking at monuments. Many of these gothic churches I had to see also at home.'

This lukewarm enthusiasm was deemed enough encourage-
ment for Sinclair. It occurred to me I might be invited to join them,
to keep me away from the tollbooth, but no mention was made of
my going, even by Pierre. It was not till Mr Sinclair's visit was
ending that this possibility occurred to either of them. 'Would you
care to come with us, Miss Ford?' Welland inquired.

'No, thank you. I have other plans for tomorrow, you will
recall.'

He stood, glaring, for several seconds, then turned to Aunt Loo.
'Will you excuse us for a moment,' he said, bold as brass, then
took my hand and drew me out the door. I never saw such a
brazen display of bad manners in my entire life. My aunt was too
shocked to object, and Pierre too confused to know what to do.

'Let us hope Pierre does not decide to copy your manners,
mistaking them for those of a *gentleman*,' I said, when we were
standing alone in the cavernous hallway.

He consigned Pierre to hell's flames, and continued walking till
we were in a dark room occasionally used by the butler to rest his
bones at visiting hour, when he wishes to be near the door. He
took up a brace of candles from a hall table into the room. 'I want
you to promise me you will not attempt this jump while I am
away,' he said, under the misapprehension that he had anything
to say to my behavior.

I laughed in his face. 'I can promise you I *shall* attempt it, God
willing.'

'Very well, if that is the way you feel, I have done what I feel
compelled by conscience to do. Let it be on your own head. I
should think your concern for a *borrowed* mount, if not your own
limbs, would show you the wisdom of reconsidering, but I come to
realize wisdom forms no part of your makeup.'

'Neither has interfering in what does not concern me, Mr
Sinclair. I shall say good-evening to you, before I say something
less polite.'

I made a sweeping curtsy, and arose to see him standing with his arms crossed, leaning against the edge of the table. He appeared to be regarding his boots. When his head came up, his face wore a new expression. It was a conning smile.

'Wait till the next day. I'll jump with you,' was his offer, or his manner of delaying the feat at least. 'If Nancy really made that jump, Diablo could do it off his hocks. I remember hearing some tale of William Pitt doing it. If a Cornish tin dredger could do it, a St Regis certainly can.'

'Very likely, but I don't suppose St Regis would approve of your risking the mount he gave you – or is it *borrowed*? He does mount you, if I understand aright?'

'That's true. He'd have my head in a basket if I crippled Diablo,' he backtracked at once. 'It's not worth the risk. A mad idea; I *must* have been mad to have considered it for a second. You intend to go through with it?'

'Would you like me to put it in black and white, so you can reassure yourself every minute, instead of repeating the question? I am going through with it. And I shall be at your party tomorrow night, sir, with my two legs intact.'

'If you survive,' he said, in a tone of the utmost indifference, 'I would like you to do something for me in the afternoon.'

'Gladly, since you express your desire as a wish, and not a command.'

'See what you can find out from your aunt about the first Lady Sinclair. Alice Sedgely, I mean, not the first ancestor ever recorded by history.'

'I'll see what I can do. What, specifically, do you want to know?'

'Everything.'

'Hill might be of some help. You can ask him tomorrow evening. Alice was some kin or connection to Hill's wife, he tells me.'

'Really? I never heard that.'

'You have played the role of recluse too strenuously. You don't discover much about people by standing off from everyone.'

'That is precisely why I decided to go social, tossing these little soirées. I never knew Hill was connected to the Sinclairs by marriage. That figures though.'

'What do you mean?'

'Just that he has been around here for eons, a close friend of Sir Edward in the old days. It stands to reason he would come in contact with the mistress's kin, and if he were ambitious at all, it was a way for him to advance himself. His wife, you mentioned, was the original possessor of the decent pieces in his cottage. She would have been a step above him socially. Where else would he meet the high and mighty, but at Troy Fenners?'

'He had a fashionable practice on Harley Street in London.'

'*Ladies* don't marry their doctors and tooth drawers, Miss Ford.'

I exercised great self-control in not mentioning that *some* ladies married clerks and errand boys for the aristocracy. I know he appreciated my restraint, for he added, 'And he did not have a noble cousin to set up a good match for him, like some lucky fellows. He must have retired rather young from that Harley Street practice you mention. I wonder why he did so?'

'He did not like the city.'

'He must have made a good bundle all the same. He does not do much in the way of medical work hereabouts. I believe Loo is his sole patient, and she is not really ill. My house-keeper was at the local modiste the other day, and heard from her a Dr Bellanger is the local sawbones, the one everyone goes to. Mrs Harper had a strained back.'

'She must have been doing some housecleaning, lifting heavy boxes out from under beds.'

'She is privy to all my dark secrets. She comes from Tanglewood, you see.'

When he was about to leave, he wished me luck on my coming jump.

'Say a prayer for me. You will be at the cathedral, you know.'

'Cathedral? Oh – Winchester, yes,' he added quickly, but his first question made me wonder if he had any notion of going to the cathedral at all. 'Will you wish Lady Sinclair and Peter goodnight for me? I am feeling very tired, all of a sudden.'

'It would be the strain of holding your head and shoulders up straight for a whole ten minutes. Your voice too was hardly whining this evening. You must be careful not to overdo it, Welland.'

'The salubrious country air is having the desired effect.'

'What did he want?' was my aunt's first question when I rejoined her.

'He wanted to badger me not to jump tomorrow.'

'He takes a great deal on himself to *forbid* it,' she said, allowing herself to become angry, now that he had gone. 'He reminded me quite forcibly of old St Regis. They are like that, the whole family. Top-lofty. Sir Edward the same. *He* would not take no for an answer either.'

'He forced you to have him, did he?' I asked, knowing it was not the case. Louise was considered to have done very well for herself to have got him.

'He forced the wedding on faster than Mama liked. So close, after Alice's death, you know.'

I found that, in fact, I knew little about either Alice's death or her life. As Pierre had taken to his bed to recover from the chills, this was a good private opportunity to quiz Loo on those matters Welland had mentioned to me.

'Was he not heartbroken when she died?'

'It was not a love match, my dear. Parents had a good deal to say about making matches in those days. His cousin, St Regis, arranged it. That is, the late St Regis, not the present one. Actually, it was the one before the late one, if you follow me. The present St Regis's grandfather. Alice Sedgely was an heiress, some connection to the family, like Mary Milne in the present case. St Regis is foisting that match on to Welland. He admitted as much today, poor fellow. One cannot but feel a little sorry for him.

Anyway, there was not an atom of love lost between the pair of them, Edward and Alice. *I* think she meant to desert him, was running away to America with Arundel, and not going to visit Cornwall at all. Why would she go by ship to Cornwall? Though the *Princess Frederica* was certainly stopping there. It was named after the king's eldest daughter, you know, the ship.'

'Could you tell me that again, Auntie?'

'It is just as I have explained, Valerie. The young don't bother to listen today. Alice and Edward were not getting along well. She was seeing more than she should have of James Arundel, a distant cousin of her own, and no relation to Edward. They had some relations living at Cornwall, who invited her to visit them. Arundel decided to go at the same time to accompany her, along with an older relative, you know, to act as chaperone, but who is to say Aunt Gertrude was not in on it? She was the chaperone, if I recall aright. Edward and Alice were at Bath at the time, with Edward's mama. They went every spring, and that is how I came to meet them. Bath was fashionable in those days, not the dreary spot it is now.'

'The Fords never lived at Bath, did they? I don't remember hearing Papa mention it.'

'Your great-grandmother made her home there for several seasons. She retired there for the waters and because she hated her son's wife. That is my mama, who was an angel really, but Grandmama did not rub along with her. It had to do with raising the children like savages, which is not at all true, but only what Grandma said. Edward was trying to set up a flirtation with me the first year I met him, but Grandma was a Tartar. She would have none of it. He used to visit us every spring, however, despite her glowering and snapping at him.'

'Did Alice visit you too?'

'No, she never did, which is why Grandma disliked it so. Then Alice announced she was going to visit Cornwall, letting on she did not care for Bath. Arundel popped up out of nowhere with his

Aunt Gertrude to go with her, and they took the decision to go on the *Princess Frederica*, since it was leaving just at that time for America, but stopping at St Agnes in Cornwall to pick up something or other. The ship ran into a dreadful storm just off Trevose Head and sank. Nearly everyone on board was drowned, but a few sailors made it to shore, and told the tale. They could *swim*, you see. I believe you told me *you* swim, Valerie? I wonder if Gloria could. . . .'

This was no time for *Tenebrous Shadows*. 'Alice did not make it to shore?'

'None of the passengers did. It was from one of the sailors Edward got the hint that Alice had no notion of getting off at St Agnes, or Arundel or Gertrude either. There were *no* passengers aboard for Cornwall. The shipping company did not hire space out for such short jaunts. They wanted customers paying the full fare to America. And *that* is why Edward refused to keep up two years of mourning in the regular way, but married me out of hand, as soon as he was sure Alice was dead. Grandma raised a wicked row. Called me an ungrateful girl, and a wanton and conniver and I don't know what all else, but I *never* was making up to Edward while Alice was alive. *He* was the one who did the flirting. He told Grandma he meant to marry me at once, with or without her approval, so she did not disallow it, but she would not come to the wedding. Was not that *spiteful* of her? She knew as well as I that if I let him get away, I'd never land him, for there was mention of some lady around the village here he had in his eye too. But I do not mean to imply he was a *womanizer* exactly. It is only that he *appreciated* women a little more than most gentlemen. I see you smiling out of the corner of your lips, sly puss! I know what you are thinking!'

'What am I thinking?'

'That I could not manage him, but I could. What you do with a man like that is agree with him that *every* saucy baggage who walks through the door is a perfect beauty. Praise her a little harder than he does, and within two minutes he will be finding a fault in her. Edward liked *looking* at all the pretty girls, and flirting with them, but he liked dogs and horses too. He admired pretty *things*, that's all. We had a very quiet wedding. Too quiet, and then came straight home to Troy Fenners. All the neighbors were very nice about accepting me, for Alice was not at all popular, always feeling herself above the country people, and trying to draw Edward off to London twice a year, and in general acting like a queen when she was at home.'

'Dr Hill married some cousin of hers, I believe. What was the cousin like?'

'Quite different. Alice would never have married a doctor. She was too proud. But Walter's lady, you know, was getting a trifle long in the tooth, and was happy enough to take the first one who asked her. It was a good match for them both. It did not bother Walter that she was old and plain, and it did not seem to bother her that he was countrified. He let her smarten him up. Was happy to do it, for he was a little ambitious, you know, as a young man will be.'

'Now he is smartened up so much he will be making an offer for *you*, I fancy.'

She blushed and giggled like a schoolgirl making sheep eyes at her dancing master. 'I won't say he has not *asked* me. I expect St Regis would throw a fit. The fact is, he has some aging uncle he keeps threatening to send down to Troy Fenners for a visit. A retired colonel, a widower, who expresses a keen interest in turning country farmer. He has not *said* so, but he thinks I will marry the man. He is a regular matchmaker, St Regis. I don't know why he does not make a match for himself. He is of the age.'

'He probably has some heiress in his eye.'

'Yes, and will soon have her estates in his hands. Well, my dear, I think we should have some cocoa and go to bed. We have a busy day tomorrow. Chapter eighteen – I have been looking forward to getting at it.'

As I could think of no more questions, I agreed to cocoa, and an early bed in preparation for chapter eighteen.

Chapter Sixteen

$\mathcal{B}$y having Pinny spy for me. I was able to ensure missing Pierre at the breakfast table. My spirits were in enough turmoil without having to fight him off this morning. I ate more lightly than usual. I had only coffee, while awaiting Aunt Loo's descent, becoming more chickenhearted by the minute. I should have gone to the stable, got Nancy saddled up, and taken the jump the minute I came down, without thinking too much about it. It was nine o'clock when she entered, wearing not one of her ghost-hunting outfits, but a decent blue cambric gown. She would go in the carriage to the tollgate to watch me commit suicide, for that was about the way I viewed the project by that time.

'I want to see how Nancy looks, as well as learn how you feel, Valerie,' she said. 'How the tail flies out, you know, how the sun moves on the ripples of her muscles, the wild, frightened eyes of her. All that will make good reading. I mean to stretch the jump out to a couple of pages at least. I want a page of Gloria's thoughts and feelings, so be sure to remember how you *feel*.'

'Nauseated,' I told her, as a prelude.

'Now pray *don't* go and be sick on me. It must be done today. I hate patching up a story, leaving a blank here and there, and going back over it like a carpenter mending a broken chair. It must be done in sequence, or the flow is interrupted. And I shall describe how beautiful you look too, my dear, with the fear pulling your facial muscles taut, and your fingers clutching at the reins.

You will enjoy to read that, eh? But you must never reveal to your papa that it is you, or that I am Mrs Beaton.'

'Let's go.'

'I ain't ready. I have not had a cup of coffee yet, and we cannot make the jump till ten-thirty. You will have plenty of time to pull yourself together. You look a trifle pale. Where is my toast? I want toast and marmalade.'

While she dawdled over the meal, I went along to the stable, praying Nancy would have a sprained ankle, a pulled tendon, or a bad cold, that I might delay the jump another day. Upon seeing her empty stall, I felt a surge of hope. Dr Hill had taken her back, needed her for some reason. His own mount must have been crippled. 'Where is Nancy?' I asked the groom.

'Mr Sinclair took her, miss. Rode over to Winchester this morning he did, with Mr St Clair. He said you would understand.'

'Did he indeed!' I declared, caught in the grip of a powerful and fast-rising fury. 'How extremely thoughtful of him.'

'Did you not give him permission?' the man asked, fearing he had done wrong.

'No, I did not, but a lack of permission has never stopped Mr Sinclair from doing what he wanted.' I turned and stormed from the stable, plotting my revenge. It is strange it took me so long to realize what I must do. I hold my demented state of fury accountable. It was not till I got back to Aunt Loo that it occurred to me. I phrased it in a manner that I hoped she would find acceptable.

'Sinclair has exchanged mounts with me for the day, Auntie. He has taken Nancy to Winchester, and I am to make the jump on Diablo. I hope it will not interfere with your story.'

'Not at all, but do you think you can handle that wild stallion?'

'Diablo is a gelding. Sinclair must think I can, or he would not have made the exchange, would he?'

'Are you sure. . . ? But of course if Diablo is in the stall in Nancy's place, it is obviously his wish that you use his mount. He was afraid Nancy could not make it.' This rearranging of the facts satisfied her, and me. 'I know you will not come to any harm. It would be a pity if you destroyed St Regis's mount, for it is a valuable one, you must know.'

Not a single word of concern about destroying myself. It was the horse that worried her. 'I'll drive with you in the carriage to the gatehouse. I am to pick up Diablo there.'

'Very well. Let us go. I have got my pad and pencil and telescope. I don't want to miss a single detail.'

'Pity Dr Hill is not here,' I said forlornly, thinking I might have need of him.

'He would enjoy to see it, but it would mean more to him if it were Nancy that was to do the jumping.'

I got down from the carriage and walked round to the gatehouse stable, a small affair with stabling for only four animals. There were three there – Sinclair's team of grays used with his curricle, and Diablo. The animal was large. He stood sixteen hands high. His long silky, black tail switched back and forth. When I reached out to pat his haunch tentatively, he lifted his head, his black mane shaking, and turned to stare at me, just as though he were a person. He had fine, large eyes, the bulging forehead and small concave nose of the purebred. He dilated his nostrils and whinnied, giving one a good explanation for his name. He did indeed look diabolically mischievous.

While I tried to make my peace with the animal, Sinclair's valet-cum-groom, Napier, came up behind me. 'That there is a purebred Arabian,' he boasted.

'Very nice.'

'St Regis bred and trained him at his own stables. He's a goer.'

'Manageable?' I dared to inquire.

'If you know how to ride him. Nobody ever has, except St Regis. And of course Mr Sinclair,' he added.

This conveyed to me what I was afraid to hear. The groom was going to be difficult about letting me take Diablo out of the stable. 'You must be Napier,' I said. 'I have heard my woman, Miss

Pincombe, speak of you, I think. She asked me to see if you have a moment free this morning. She most particularly wished to speak to you about some matter. She is free now.'

'Is she? I'll take a run up to the house now, then, as soon as you're finished looking around, ma'am.'

'Don't let me detain you,' I responded at once.

He stayed for a few more minutes, but eventually romance won out over good manners, and he was off. I let him get well up the hill to Troy Fenners before I untied Diablo's rope and led him, frisking merrily, from his stall. I am neither so short nor so frail as to have any difficulty getting a saddle down from its perch and buckled over a horse's back. It was, of course, not a lady's saddle, but I had used a man's before. I preferred it, and preferred riding astride as well for such a jump as awaited me. To get into a footman's trousers, however, would take time, and I had to get Diablo out before the groom returned. I could hardly ride down the public road astride in skirts either. I would take the jump sidesaddle.

Diablo seemed a compliant enough animal, so long as I patted his withers and flanks, and spoke in soothing tones. I led him to the mounting block, clambered up, and very carefully got on the beast. We generally assume animals lack intelligence. This one had the wits to lull me into a false sense of security till he was safely out of the stable. It was not till then he began living up to his name. He reared up on his hindlegs in an effort to be rid of me, his mane floating out on the breezes, while he whinnied in exultation of the fine day. He wheeled his crazy circles, cantered a few yards, then stopped suddenly. He backed up a couple of steps, then flew forward suddenly again; he did everything but get down on his knees and roll over to dump me in the dust.

The more antics he played off, the more determined I became he would not throw me. I held firmly to the reins, without jobbing him. When he had worked off his fit of fidgets, I patted his neck and called the soundrel a good boy. The performance led Aunt Loo, observing us from the carriage, to suggest I could not handle the mount. Diablo was completely amenable to flattery; a few more words of praise, and we went along fairly well.

'I can handle him,' I told her boldly.

Diablo looked over his shoulder with a sly smile, rolling his great shining eyes at me. I urged him forward at a trot till we reached the road, then let him out gradually. Not till the tollbooth appeared in the distance did I give him the office to fly. I had a sneaking suspicion Diablo had wanted to take that booth ever since he first laid his eyes on it. He went for it with a vengeance, his head lowered, neck stretched, hoofs flashing. I rode in rhythm with him, swinging my body forward as we approached the booth, to lessen the weight. There was none of the anticipated terror. I enjoyed every second of the flight, and flight it was, clearing the building by a safe margin of inches. It was a smooth landing too. Diablo's head came up, I relaxed somewhat, only then realizing how tense I had been.

If I seem to be emphasizing the victory with Diablo, drawing it out to a page like Mrs Beaton, it is to counterbalance the remainder of the ride. From the moment we hit the road on the far side of the booth, affairs took a sharp turn for the worse. I do not blame it on either rider or mount, but the mount's regular rider, Sinclair, who should have been half-way to Winchester, instead of jogging down the road from the opposite direction. I thought I must be seeing things, for to tell the truth, I had wished he had viewed my performance.

I suppose it was the unexpectedness of seeing Diablo flying over the rooftop that caused him to behave so foolishly. He stood up in Nancy's stirrups and shouted at us, waving his arms and generally acting like a Johnnie Raw. Diablo – I am convinced that animal possessed a human brain – was thrown into a pelter by the display, and feared for his hide. Why else would he take into his Arabian head to go tearing down the road at fifty or so miles an hour? I tried to rein him in, without quite ruining his mouth. Before too many yards, I forgot about his mouth and turned my worries to saving my own head. On we galloped, past astonished riders and staring drivers, nearly overturning a dung cart that was coming toward us, leaving any drivers going in our direction in a cloud of dust behind us. The easiest, indeed the *only* course open to me was to let Diablo run himself to a standstill, though I did keep jobbing mercilessly at his reins. Eventually he began slowing down to a mere thirty or forty miles an hour, allowing Sinclair, following behind on Nancy, to draw up beside us, and shout various curses and imprecations in our general direction.

When at last I drew Diablo to a halt, I was utterly spent, exhausted from fear and excitement and plain hard work. I looked down to see Sinclair striding angrily toward me, while Nancy turned aside to search for grass at the roadside, all unaware of the scene about to be enacted before her. Diablo, more interested in human affairs, looked quizzically to his master, to see if he was going to get the whipping he knew full well he deserved. My fingers went limp; the reins fell from them, and I slid down from the saddle. When I tried to stand up, my knees had turned to jelly, and I began sinking to the ground. Trees and barns and fields spun in giddy circles. Welland's face was an angry black and white smear before my eyes. I was quite sure I was going to be sick to my stomach.

Before I had quite sunk into the dust, Welland was galvanized into action. He grabbed me tightly to prevent my falling. I heard his short, shallow breaths in my ear, felt his heart pounding and hammering against my breast, could feel my own heart, which had mounted up into my throat, beating wildly. I closed my eyes and emitted a shaky, uneven sigh. A soft, violent curse was whispered into my ear. I shan't scandalize you by repeating it, but it had to do with insanity in the canine kingdom, female branch. I rested my head against his shoulder till the nausea passed, then a moment longer to give him time to worry about me, before I looked up. All the while we were under the observation of passersby, with carriages slowing to a crawl, and one outsized man on a small mule stopping entirely to stare.

'I did it!' I said triumphantly.

More profanity followed, heavy, professional, mouth-filling profanities. I expect he learned such heady language at Oxford. 'I should have known better!' he shouted when he had simmered down to a bubbling fury. 'How dare you subject a valuable mount that does not belong to you to such a risk!'

'Risk? You assured me he could do it.' My throat was too dry to say more.

'There's an inn,' he muttered. It was only a few hundred yards beyond.

'A glass of ale,' I replied, swallowing painfully with my dry throat.

He submitted, still trembling with anger, to this idea. I took one step and tumbled against him. Only then did he bother to inquire whether I had hurt myself, did it in a curt, abrupt way that did much to return my circulation to normal.

'Not in the least. It was delightful, till you came along and upset Diablo.' Diablo, listening, whinnied in offense as Sinclair took up his rein to lead him along with us.

'You're going to get a good beating too, when I get you home,' the gelding was told. You will find it difficult to believe the animal laughed out loud, but his snort sounded very humanly amused at the threat.

I wrenched my arm free of his grudging support and increased our pace. When the mounts had been stabled and we were ensconced in a private parlor, some semblance of rationality crept into our discourse. 'What were you doing coming from the west? You were supposed to be at Winchester.'

'We changed our minds. Peter remembered he had already seen the cathedral, and we went west instead.'

'Where did you go? Where is Peter? Why did you come back?'

'We were going to see a cockfight. It occurred to me about an hour after I left that you might decide to use Diablo for the jump, and I came straight back. Peter went on to see the fight. Now that we have *that* straightened out, I would like to hear the explanation for your audacity in taking Diablo without my permission.'

'Why, Welland, how obtuse of you. I took him for the same reason you took Nancy, *without permission.*'

'*Not* for the same reason. I took Nancy to save your life.'

'That's why I took Diablo, to save yours. I was ready to *kill* you, you see, till I realized you had left Diablo for me to use instead. You assured me, if you will hark back to last night, that he could do it from a standstill. I can't verify the point. We took a good run at it.'

'If that horse is injured in any way. . . .' he began, with a menacing scowl.

'Do you take me for a flat? We dealt famously together.'

'You were yanking at the bit so hard I'll be surprised if he hasn't got a split mouth.'

'He was just a little rattled toward the end, when you made such a foolish commotion, and frightened him. Pity, really. It went so beautifully till then.'

'What was I to think, to see a woman on a horse come sailing through the sky, about to land on my head! You should have had a scout on the other side, to be sure the coast was clear. And you should not have tackled it sidesaddle either.'

'I would have preferred to be astride, but I was afraid Napier would be back too soon.'

'How did Napier come to allow you to take Diablo out?' was his next angry question.

'Don't blame Napier. I lured him off to Troy Fenners by inventing a message from Pinny.'

'Lies and deceit at *every* turn!'

'Quite true. Deceit on *all* sides, including your own. I don't exclude Diablo either, letting on he was as tame as may be, till I got him out of the stable.'

A smile peeped out to hear this hint of trouble, so I was quick to minimize it.

'I am greatly surprised, astonished he would let you mount him at all. No one but me has ever ridden him before.'

'I can't believe my ears! You have forgotten the great and wonderful St Regis for a whole second. Napier assures me you and your patron are the sole riders. He has done your boasting for you. Now you see you have been overly cautious, and can recommend him to all your friends.'

'At least it is over. I can stop worrying about it. How was the jump?' he asked, unable to contain his curiosity longer.

'Perfect! I can't begin to describe the exhilaration. You should have been there, Welland. It was like *flying*. I bet he cleared the roof by three or four inches. Auntie will know.'

'Lady Sinclair? Was she there?'

'Why, yes, she was,' I said, wondering what had become of her.

'Imagine that woman allowing you. . . .' He stopped and shook his head ruefully. 'As if she would have a word to say about it.'

'Or *against* it. You are behind on your snooping. Get into the scriptorium and read chapter eighteen at the next opportunity.'

'Her readers will never believe it,' he said, but really he was more interested in the jump and was soon back at it. 'Did Diablo shy off at all, show any disinclination to taking the booth?'

'Not a bit of it. He has been wanting to do it for an age, I am convinced. He simply gobbled it up.'

'You are a lighter load than I. I wonder. . . .'

'He could carry you over easily.'

'I believe the toolshed at home is as high, and certainly a foot wider. He took that without flinching. When do I try it?'

'Choose your day, and I shall be there to terrorize him for you when you land on the other side.'

'I am sorry. It was a damned idiotic thing to do, but really, it took me by surprise, and when I recognized you, I was afraid you'd break your head wide open. I hoped I would get back before you tackled it. I thought you would have more organization – men to clear the road, and preferably a doctor standing by.'

'Good God, it was only a jump, not a duel!'

'It's a duel now. You are not going to outdo me.'

'Rubbish. I am undertaking arrangements to jump Nancy over St Paul's. But first I must find Auntie. She will be worried.'

'Not she.'

Before many minutes, she came bustling into the parlor, not at all worried, but only peeved that I had forgotten her. She was afraid I might forget those unforgettable sensations before she committed them to paper. Knowing she would be eaten up with questions that could only be posed in private, I suggested we leave at once.

'Right, and *I* shall ride Diablo,' Welland declared with an irate look.

'Go ahead, I have tamed him for you. You should not have any trouble.'

Auntie drove home in her carriage, while we went in advance on our mounts, discussing the morning's events. It was clear from his questions that Welland intended to repeat my act. It galled him that I had done what he hesitated to. 'Just do it,' I advised nonchalantly, making little of it. 'I shan't wait so long next time. It is the anticipation that is misery, not the doing.' He didn't say a word.

'There, you see, it is not so very huge after all,' I mentioned, as we approached the booth.

'See if there's anyone approaching on the other side,' he ordered, in his customary brusque manner.

I was delighted to comply on this occasion, for I had some hopes Diablo would be tired enough to balk at it a second time. There was no one coming. I rode up on the hillside to get a good view, to describe the sight for Aunt Loo. It was beautiful. I wish I were a painter, to have caught forever the graceful flowing form of steed and rider, sailing over the roof, with the tall willows swaying so peacefully behind. Diablo's mane stood straight up, while his tail was flat out behind him. Auntie would like to have these details. Welland's landing was rougher than my own, but I would not tell him so. I did not wish to spoil his moment of pure pleasure.

'Now that is what I call living,' was his simple statement when it was over. 'I am sorry I waited so long.'

Diablo whinnied in agreement, with one of his peculiarly human sounds.

Chapter Seventeen

I made my account to Aunt Loo as soon as we got home, omitting nothing of either actual jumping or observations of Welland's repetition. 'I wish he had waited till I got up to you. Why did you not ask him to, Valerie? You knew I wished most particularly to see it. I was not in position in time to see you go over either. Fancy Welland being so dashing! The tail straight behind, did you say?'

'Straight as a ruler, and the mane standing up.'

'That does not sound convincing about the mane. Are you sure it was not flying out behind, like the tail, whipping Gloria in the face, and causing her to loosen her grip?'

'Straight up. Gloria did not loosen her grip.'

'You were not frightened at all, you say, when you actually left the ground?'

'I was exultant, Auntie. It was pure bliss. Like being, kissed by someone very special.'

'Gloria would not know *that* before the last chapter, my dear! Though there is no reason she could not think of the jump when he kisses her at the end. No, I don't like it. She should not be thinking of a horse when her hero holds her in his embrace. She ought to be thinking of stars and flowers and eternity, feeling just a little vaporish, but not falling into hysterics. That would not do. The sense of inevitability will be her saving. She will know this has been her fate all along.'

'Her hero would give her a good shaking, or a slap to smarten her up if she went off into hysterics.'

'Oh, no! FitzClement would never *shake* her, and never, *never* strike a lady! My readers would not like it. The villain might be allowed to do so; not the hero. Not in anything but a fast French novel. We have our *standards* to maintain, Valerie. I cannot think you are reading as many gothic novels as you should be.'

I promised to do better, and escaped out into the hallway, thence to my room to be quizzed by Pinny as to why I had sent Napier to her.

'I disapprove of the lackadaisical way you are managing your young man, Pinny. You must make a push if you hope for an offer before he leaves. He shan't stay long, you know.'

'That's true, miss. He says Mr Sinclair has promised they won't be here but another week at the outside. He has to get back home to get ready for his wedding himself.'

'That soon! He did not say so!'

'Happen you should be making a bit of a push yourself, miss,' Pinny said, with a frightened glance at her temerity. I glared. 'Just joking, miss. I know you don't really care for him, but Napier, he says Mr Sinclair is always singing your praises. He thinks his master has *feelings* for you, miss, but we know he's engaged, so there's nothing to be done in that quarter. Will you be changing out of your habit now, miss?'

'Yes. I must wash up. I'll have the white spencer and yellow skirt.'

'I've been aching to see them on you, miss. Are you going visiting, that you're wearing that special outfit?'

'It is not a special outfit,' I objected, though I liked it better than most of my gowns. The spencer fit closely, looked well with the bouffant skirt. It was not in the latest fashion, but what enhanced the appearance was preferable to the latest fad. Romantic was the word Mama used when I had it made up. It seemed a proper outfit in which to go courting Miss Milne's fiancé. I had not realized time was pushing so hard at my back. Only a week in which to steal him from her. I hadn't a moment to lose.

As soon as lunch was over, I had the whisky harnessed up to go down to the gatehouse. Auntie, having missed her morning writing session, was to lock herself into the scriptorium to put Gloria through her paces at the tollbooth. I met Welland on the road, coming up to call on me. I had been too quick to go after him. I would have preferred to let him come calling, but was by no means sure he would do it, so pretended instead I was just going for a jog down the road in the whisky.

'Too bad you have changed out of your habit. I was looking forward to a good ride this afternoon,' he said.

There is not much I prefer to riding, but it is not the best means of advancing a romance. You have to wait till you find some secluded spot to dismount, and there is no saying one would be found in this territory that was still not too well known to me.

'Give Diablo a rest. He's earned it. I'll take you for a spin in the whisky instead.'

'I'll accept your offer, before you talk me into driving my grays.'

'What a splendid idea, Welland!' I said at once. 'Why did I not think of that?' Had my mind not been full of other more intriguing things, I would have done so.

'After the tongue-lashing I have just given my groom, I would be ashamed to let you drive them out of the stable, though I make no doubt you could handle them with one hand.'

He was sorely mistaken here. I had little experience handling the ribbons. The sole extravagance allowed me at home was my mount. I did not possess a phaeton, or anything of the sort. My experience was limited to the few times I had conned gentlemen into letting me drive their rigs: 'Let's walk instead,' I suggested. 'I'll leave the whisky at your stable, and we'll go for a stroll through the park.'

When he accepted this tedious pastime with great alacrity, I felt Miss Milne was in some danger of losing her beau. When he took a firm grip on my elbow as we strolled off to the west, I began to hope a week would be sufficient to detach him from her completely. The initial talk was not romantic, but then we did not have to rush things *that* much.

'Did you find out if Hill ever proposed to your aunt?' he asked, pretending not to notice that his hand had slid down from my elbow to grab my fingers. Holding hands is much more satisfying than having the elbow taken. His grip too was firm, as though he did not mean to let me slip away.

'He has offered. I wouldn't be much surprised if she takes him up on it.'

He nodded, then asked, 'How about the people from Suffolk? Anything there? Did she tell you anything about the other Lady Sinclair – Alice Sedgely?'

'I have the whole history at my fingertips,' I said. As we walked on, my eyes peeled for a private spot to stop, I recounted my aunt's Bath tale, including such items as Mr Arundel, the *Princess Frederica*, and America. 'It is only what is to be expected, of course, when a marriage of convenience is arranged for a couple.'

There was a nervous increase of pressure on my fingers. 'Let's keep this impersonal, shall we?' he asked.

'What do you mean? Welland, you cannot think I meant *you!*' I said, batting my lashes shamelessly.

'I don't think for one minute you mean anybody else. The fact is, I have been considering what you said about my marriage to Mary. A gentleman cannot call off without good reason, but as the whole affair was St Regis's doings in the first place, I have written asking him if it might be possible to work something out. Find someone else for Mary, I mean. Her heart will not be broken. She *likes* me, was agreeable to the match, but not – well, not in *love*, as you novel-reading ladies would say.'

'I don't read as many novels as I should,' I answered, weighing his statement, and deciding to take offense at his half-hearted attempt at disengaging himself. 'As to seeking St Regis's *permis-*

sion to lead your own life, it is disgusting. You're not a child.'

'I am not independent either.'

'We have already had this discussion, have we not?' I asked sharply, snatching back my hand, or trying to. He not only maintained his grip, but tightened it, which was about the most satisfactory thing he had done thus far.

'Yes, the night I kissed you.'

'Why do you raise the specter of *that* piece of poor behavior at this time?' I asked, my heart thumping.

'Because I feel a repetition of it coming on.'

'Don't think I am going to sneak behind bushes and doors to dally with you, Welland. That is not the way I carry on. Either your intentions toward me are honorable, or your conduct is unforgivable.'

'You knew all along I was engaged. It didn't bother you before.'

'Yes, it *did* bother me. Engagements have been broken before. This would not be the first time.'

He emitted a weary sigh. His fingers released mine and fell to his sides. His damned shoulders were drooping again. They had been much straighter when he was courting *me*. 'I must wait and see what St Regis has to say in answer to my letter.'

'I pity poor Mary Milne is all I can say. She's not marrying a man; she's marrying a – a – a puppet, who allows himself to be danced at his cousin's whim.'

'He's not really. . . .'

'Don't say another word in his defense. He is an interfering nipcheese, and a *woman* to boot, arranging matches like a bored spinster. I suppose he will order your jackets and linens and china for you as well.'

'This discussion has become not only pointless but demeaning to us both. Though before we part, I really must thank you for your blatant efforts to steal another lady's fiancé. I am flattered.'

'You should be!'

'I am. You could steal a much wealthier gentleman, if you had your wits about you.'

'You don't need those glasses either!' I said angrily, for I was curious to see his eyes, to see if he was at all impressed at my fine rant.

'Oh, but I *do*, Valkyrie! I must cast a shade over your vibrant charms, or I shall succumb to temptation again. I adore those spencers, by the by. So much more revealing than the high-waisted gowns the ladies favor this year. It suits you admirably. What is its real color?' he asked, reaching up to lift off his spectacles. He looked at me for about half a minute, the spencer and skirt, that is, nodding his head in approval. Then he looked me in the eye, with a laughing spark in his own. 'Do I put them back on, or do I kiss you?' was his bold question.

'Why don't you run home and write St Regis a letter, asking his opinion?' I asked helpfully. Never let it be said I was forward in hounding a man to the altar.

'I know what he would say,' he replied sardonically, sticking them back on his face, while I tried manfully to hide my rage. 'Do you really think I ought to shake free of him?'

'Only if you are interested in *growing up*, Welland.'

'I am not sure I'd ever be up to your weight. I ain't a thorough-bred Arab, you know.'

'No, I am convinced there is a strain of mule in there some-where.'

'Mules do not breed; they are sterile. Fancy a horsewoman like you not knowing that.'

'A slip of the lip. I meant jackass, of course.'

He made a convulsive movement toward me. I thought I had goaded him into action at last, but he pulled himself back, straightened his shoulders, and suggested we return to the stable, to let me continue my drive alone, since I would not like to have so asinine a companion cluttering up the whisky.

'An excellent idea,' I agreed, stiff with anger.

There was no hand-holding on the return route. We strode

briskly, not saying a word. I climbed unassisted into the gig and left, more or less forced to take a drive. In about two minutes he shot past me in his curricle, going fifteen or sixteen miles an hour. He pretended not to notice me. I turned around at the first farm I came to and went home, in a thoroughly wretched temper.

I was a pattern-card of civility at Welland's dinner party that evening. Dr Hill came to call for my aunt. I went with Pierre, who had returned from the cockfight just in time to change for the evening. 'How was the sport?' I asked him.

'Very much fine sport. Excellent.'

'I am glad you enjoyed it,' I said, wondering where he had actually gone. Had he been at a cockfight, he would have had more to say. I concluded he had spent his day chasing some girl or other, but his first speech to Sinclair, said while still at the front door of the gatehouse, caused me to wonder.

'I do every things like you tell me,' Pierre assured him. 'Spoke at the. . . .'

'Good. We'll discuss it later, Peter,' Welland said. 'Come in and take off your wrap, Valerie.'

I bowed coolly, said good-evening, and sailed past on Pierre's arm. I allowed Peter to help me off with my pelisse, made no objection when he reached up to nuzzle my neck, and only set him down when he followed that up with an arm around my waist. I refused to enter the saloon actually in his arms. Pierre was still at my elbow when I stopped to adjust my hair in the mirror. I caught Welland out in the act of frowning at us, saw him reflected in the mirror, I mean. He turned quickly away, pretending to be interested in something else.

I had some hopes Pierre's attentions might goad my lagging suitor into a fit of jealousy. I am sorry to relate it was not the case. Welland elected to sit with Aunt Loo and Dr Hill. The subject, when I managed to lend an ear, was archaeology again. The interval was put to use by me ferreting out where Pierre had actually spent his day. 'Was this your first cockfight?' I began.

'I never seed. . . .' he answered quite spontaneously, then with a guilty glance to his cousin, he changed his tack. 'The cockfights is not to talk to the ladies about. Very much blood and gory.'

'You would not have liked that. I wager you did not stay longer than half an hour. Come now, confess you were out chasing the girls.'

'Mom is the word. I can keeping the good secrets. I don't tell you who I am speaking at.'

'Now you are making me jealous, Peter. Who was she, eh?'

'No ladies are doctors,' he pointed out. 'The ladies' places is in their house.'

'Doctors' brought to mind Dr Hill, which soon brought to mind the sanatorium he had been at, which had another doctor in charge. 'You went to Southampton with Dr Hill, did you?'

He closed his lips hard, blew out his cheeks, turned scarlet, and glared at me. 'Please not to be saying nothing. It is the most great secret.'

His antics brought Welland darting to us. 'Pierre was just telling me that he was at the sanatorium, speaking to the doctor there,' I mentioned casually, though a little note of triumph intruded. 'I understand now how it came you were returning from the west, when you were supposedly headed to Winchester. Sorry to have interfered with your plans, Welland. And if you don't tell me *everything* this very instant, I shall ask Hill what is going on.'

He wanted to murder me. 'We'll speak of it later. Don't say a word.'

He was saved by the dinner bell. I entered the dining room wedged between my two guardians. 'If I feel so much as a toe molesting me under the table, the offender will get my soup poured over his head,' I warned. The two gentlemen exchanged offended glances, escorting me to the table in silence, where they took not the least heed of my warning. I tucked my feet safely under my chair, from which safe point it would take a contortionist to get at them. I enjoyed a lovely dinner.

The subject of Suffolk arose while we ate. Welland, in his own way, made the opportunity. 'So your father is off to Suffolk, is he, Valerie?' he asked, with a demanding look at me.

It was time to grill Dr Hill. 'Yes, to visit an exhibition of new farm equipment. Blaxhall he is going to. I have never been there. I hear it is not spectacularly beautiful. But then I am spoiled, being from Kent. Have you been to Kent, Dr Hill?'

'I certainly have. I admire it. It is justly called the Garden of England. A delightful spot.'

'How does it compare with Suffolk? Or have you been there at all?'

'My wife was from Suffolk,' he admitted readily. 'She was a Fowler. I have often visited her people. I still go once a year. Her parents are dead, but her sister and brother are alive. You know the Fowlers, Lady Sinclair. You met them once at my place, if memory serves.'

'Yes, Elizabeth sets a beautiful stitch. She promised me a pattern for a cushion cover, but never sent it. Hit her up for it next time you visit her, Walter. My eyes are beyond stitching, but Miss Brendan in the village could do it for me.'

'Do you happen to know the Sedgelys at all?' Welland asked, his face never lifting up from his plate to indicate any particular interest.

'I was well acquainted with Alice, Sir Edward's first wife. I do not visit the family, but I know them, due to my own wife's connection with them.' This readiness to trot out the kinship was disappointing. It would have been more interesting had he denied it, but he could hardly do so with Auntie at his elbow. The elders went on for a disconcertingly long time discussing past events and memories that meant nothing to the rest of us.

When she tired of this topic, Aunt Loo said, 'We must have another séance one of these evenings.'

'The Franconis are going away on a holiday, are they not?' Hill asked.

'They did not say a word to *me!*' Loo objected.

'I heard nothing of it either,' Welland added.

'They mentioned it when I drove them home the other evening,' Hill went on. 'They do not usually stay long in one place. Outside of us and Lady Morgan, I don't believe they get much business here. I fancy they are scouting out new headquarters.'

'That is a great pity,' Welland said sadly. 'Madame is so very talented. She never *did* expand on that curious statement about justice for the lady, did she, Lady Sinclair?'

'Indeed she did. That is all taken care of,' Loo said quickly, then she looked up with a conscious start and began praising the strawberries. 'Such a treat. We had a lovely crop, but forgot to cover them, and the birds ate them all up.'

'I expect we have overrated Madame's talents,' Dr Hill said, setting down his dessert spoon. 'I for one am not particularly sorry to see them go. One can become obsessed with this spiritualism business. I find myself peeping behind doors and under tables for ghosts. When medical men reach such a state, it is time to leave off playing with the spirit world.'

'I would like to have one last séance,' Welland persisted. 'Madame felt my mother was on the very verge of contacting me, through Anastasia, you know. I would be very interested to hear what she might have to say.'

'Stick with your literary ghosts, Mr Sinclair,' Hill advised. 'I was wondering if you had included the recent literary spirits in your treatise. *Otranto*, for instance. . . .'

'Yes, I included Walpole's novel. What I mean to do next is a tract on the ghostly legends of England. The Green Lady's Walk at Longleat, Beaulieu positively haunted to death, the ringing bells and the dark monk of Burford Priory, our own armless ghost at Tanglewood, the knight who lost his limbs in battle. The spirits that return are generally those who died a violent death, who have revenge, a demand for justice weighing on their minds. Murder victims, blighted lovers, that sort of thing. Do you have any such ghosts at Troy Fenners, Lady Sinclair?'

'Edward was used to speak of a ghost in the oubliette, but it turned out to be a cat. It got locked down there somehow and lived on mice and drank from the puddles of water. It went quite mad. He had a ghost hunter in once, a fellow named Gerard. He thought there was a presence in the feather room, but nothing came of it. You were there that weekend, Walter. You remember Gerard?'

'The fellow was a jackanapes,' was Hill's opinion.

'Has anyone in the place's history met a violent end?' Welland continued.

'Edward's great-grandfather fell off a gargoyle when he was trying to do a sketch of it close up,' was the best she could come up with.

'Alice Sedgely – she met a sudden and tragic end. It is possible she might return,' Welland suggested, looking around the table.

'Oh, no, that is impossible!' Loo said at once.

'I would not encourage Lady Sinclair to dwell on such a disturbing possibility,' Hill said, drawing his shaggy brows together in disapproval. 'A highly imaginative woman, spending a great deal of time alone – the worst thing for her.'

Welland heard him out, then turned to Loo. 'Why is it impossible, ma'am?'

She blinked her eyes, but before she could reply, Hill intervened. 'Because she drowned at sea. She did not die at Troy Fenners. Now we must have a toast to Miss Ford for that jump she made this morning. I wish I had been here to see it. You did not use Nancy after all, your aunt tells me,' he said, speaking in a large voice. He continued talking to include Welland in the toast, then went on to give a history of Nancy's first jump. As the subject was allowed to be changed, I judged Welland had heard what he wished to hear. As he drew out my chair at the meal's end, however, he said in a low voice, that I should 'see if I could find out anything from Loo' while we waited for the gentlemen in the saloon.

When I made an effort to do so, I came up against a wall of vagueness. 'Why should I be afraid of Alice Sedgely's ghost? I never did her any harm.'

Similar comments were made, quite a few of them, but my aunt's heart was not in it. She had her *Tenebrous Shadows* look in her eyes. I feared to hear what new challenge I must face, but it turned out to be a matter that did not require my large size. She was dickering with the notion of introducing a ghost into her novel.

As we drove home a few hours later, I with Aunt Loo and Hill, for Welland and Pierre wished to have a chat, I could not but wonder why that dinner party had been arranged. It had not accomplished much. The only new element introduced was the idea of ghosts. Was Welland hinting there had been a *murder* at Troy Fenners, with his talk of violent ends and revenge? He had mentioned Alice Sedgely Sinclair in that context, but she had died on the *Princess Frederica*, hadn't she?

Chapter Eighteen

Sleep was difficult for me that night. I don't really know why, because I had had a very tiring day, jumping Diablo over the tollbooth, fighting with Welland, and attending a dinner party in the evening. I was by no means despondent that my theft of Miss Milne's fiancé was going so poorly. I still had six days left to steal him away from her. The idea was already in his head, and the morality of it occurred only to be dismissed. Every sport has its rules. A good hunter does not kill a fox in covert, a good bruiser does not kick his opponent when he is down, and a good husband-hunter catches her own husband. To sit at home and have a match 'arranged' by an outsider is not playing fair. Prizes won in such a fashion are still fair game in my opinion. I would *never* go after a man won fair and square by some enterprising female. 'Fair' is the idea I wish to present, in case three repetitions slipped by unnoticed. It is the sportman's code, which I have adopted for my own. A marriage of convenience is not a real marriage at all. Had Welland loved her, perhaps that would make a difference, but if he loved her, he would not be capable of being stolen away. With Pierre around to incite him to jealousy, the thing was by no means hopeless.

With this settled, I turned to ponder what my two suitors had been up to that day. They had set out for Southampton, to check up on Hill and the sanatorium obviously. Hill had known Alice Sedgely, and we had deduced, or at least decided, that Alice was the mysterious lady whose case demanded justice. It is difficult to do justice to a corpse, and Alice was dead. Who, then, was at the sanatorium? Alice had no children. A legitimate one would have been announced in the normal way, and if Arundel had pulled such a stunt on her, there would be no 'justice' at question. Alice would be the deceiver. Again then, *who* was still alive to require justice, and Auntie's money?

After a futile hour of this puzzling, I was wishing I had taken a draft of laudanum, like Loo. Hill thought it a good idea, lest she be bothered by thoughts of ghosts, after Sinclair's foolish talk. As my eyelids became heavy at last, I decided I had been correct all along, and it was the Franconis who had been relieving Auntie of her fortune. I was glad they were leaving. Was not it odd they had told no one but Dr Hill of their departure? I wondered if he had not hinted them away because Loo was becoming too much taken up with ghosts. He had a protective way in his dealings with her. Was it possible his trips to Southamptom were directed to the same end? Who could he be keeping there, not wanting her to know about it?

This intriguing idea had the unwished-for effect of rousing me from any thought of sleep. Doctors tended births and deaths and accidents and illness. Had he delivered a child? Alice had none, but if *Edward* had sired an illegitimate child on some female and never acknowledged it. . . . Yes, this was more like it! My aunt had spoken angrily of his 'stunt,' said if he were alive she would kill him, or something of the sort. Either the child or mother might be at that sanatorium, and that could be the lady for whom the Franconis demanded justice. Some justice *was* due, but with an income of ten thousand a year, it ought not to have bankrupted her. A couple of hundred annually was the usual maintenance fee. More than one child, then? The Duke of York with his dozen or so illegitimate offspring popped into my mind. How was it possible Edward could have populated a whole orphanage, and my aunt not know of it before now? He had been dead for a decade.

Loo *had* spoken of debts he left when he died.

Or was it a death and not a birth the good doctor was involved in? Some violent death, perhaps even murder, that Hill had covered up for his good friend, Sir Edward? The body buried in the oubliette, the bones removed – she had mentioned that! If someone had discovered the fact, Hill would be wide open to blackmail, and as it was Sir Edward who was responsible, he *must* turn to Loo for the money. He hadn't any to spare. So who had Edward killed, a man, or a woman? An irate husband probably. The Sinclairs were philanderers, and the woman requiring justice was the widow. For what earthly reason would she have waited so long to demand her justice?

It is impossible to solve anything in bed at night. By yourself, I mean, for I fancy many a marriage squabble has been settled there very satisfactorily. I would ask Welland point-blank tomorrow what he was looking for at the sanatorium, and insist he accept my help in the affair. It was my mystery too. She was *my* aunt. I counted one hundred and eighty-seven fat-bellied sheep jumping over a fence, but they were no more than sheep that passed in the night. I could not sleep.

Another hour, perhaps as much two, passed before I dozed off, only to be awakened by an ear-splitting scream. It came from the direction of Loo's chamber. Without waiting to don a dressing gown, slippers, pick up a candle, or do anything but throw back the covers, I went careening down the hallway. It was pitch black, with only a rectangle of paler darkness where an open curtained window at the far end of the hall threw the window's shape on the floor. It was enough to allow me to pick out my aunt's doorway. It had crystal knobs, that emitted a sliver of light. Throwing open her door, I was greeted by the horrible vision of my aunt sitting bolt upright under the canopy of her four-poster with her hair done up in papers, her eyes popping in terror, her chins sagging, and her mouth hanging open. She had lit a single taper, which she held so close to her chin I was afraid she would cook her own flesh with it. The shadows lent her face the appearance of a gargoyle. She was gibbering, clutching at the counterpane.

'What's the matter? What is it?' I demanded, looking to the far corners of the room for signs of an attacker.

She relaxed a little to see me. She began flapping the ends of the counterpane against her chest as she babbled quite incoherently. 'Nightmare. I had the most wretched dream,' she gasped.

'Is that all? You frightened the wits out of me. Let us have more lights.' I lit two lamps. She was too overwrought to hold the tinderbox. The room sprang into its usual state of ugliness, the old Chinese wallpaper dim and fading, the cluttered dressing table holding some remnants of her evening's toilet. She needed a Pinny herself. 'What was your nightmare about?' I asked.

'Alice. I dreamed she walked right into my room and demanded. . . .'

I kept silent, hoping she would meander over the edge of revelation, but she only began fanning herself with the tip of the counterpane. 'Yes, demanding what?' I asked, trying to sound nonchalant.

'Demanding Edward back,' she said, laughing in giddy consternation.

'An odd dream. She must have him back now.'

'Yes, it was very odd. I am all right now, Valerie. Sorry I disturbed you. It is the laudanum. It puts you to sleep quickly, but gives dreadful dreams, and you don't sleep through the night either, unless you take a great dose that leaves you weak the next day. I shan't take it again. Walter *tries* to be helpful, but I shan't accept any more laudanum.'

'Does he *urge* it on you?' I asked, frowning, for at home Mama is a stern foe of the stuff.

'Not *urge*, exactly, he only suggests it. Would you mind closing the curtains, my dear. I was so groggy I forgot to have it done before I went to bed. My woman don't know enough to hang up a gown unless I tell her. How is Pinny working out?'

'She's a wizard,' I said, as I went to pull the curtains together, just glancing to the lawn below, where the pale moonlight, etched the tops of elms and oaks against the gray sky. Vision was not at all good, but good enough to pick up the outlines of a man darting like a hare down the slope toward the gatehouse.

'Are you sure there was no one here?' I asked in alarm.

'It was only a dream. So foolish, Alice crawling out of the cubbyhole where the secret passage opens.'

I looked to the cubbyhole door, to see it standing ajar. A shiver started at my heels and inched its way up my legs to my spine, increasing in intensity as it climbed, till I felt my hair might stand on end by the time it wiggled up my neck. She noticed where I looked, saw the fear on my face.

'Good gracious, how did *that* get open?'

'Was it closed when you went to bed?'

'It is always closed. No one wants to look at an ugly black hole. You don't think. . . .'

I went to the door, bent down, and opened it wide to look inside. There was only the darkness. I was not in a mood to investigate further alone. 'I'm going to rouse Pierre to help me look,' I said.

His room had wisely been put at the far end of the hallway from my own. I picked up my aunt's peignoir, a lamp, and hastened to his room. A sharp rap did not rouse him. I opened the door and started in, only to see his counterpane had not been disturbed. He was nowhere about.

I could not like to disturb Loo more than she already was. 'He's sleeping so soundly I cannot waken him,' I told her. 'Would you mind if I slept with you tonight? I'm frightened to go to my own room alone.' My real fear was to leave her unguarded.

'A good idea. I'll sleep better knowing you are here.'

I extinguished the lights, removed her peignoir, and climbed in beside her. After a few weary sighs, she settled down. Just as she was about to doze off she said, 'Imagine Alice creeping out at me from the secret passage, and then the door being open.' On that disturbing statement she settled into a good snooze, leaving me with saucer eyes to contemplate this matter. On the edge of awakening, she had heard the door open, and her dream had adjusted to take the matter into account. Just so had I dreamed I was jumping into the lake when Elleri poured a glass of cold water on me one day, when I had dozed off in her room. Someone had come creeping through the passage, planning to enter this chamber, and been frightened off by her screams. Was it her jewelry, or her life the scoundrel was after? I must urge her to either hammer up the secret passage, or change her room. The former, in fact. The jewels would be all the more vulnerable without her sleeping here, and they were not *all* paste. The tiara and some of the others were genuine.

As sleep was out of the question, I lay there wondering who had been at the cubbyhole door. Hill had prescribed laudanum for her, which was suspicious, but then he often did that. Welland knew the passage opened here, possibly Pierre knew it as well, though I had not told him so. Was it Pierre I had seen darting across the lawn to the gatehouse? The form had not moved with his customary sloth, was not low set like a badger. The shadow had moved with more speed and agility, more like Welland Sinclair is what I mean. The two of them? They had been together, and Pierre was not in his room. Before many more minutes I heard a creaking along the hall – Pierre going to his room. I thought he had been with Welland in the passage, gone downstairs with him, then waited till silence reigned above, before he came up, while Welland ran home. What could they have been doing? Was it possible Alice had been not a nightmare, but a calico sheet danced across the room? I would investigate the passage in the morning for any signs they may have left behind in their haste.

Despite my poor night's sleep, I was awake early in the morning. I have an internal bell in my head that awakens me whenever

I wish. I set it for seven-thirty that I might get into the secret passageway before Pierre or Welland went to check for any tell-tale clues left behind. Pinny was completely mystified by my absence from my own bed. She stood in the room staring at an empty bed when I entered. I told her I had slept with my aunt, since she was having bad dreams.

'I thought I heard something in the night myself, miss, and was afraid her ladyship had got the doctor to give her another black drop. She howled like a banshee for two days straight when she took that, with Dr Hill sitting by her side the whole time, feeling guilty he'd let her talk him into it. He wouldn't want another scandal on his hands.'

'*Another* scandal?' I asked, coming to sharp attention. 'What are you talking about, Pinny? What scandal?'

'Why, miss, it's no secret he had to give up his London practice for nearly killing some lady he was giving dope to. His business fell clean off, and when he came back here, the local folks were all afraid to go near him too. It was only his wife's dowry was all kept him going. She had some money, and when she died, she left it to him.'

'How did she die?' I asked, fearing another dose of bad medicine, either accidental or intentional.

'She was dancing a jig at the assembly when she fell down dead on the floor. The heart it was, miss. I had the story from my ma, who knew all about it from Lady Sinclair, the other Lady Sinclair I mean. She was her woman from away back, came with her from Suffolk when she got married to Sir Edward.'

I looked at her with a totally new interest. 'Your mother worked for the first Lady Sinclair?'

'Yes, miss. She came here with her ladyship when she got married, and then she married Sir Edward's head footman herself. I've been here from day one, born and bred here. My folks are dead now, but I have a good home.'

'Now isn't that interesting!'

'I don't know, miss. Napier says my life has been as dull as dish-water, but I don't see that his own has been much more interesting, working for St Regis and Mr Sinclair all these years.'

'Do you remember anything about your mother's mistress, anything at all?'

'I only remember them talking about her. I was born after she died, so I have no memory of it. She was pretty, they say, but not near so nice as your aunt. The servants all liked your aunt better till . . . till lately.'

'What do you mean?'

'It's the wages, miss. She keeps putting them off. She's paid a little something on account, but there's a full quarter still owing. People need their money,' she said simply.

I continued quizzing her while I dressed, but Pinny was too young to know anything of interest about Alice Sedgely. Still it was odd, her being in the house all the time, and my never realizing we had a representative from Suffolk. Upon further questioning, I learned the seamstress in the village, Miss Brendan, had done considerable work for the first Lady Sinclair. I decided it was time I had a new gown, and would have Miss Brendan make it up for me. If there was any local scandal, a modiste was as apt as anyone to know about it.

But first I would investigate the secret passage. Occasionally the gods smile on us. More usually they laugh in our faces, but on this occasion they were benevolent. They led me to Welland's green glasses, fallen from his pocket in his mad dash through the passageway, for he would not have been wearing them in the dark passage. He would want all the light his unshuttered eyes could give. They had fallen just at the foot of the stairs. I nearly stepped on them, for they had fallen half under the bottom step. My candle flame picked up the twinkle of the metal frames. I went on up to the top of the passage, very carefully, so as not to awaken my aunt. If they had been pulling a sheet before her eyes, they left no trace of it, but I remembered very well seeing Uncle Edward in

Welland's closet. He knew how it was done, and if he had not been instrumental in the Franconis initial apparition, I would be much surprised.

His whole behavior was taking on a menacing flavor, in light of last night's prank. I had been too easily hoodwinked by his facile explanations. As I tallied up the evidence, I realized that it was he, and no one else, who stood out as being guilty. *He* was the one who championed the Franconis, *he* had the sheet with Edward's picture on it, *he* had that stack of money and jewels, and a glib story to account for them. He *said* he was working for St Regis, but no one had checked his story. He might have brought the letter of character with him, written by his own hand, for all I knew. And even if he was St Regis's secretary, who was more likely to know the family's background, to be aware of family secrets that laid the members open to blackmail? St Regis took a keen interest in the family; a careless word to an unscrupulous and impoverished cousin who was as sly as a fox and as poor as a churchmouse might put ideas in the fellow's head. He might even have suggested his coming here to St Regis to discover what was amiss, but in reality have a different intention at the back of his head. Who was he anyway? 'Cousin' was a blanket term that covered everything from actual blood cousins to tenuous connections; even illegitimate kin were sometimes honored with the term. His actual living *with* St Regis indicated he did not have a parental roof over his head. Outside of his made-up story about his mother's locket, he had been marvelously mute on the subject of his parentage, as I considered it. Did he have any brothers or sisters? How often I had mentioned Elleri and Marie – all of my family – to him, with never a single word of any kin but St Regis from him. It seemed as if he had dropped full-grown into Tanglewood, with no family strings but his patron.

I was a ninnyhammer. Like any foolish, gullible, half-in-love girl, I had swallowed his stories holus-bolus, because I was a little infatuated with him. He had been at pains to see I should be too. It was suddenly crystal clear to me that his green glasses were worn to hide his real appearance. What other possible reason could there be? His eyes were healthy, untinged with red or weariness. A criminal, of course, would have some interest in hiding his phiz. Too clear a description of him after he had done his dirty work and left the neighborhood would make his capture easier. And if there was one thing on that man's face more noticeable than any other, it was his damned melting chocolate eyes.

Chapter Nineteen

I hastened straight to my desk and wrote a lengthy letter to St Regis. It was full of questions. Did Welland Sinclair wear green glasses? Had St Regis sent him to Troy Fenners to investigate the matter of Aunt Loo's fortune, and to buy back the family heirlooms? Was there any reason at all to suspect the man's character? All these and a good many queries were scribbled down. At the end, I suggested rather urgently that St Regis himself come *at once* to see what he could to straighten out the imbroglio here. This done, I sealed it up for posting in the village.

But before I set one toe out of that house, I convinced my aunt to have a servant hammer her cubbyhole door closed on the inside of her room, so that no one could enter it via the secret passageway. It took a little convincing, but I said I had seen a very dangerous-looking man sneaking off through the park the night before after she had been disturbed.

'Why did you not tell me at the time?' she asked.

'I was afraid you would not get any sleep. That is really why I slept with you.'

'How sweet of you, my dear. That was very courageous, but are you sure it was a *man*?'

'It was certainly not a woman, but whether one would care to dignify such a low person with the title of man is a moot point.'

'I wonder who it could have been.'

'He was headed toward the gatehouse.'

'You don't think it was Welland?' she asked, frowning.

'It rather looked like him. Who is he? Other than being St Regis's cousin, I mean. Is he a cousin on the wrong side of the blanket, or how does it come he has no patrimony, no family ever mentioned, outside of St Regis himself?'

'He is an orphan,' she said, in a commiserating way. 'I could not tell you precisely what the connection is. He was just always *there*, you know, accepted as part of St Regis's household.'

'Did Edward never mention who he might be?'

'Edward was very fond of him. I remember that. Used to write him little letters when he was at school, and send him a few guineas. Edward knew his mama, I believe. He was used to speak of Lavinia in a fond way. I never met the woman myself. She was dead before I married Edward. Welland's papa was a cousin to Edward, I know that much at least. They made the grand tour together. I seem to remember they were both in love with Lavinia, but then St Regis arranged the match with Alice Sedgely for Edward, and so it was the cousin who got to marry Lavinia. I think Welland must get those weak eyes from his mama. The Sinclairs never had any eye trouble.'

'Do you know his father's name?'

'It was Welland. The son was named after his papa. Old Welland was scholarly too. Not terribly well to grass, of course, but Lavinia had some dowry. I wonder what happened to it? Young Welland hasn't a sou to his name. He is completely dependent on St Regis, but of course when he marries Mary, that will be all taken care of.'

I considered this, a theory forming in my mind that was wild, farfetched, and perfectly reasonable for all that. 'How many years ago would it have been that Lavinia married her Welland?'

'Oh, mercy me, you are getting into ancient history. What do you care for all that old stuff? Welland is about twenty-eight or nine. It must have been thirty years ago.'

'It was a marriage of convenience, was it?'

'It must have been. The Sinclair marriages usually are, and certainly Edward was in love with Lavinia, but whether she returned the attachment I could not really say. Memory is selective. Edward used to *imply* she was, but we mostly remember the good parts of our past, and if some details are unpleasant, we manage to change them a little to make happier daydreaming.'

'I wonder why St Regis insisted on Edward marrying Alice. Lavinia cannot have been so terribly ineligible, or he would not have allowed Welland to marry her.'

'Alice would not have Welland. She did not *like* Edward, but she positively loathed and despised Welland. St Regis was determined one of them would have her, for she was very rich, and since she would not even consider Welland, in the end they made her marry my husband.'

'I am a little surprised St Regis would permit Welland to marry Lavinia. He seems to have had *no* fortune, and Lavinia very little. I wonder why he did not find another heiress for Welland.'

'Yes, that is odd, now you mention it. St Regis not only *accepted* the match, but even *sponsored* it. He must have, for Lavinia lived in the dower house. I often wondered if she was not St Regis's lover.'

'And Welland St Regis's illegitimate son?' I asked, with a stir of excitement.

'They don't call it illegitimate when they get someone to marry the girl in time,' she pointed out. 'Adulterine, I believe, is the word. I do not think it can be the case, however, for Edward would not have been fond of St Regis's son. He would have hated him.'

'But he loved Lavinia.'

'Yes, but he would have hated her having St Regis's child, you see. When they married her to Welland, it was only natural they have a child, and Edward did not seem to resent *that* so much.'

'Does the present Welland have any brothers or sisters?'

'No, he was the only child. I think I must return to my scriptorium now, Valerie. I have wasted I don't know how much time with this business of nailing up the cubbyhole door. Oh, just before you go, my dear, would you mind telling me how the gentlemen kiss nowadays? I am getting to the last chapter. Of course I remember kissing, but styles and customs change, and I don't want to make it too old-fashioned. They used to ask permission in the old days. I hated it. One seemed so fast to say yes, and so prim and proper to say no. Do they still ask?'

'No, they don't. What did you used to say, Auntie? Yes, or no?'

'I made it a point never to answer at all, but only to look shocked, and willing,' she answered.

Looking shocked would not have been difficult, with those eyes. She looked perpetually shocked. 'I am going into the village to post a letter. Have you any errands for me?'

'No, dear,' she said, already preoccupied with the trials of Gloria. She had her 'story' look on her face.

I went over our conversation as I jogged into the village in the whisky. I expect you have some inkling what was in my head. I was wondering, not whether Welland was St Regis's adulterine son, but whether he was not Edward's. Edward had loved Lavinia; he was a bit of a philanderer; she was hastily married off to a poor cousin and supported by St Regis himself. St Regis had arranged it to cover up the disgrace, and to settle a proper match for Sir Edward, who was too high in prestige to marry a nobody. Naturally Edward would take an interest in his own son, would send him money, be fond of him. Equally naturally, the son would feel mightily gypped if he learned, at some latish date in his life, that while he was a pensioner, his own papa had left a good estate.

I wondered how it had come about he only learned it at this late time in his life, for I assumed if he had known it before, he would have acted sooner. But a child would hardly be aware of such goings on, and when Welland began to grow up, he had been much away at school. It was only after he returned from university and began working as St Regis's secretary that he chanced upon the discovery, in some letter or document. Yes, rooting through old family records had occurred to him as a source of information. What must his reaction have been to learn that while he scribbled for a living, his own father had left a fortune in the hands of a silly widow who did not even know of his existence, except as a poor family cousin?

There had even been talk of St Regis giving him Troy Fenners after my aunt's death. But Auntie was not old; her death was eons away. An impatient young man might decide to take some of his father's patrimony *before* she died. For a frightening moment, it even occurred to me he might try to kill her, though there had been no evidence of that. There was pretty good evidence he was getting money, however, and the last remaining mystery was what he was using to blackmail her. She seemed genuinely unaware that Welland was her husband's son, so that could not be the tool for blackmail. No, it was something else. Something involving a lady, a mystery, and justice. I could not see how Alice fitted into this version at all. Auntie had asked me if I was sure it was a man I had seen scuttling down the hill last night. She had spoken of Alice, seen in the nightmare, which suggested to me she thought it must be a woman. But it was probably a ghost she meant.

I got to the village, posted my letter, and returned to Troy Fenners without bothering to see the modiste. It was while I drove up through the park that I was accosted by Welland. He pretended to be out exercising Diablo, but his exercise would not have occured so close to home if he had not wished to see me. This was no longer construed as having anything to do with romance. He wished to discover whether his trick last night had been discovered. He would know he had lost his green glasses somewhere along the way, and be afraid I had found them, knew he had been in the secret passage, scaring my aunt to death. I would feign ignorance of the whole thing. I would not reveal by so much as a blink that I suspected him of any involvement in the affair other than his involvement as St Regis's ambassador. He must be lulled along into a sense of security till St Regis arrived.

'Good morning, Valerie. Been into the village, have you?' he asked, riding up to me. I reined in for a chat, hoping to discover something of his plans.

'Yes, just posting a letter. What are you doing today?'

'I am giving you a lesson in curricle-driving this afternoon, if you are willing.'

By this time, I had formulated other plans for my afternoon. 'I'm afraid I cannot. I am to help Auntie with some work – she wants to read me a few chapters from the *magnum opus*, to see how they appeal to me. But while we are talking, I must ask you to return the carton of family papers. Auntie was looking for something this morning. Could you bring them up to the house now?'

'What was she looking for?' he asked swiftly.

'Some letters from her husband,' I answered, purposely vague.

'They're not in that box. I've been all through it.'

'Well, she was looking for the box in any case, and we had better put it back, or she might become suspicious.'

'I'll leave it off at the kitchen door, and trust to your ingenuity to return it to the scriptorium.'

'Fine. You had better do it now, before lunch.'

'All right. I'll see you tonight.'

I nodded in agreement and continued on my way. My afternoon would be spent pouring over the carton's contents for confirmation of my theory. It was not till I had gone a few yards that I became aware of some incongruity in his appearance. He was wearing his green glasses. I had become so accustomed to seeing him in them that it did not strike me odd at first. But of course he had had plenty of time to lay in a store of them, in case of loss or breakage. He was really extremely interested in hiding his face. Was it possible he thought someone would trace a resemblance to Edward? This was not likely. His resemblance to my uncle was not so startling as that, and his father had been a Sinclair after all, to account for some family traits.

The carton was returned to the house, noticeably lighter than before. Some items had certainly been removed, but it was impossible to imagine what they might be. I had not made that close an examination of them before they left. What remained was innocent and useless stuff. I was downstairs within an hour after luncheon, rather wishing I had accepted Welland's offer for a driving lesson. There was no reason he could not be put to use, and I *did* wish to learn to drive a curricle. When Dr Hill popped in later on, I was happy I had stayed home. I would find a moment for a private chat with him.

'Where is Pierre today?' Hill asked.

'He took lunch with Welland. They will be doing something together this afternoon,' Loo answered. 'Did Welland ask you to join us this evening for the séance?' was the next question.

'Séance? The Franconis have left,' he answered, startled.

'It is not Madame Franconi who is to lead us, but another lady Welland heard of who lives a few miles away. She is either a gypsy or a witch, or both. He says she has an excellent reputation. He has been to her for a fortune reading. She knew all his future – his marriage she forecast, and he is to be married soon, you know, to Miss Milne. He has arranged a séance for this evening, right here in our feather room. He wants you to attend.'

'I don't think we should,' the doctor said at once. I was vastly relieved to hear this sensible opinion. *I* did not think we should attend either, though I was curious to learn what the purpose of it could be. He was leaving soon. Was it some final wind-up, some terminal appeal to Loo to give him money?

'Truth to tell, Walter, I should like to have a second opinion on – that matter, you know, that I have often discussed with you,' she said.

'I rue the day we ever let Madame Franconi into the house. Nothing but mischief has resulted from it.' He stopped short, with a conscious look toward me. The look told me he was privy to all my aunt's secrets. I had to talk to him. As my aunt was receiving such good advice, I was happy to leave them alone.

'Could I see you for a moment before you leave, Dr Hill?' I asked. 'I gave my wrist a jolt in that jump the other day, and would like you to have a look at it. It is sore, and a little swollen.'

'I would be happy to, Miss Ford,' he agreed. 'I shan't be long here. Your aunt and I have a few matters to discuss.'

He stayed half an hour with her, which gave me time to weigh the wisdom of taking him into my confidence. I felt the need of mature guidance in this weighty matter. Who better than my aunt's best, oldest friend? I hoped too that he might know something of Lavinia, and her affair with Edward.

He came to me in the parlor before he left. 'Let's have a look at that wrist,' he said. 'I can put a tight bandage round it if it bothers you. It cannot be broken or you would have been complaining long since.'

'There is nothing wrong with my wrist, Doctor. I want to talk to you about something else entirely.'

'What is it?' he asked, shocked and curious.

'About my aunt, and her being blackmailed.'

'She told you? I wish she had not. There is no need to worry a young visitor in her home.'

'She told me nothing, but I have been at work, and think I know something about it.'

'What is it you think you know?' he demanded.

'I believe Welland Sinclair is involved, deeply involved. In fact, I believe he is behind the whole affair. Do you know anything about the man?'

'He came with St Regis's blessing. I know *that* much, and one cannot credit St Regis would have anything to do with a crooked scheme.'

'He would not have to know. Indeed I don't believe he *does* know. Do you know anything of Welland's parents?'

'Very little. I never met them, though I know well enough Sir

Edward once fancied himself attracted to the wife, before she married. Why do you ask?'

'Madame Franconi mentioned a lady, the mysterious lady demanding justice. . . .'

'Yes, but she did not mean her.'

'How do you know?'

'Well, I . . . I don't actually *know*, of course. The whole thing was nonsense, in my view. But why do you think Sinclair is behind it, and even if he is, how should he be using his own mother, dead and in her grave for a decade?'

'*I* think Sir Edward was Welland Sinclair's father,' I said, to get it all over, let him take the shock and assimilate it, before further discussion.

He sat back, speechless with amazement. 'This is incredible,' he said at last.

'No, it isn't, Doctor. Sir Edward had an affair with Lavinia, then suddenly it was necessary for someone to marry her. St Regis engineered a match with Welland Sinclair, the old Welland I mean, and practically supported them for the rest of their lives, so far as *I* can see. Sir Edward knuckled under to him in marrying Alice Sedgely's fortune, and in return, he hushed up the other affair. Now young Welland has found it out somehow and come down here to see how he could weasel Auntie's fortune out of her.'

'But what of Alice?'

'What about her? The mysterious lady need not be *her*. Is that what my aunt thinks?'

'She has intimated something of the sort,' he admitted.

'What was the injustice done to her? She agreed to marry Sir Edward, then treated him very badly by running off with Arundel.'

'You *have* been busy,' he laughed. 'Got that old tale out of your aunt, did you? Well, I must say this throws a new light on the whole thing. What can young Sinclair be up to, having this new gypsy coming to hold a séance?'

'*You* frightened off the Franconis on him, I think?' I asked, with a knowing look that caused him to blush.

'I felt they had done enough mischief.'

'They were here some time *before* Sinclair's coming, I think?'

'Yes, several months before. Just after Pierre arrived, it was.'

'Pierre. *He* could not be involved, could he? He is about the same age, but he has been in France the whole time, was born and bred there. It cannot have anything to do with him.'

'He is very French, is he not? Almost determinedly French, I would say. He makes little progress for a fellow who has been here half a year, with nothing better to do than learn the language.'

I considered Pierre only to dismiss him. Welland's history dovetailed too well to be dragging in another suspect. 'Pierre is wealthy. Everyone says so. I don't think he is involved. What I am wondering is what tale Welland had the Franconis tell my aunt to get her to shell out so much money, for I don't believe she even realizes Welland is Sir Edward's son. I know *why* he is doing it, but I really cannot imagine *how* he is getting her to pay up. What tale can he have told her?'

Hill cleared his throat a couple of times, scuffled his feet, and kept looking at me, wondering whether to say anything.

'I believe you know what it is, Doctor, and I wish you will tell me. It has to do with Alice, has it not? Some story he fabricated about her?'

'Her body was never recovered,' he said, looking at his feet.

'I see. And from that acorn he has grown an oak, letting on she is not dead. *Now* I know why he was in the secret passage. Oh, yes, don't *stare*, Doctor. He was there last night, and whatever he did, or said, he caused Loo to have a nightmare about Alice. If she had not had that dose of laudanum, she would no doubt have held communication with some woman dressed up to pretend she was Alice, grown old and poor. We must stop him.'

'I'd give an ear to know what he plans to do tonight.'

'I don't care what he *plans*, it will not succeed. We are on to him, and will catch him out.'

'I have a mind not to come at all.'

'No, do come. I may need your help.'

'I never took the fellow for an outright scoundrel. I daresay you have got it all wrong, Miss Ford, and he means no more than to say good-evening to Lavinia. He really does put a deal of faith in this spiritualism business, you know.'

'I don't think so, Doctor. He puts a deal of faith in my aunt's belief in it. I wish I had thought to contact St Regis sooner.'

'You have written him?' Hilled asked, displeased. 'Your aunt won't like that.'

'The letter has already been mailed.'

'When?'

'This morning. He won't be here for a few days. We can lull Welland along till he gets here, but we must not let him get any more money.'

'I am very happy you consulted me, Miss Ford. We'll keep a sharp eye on him. He seems very cocksure, doesn't he?'

'Yes, he thinks he has conned us all.'

Hill left very soon, and I went on thinking about it. I found it odd Welland would agree to marry Mary Milne when he was about to get his hands on a different fortune, but he probably loved the girl. He had said so at first, till it became necessary to make up to me, to distract me from the truth.

I continued fretting over the problem long after Dr Hill left. I was like a dog with a bone; I could not let it go. In one version Lavinia had in fact been married to Sir Edward, so that Welland was the rightful heir to Troy Fenners. In another, Pierre was deeply involved in it, all having in some unclear manner to do with the war going on with France. I even spared a moment to consider if it were possible Alice was indeed alive, which would make my aunt not only a bigamist, but destitute, for all the estate and income would belong by rights to Alice.

All this was a sheer waste of time. I knew who our culprit was, and must be busy to catch him. I went to the feather room to see if he had any calico hidden in the secret passage, any lamp or ropes. There was nothing. He was either leaving his preparations till the last minute, or planning some other trick for this evening. I toyed with various manners of exposing him during the evening's performance. Should I arise and stalk to the panel, rip it open, and show my aunt that some hired person was manipulating strings? That should prove quite unequivocally that the whole affair was a sham. There was some question in my mind whether Welland would use that same stunt, when I was on to it. He was clever enough to come up with a new one, but no amount of figuring gave me a single clue what it might be. I would not be dissuaded to stay away from the séance, no matter what aura the gypsy discerned around my head. I would be there, and I would expose Welland Sinclair for the conniving crook he was.

Chapter Twenty

*O*ur only company for dinner was Dr Hill. Even Pierre was not at home. He was dining with Welland, and probably being talked into some scheme that would remove a part at least of his fortune from his pockets. Immediately after dinner I left Loo and Dr Hill alone while I went to the feather room for a last check of the secret passage. I could discover no evidence of chicanery. It was during the few moments the medium was being introduced to us in the saloon that his accomplice would slip quietly in and prepare the stunt. Napier I figured for the assistant; he would not trust Pierre, who talked too freely.

At about eight, the cousins arrived from the gatehouse with their new accomplice in tow. The medium's name was Ethelberta. That was the only name by which she was introduced. I cringed in my seat to look at the woman. She was a gypsy, a real gypsy, not a half one like Madame Franconi. This one had blue black hair, only the front tip of which was visible, forming a sharply etched widow's peak on her swarthy forehead. The rest of her hair was covered by a black turban. She was not a young woman, yet not quite old either, about forty-something. She had dark eyes, strangely light brows, a sharp pointy nose, and a wide mouth held in a sullen line. Her outfit was plain and dark, with a black shawl round her shoulders.

Welland introduced her but did not give the woman our names. The medium said not a single word. She only nodded and stared as if she were memorizing our features for the rest of eternity. It was an unnerving experience.

'Where does Ethelberta come from, Welland?' my aunt, asked, with a smile at the woman.

'From Barrows Woods, just outside of Alton, Lady Sinclair. She makes her permanent home there, has for as long as she can remember. She is an accomplished fortune teller, as well as a spiritualist.'

'Maybe she would give me a tarot reading tomorrow.'

'Ethelberta does not read the tarot cards. She reads palms and uses a crystal ball.'

'Crystal gazing!' Aunt Loo chirped, her eyes bright with interest. 'How nice! I never tried that. We must do it tomorrow. Set it up for me, Welland.' Then aside she whispered to him, 'Does she not speak English, or why don't she say something?'

'She does not speak the language too well, and is shy to try it before a crowd.'

I exchanged a speaking glance with Dr Hill. How extremely convenient that he had found a person who did not speak the language to use for his scheme. One could only wonder how he had communicated his needs to her.

Pierre came frisking up to my side. 'Where have you been all day, Peter?' I asked.

He was luminous with excitement. 'We have the good secrets,' he whispered. 'Much big surprise for every ones.'

I stifled the temptation to inform him that he and his cousin were in for a surprise as well when I ran to the panel and pulled it open to reveal their machinations.

'Shall we get right on with it?' Welland asked, an eager smile hovering round his lips.

'I am ready,' Aunt Loo replied, every bit as eager. As we went into the feathered room, Welland had his aunt's arm, talking to her in low, confidential tones. I walked as closely behind them as I could but overheard nothing of interest.

'Does she know anything about us?' Loo asked him.

'I did not tell her a thing. I am curious to see if Ahmad will come for her, as he did for Madame Franconi. We'll try Ahmad first, before Anastasia.'

'Has she got hold of Anastasia for you before?'

'No, not yet. She is to remain at the inn in the village overnight, and would stay longer if we wish more sittings.'

'Good. I want to try the crystal ball. A *real* gypsy, she ought to be able to tell us things. I am anxious for a second opinion on – a certain matter I have under consideration.'

There was no doubt in the world what opinion she would hear from Sinclair's henchwoman, imported to replace the Franconis. She would be ordered to give all her money to the blackmailers.

We took up our regular places round the table, which put me within quick darting distance to the required panel. Once we were seated, Welland removed his green glasses. It was the first time he had ever done so in company. He did not want to miss a single bit of the performance. The room was dark, with only the single taper burning. Both he and Pierre were too excited on this occasion to be bothered playing footsie with me beneath the table. The tension in the room was so great the very air seemed to pulse with it, all of our attention focused on the dark-gowned gypsy, placing her hands on the table, swarthy, work-worn hands, the fingers not dainty like Madame Franconi's, but a farmer's fingers.

With heads bent, we sat silent, waiting for Ethelberta to go off in a swoon. She was slower than Madame Franconi to get going. It seemed to stretch out for hours, that sitting there, pretending to feel some overpowering emotional experience. I cannot speak for the others, but for myself, the emotion uppermost in my breast was impatience to get on with the charade. Ethelberta's routine was a little different. Before she went into a swoon, she closed her eyes, held her head straight up, and emitted some sing-song unintelligible syllables, gypsy-talk perhaps. Not till she had performed thus for two or three minutes did she let her head fall back and begin speaking in the voice of Ahmad. Obliging of him to come hopping to a new mistress!

The rest of the séance, at the time, was seen by me as a true occult experience, and I can only describe it as such. A ghost appeared, not the ghost of Sir Edward, but of his first wife, Alice Sedgely Sinclair, exactly as seen in her portrait in the gallery. She came out of the secret panel, but she was suspended on no wires, neither was she painted on a sheet of muslin. She was flesh and blood, or the ghostly representation of such. She wore the peau de soie gown worn in her portrait, and had her hair dressed in the same manner. Her face glowed with an inhuman glow. It was magic – black magic – a true occult experience. My shock was too great to allow me to think of running to the wall panel. I just sat and stared, open-mouthed, like all the others.

It was my aunt's agitated poo-poohing that finally got my eyes to turn from the ghostly apparition to her. 'But – but this cannot be! You're not dead!' was her strangled utterance.

If Alice was not dead, she was remarkably well preserved, for she did not look a single day older than the lady in the picture gallery hanging beside Sir Edward.

'I *am* dead, Louise,' the apparition said, in deep, melodramatic, ghostly accents. 'I drowned when the *Princess Frederica* sank. You are Lady Sinclair now. Live up to the title. *I* did not and have suffered for it in the beyond, from whence I have been called forth.'

'But – but Walter, you said she was alive,' Loo said, turning to him. 'You have seen her, talked to her.'

Walter was on his feet, darting to the secret panel to throw it open. It was empty. There was nothing there but the floor and walls. When Hill came out, he cast one look of loathing on Welland Sinclair, then turned on his heel and bolted from the room as fast as his legs would carry him. Sinclair and Pierre were up and after him, nearly knocking over the table in the excitement. The candle fell from its holder and guttered out in a puddle of melted paraffin on the table. I ran to the door to chase after the men, till Loo called me back.

'Don't leave me alone with her!' she screamed, her voice vibrating with terror.

I went back, very unwillingly, till I remembered that our ghost had not left the room with the men. She was here somewhere, in this room. 'Lights!' I commanded, and ran with the taper to the hall to light it. When I got back, the ghost was gone. My first thought was that she had sneaked into the secret panel. She was not there. She was not hiding behind the curtains, or under the table. I looked. Neither had she left by the door. She was just gone, vanished into the air like a puff of smoke. When I stopped to glance at my aunt, I saw she had slumped over the table in a faint. There was no one to help me tend her. The men were still off, running, shouting, their footfalls echoing through corridors and chambers. I was missing wonderful excitement!

I went to the door and bellowed down the corridor till Pinny and a kitchen maid came running. 'Lady Sinclair has fainted. Get her vinaigrette, feathers to burn! Bring some wine, and for God's sake, *hurry*!'

I rubbed my aunt's hands, tried to rouse her from her faint, and all the while kept stealing glances to the secret panel, wondering how the ghost had hidden herself, for by this time I had given up believing I had actually seen a ghost. It was some clever trick played off by Sinclair and Pierre. A state of confusion was settling firmly around me. Why were they saying Alice was *dead*, even trying to *prove* it by introducing her ghost, when Dr Hill implied that they were, or at least Welland was, saying Alice had survived the ship's sinking? No, but it was Walter Auntie had said that to. *You* said she was alive. . . . How was it possible that kindly sheep dog of a man was duping Loo?

'Where did they go?' I asked the butler, when he popped his head in at the door.

'Mr Sinclair and Mr St Clair took the doctor down to the gate-

house, Miss Ford, to save him the embarrassment in front of Lady
Sinclair,' he told me in a quiet voice. '*I* took care to have all the
doors locked so he could not escape too readily.'

'Then you *knew* he would make a bolt?'

'Mr Sinclair intimated something of what was going on,' he
replied, with a modestly triumphant and knowing look.

'I'm going down to the gatehouse,' I decided.

'Don't go, Valerie. I don't want to be alone,' Auntie said, in a
weak voice.

'I want to find out what is going on,' I answered, torn by eagerness to see the excitement.

'I shall tell you what is going on,' she said, in a sad but resigned
way, her little brindled head sinking on her chest. 'Come, we shall
recover our nerves with a glass of wine, while I tell you what
Walter did to me. Let him make his confession with the minimum
of audience. Come.'

Reluctant, but full of curiosity, I followed her into the saloon. 'I
think I understand it now,' she said, nodding her head, and
strangely reminding me of a bird. 'Welland tried to tell me the day
we went for a drive, but I would not believe him, would not even
listen to a word against Walter. About six months ago, Walter came
to me and told me Alice was alive, that she had returned from
America and gone to him, for they were friends in the old days,
before I married Edward. She was destitute. She and Arundel had
escaped drowning when the *Frederica* went down, but thought it
such a wonderful chance to run away together with no questions
asked that they never came forward and told anyone of their
survival. He had all the details of how they had landed at a barren
spot of beach and stayed at a fishing shack and all that. Arundel
was supposed to have had enough money in his pockets to have
paid their fare to America, posing as a married couple. When he
died, she was left poorly off, and as she was getting old, she wanted
to come back to England to live out the last of her life. At first, she
wanted only enough funds to live comfortably. Walter got her into

his friend's sanatorium using the name of Miss Rogers.'

'Why did you not insist on seeing her?'

'I had hardly known the woman at all, would not have recognized her after all these years. Walter had known her well. I trusted him implicitly. At first, only a small sum was asked for, and I was more than willing to pay, to keep the story hushed up. But then when I paid up so readily, the fee was raised gradually, till I had hardly enough left to scrape by on myself.'

'Was Pierre involved in any of this?'

'Oh, certainly! He was very generous about lending me money. Walter suggested it. I owe Pierre three or four thousand pounds, though he don't know *exactly* why I wanted it. I told him I was helping out some poor relatives, and he could sympathize with that, though he thought I was too generous. He called me a naughty lady, but he promised not to tell anyone.'

'What part did the Franconis play in it?'

'I don't really know. They had come just a little before all this started. I fancy Walter just used them as added inducement to make me pay up. I never suspected them of having anything to do with it, and that a total stranger, in touch with the beyond, urged me to take reparations – well, naturally I knew I must. Walter always kept saying every payment would be the last, but always there was one more, and one more. Alice needed expensive treatment, then Alice had a load of debts in America that had to be discharged, then Walter thought I ought to set up a trust fund for her, a pension you know, to take care of her old age and be rid of her once for all. And always there was hanging over my head that by rights the whole thing was hers, and she could come forward and claim it all legally any time she wanted to. Walter even hinted Edward *knew* she was alive when he married me. He was Edward's best friend. He would know those things. The tarot cards too said justice must be done to the lady.'

'So you began asking St Regis for mortgages, and selling off family heirlooms.'

'I had to, to keep Alice satisfied. Then, when St Regis, odious old toad, started making such close inquiries, I had to tell him *something* to account for the money all being gone, so I told him I was helping your papa, Valerie, thinking he might approve of it, as Pierre did. I *do* hope he never checked up on it.'

'I don't believe he ever did. At least Sinclair seemed to believe it.'

'Yes, Sinclair. St Regis sent him down to spy on me, just as I thought, and discover what was afoot. I am convinced of it. He has been a great nuisance throughout the whole business, and now he has got poor Walter in *hanging* trouble, for you saw with your own eyes that Alice Sedgely Sinclair is dead as a doornail. Her ghost told us so. Was it not a powerful experience, Valerie, seeing a real live – or well, you know what I mean. A *real* ghost.'

'You cannot believe that was a real ghost!'

'Certainly it was. I realize now I was utterly duped by the Franconis. Their ghost looked nothing like the real one. It had no *substance* to it. It was all flat and colorless. Alice was a *real* ghost,' she said, quite contented. 'So of course she is dead, and Walter is a scoundrel, bilking me of thousands of pounds. I don't know how Welland figured it out, but it came as no surprise to him. He knew Walter would run, was sitting on the edge of his chair ready to go after him. I hope he will not hurt him. Walter is no longer young. The chase will be hard on him. I feel burnt to the socket myself. I shall ask Walter for a sedative before he goes home.'

'You surely won't see him again!' I exclaimed, astonished at her calm acceptance of the man's villainy.

'He must have some good explanation, my dear. I shall do him the courtesy of listening to it.'

'*I* would do him the courtesy of listening to it from the gallery at the Old Bailey.'

'It looks bad. I must own it looks black for him, but if he has a good reason, then we shall see what must be done. I wish I had married him when he asked, then he could have used my money, without all this wretched business of blackmail.'

'My dear Aunt Louise, I sincerely believe you need a keeper. Perhaps St Regis was right to send his minion down here to keep an eye on you. And I'll tell you something else, if you don't prosecute Dr Hill, St Regis will have you claimed incompetent, and put away.'

She was thoroughly shaken at this forecast, but I felt I was correct in my view. I was by no means sure St Regis was not right too, though I disliked to admit it.

'Perhaps if *you* spoke to Welland, Valerie, he would agree not to tell St Regis.'

'St Regis is probably on his way here already,' I said, but did not deem this the proper moment to tell her from whence this notion sprang.

'It would be just like the man. He will never let me marry Walter, for he has some other party in mind for me, a military man he keeps putting forward. If I *marry* Walter, I don't believe they can make me give evidence against him. Walter wanted me to sell my interest in Troy Fenners back to St Regis for a lump sum, so I could settle it on Alice, and be rid of her once for all. Then we would be married, and live at his cottage, only I am not sure I would be happy in such a tiny hole of a place.'

'Generous of him.'

'I wonder when they will come back,' was her next distracted comment.

She went back over the same story a few times, leaving me free to ponder the few details of it that were troubling me. First and foremost was the matter of the ghost, and how it was done, but of equal intrigue was how Welland had discovered Hill for the culprit, why he had been in the passageway the night before, and why he had kept the whole a secret from me. The green glasses were not explained away either. I too was eager for them to come back.

Chapter Twenty-one

$\mathcal{B}$efore they came, Aunt Loo was in such a state of fidgets she took a dose of medicine prescribed by the butler to quieten her nerves, but instead it put her so close to sleep that she was easily persuaded to retire. The wine she had been drinking might have had something to do with it too. I was alone, just beginning to contemplate the discomfort of a solo trip to the gatehouse when Welland and Pierre arrived at the door.

'It's about time you got here! Where is Dr Hill?' I demanded.

'Asleep. I prescribed him a good stiff sleeping draft,' Welland replied. 'It was that or being tied wing and leg and locked in a room overnight, for I cannot like to call in the constable in the middle of the night. I thought Lady Sinclair might like to have a word with him as well before he is turned over to the authorities.'

'She wants to see him, but you took so long she gave up and went to bed.'

'We have been having very good times. Very much exciting,' Pierre informed me. He was disheveled, his hair all askew, his jacket dusty. His companion might have stepped freshly groomed from his dressing table.

'Enjoyed beating up an old man, did you?'

'No beating up,' Pierre replied. 'Only runnings and grabbings and catchings. He catches up most easily.'

'All right, Welland, tell me all about it,' I said, settling down on the sofa for a good listen. 'I know Hill is the culprit; I know he conned Auntie into thinking Alice was alive. What I do not know is who he had in the sanatorium, or how you discovered it.'

'How about some sherries, Peter? This is going to be a long *spiel*,' Welland said.

'Now we are all sherried,' Pierre said, after pouring and passing the glasses, 'I tell you all the exciting adventures my cousin and me are having.'

I cast a defeated glance to Welland, wishing to hear the story in a less garbled version. While Pierre took a sip, Welland launched rather quickly into it.

'We knew someone was fleecing Lady Sinclair. When I found out it was not your father, I began looking around closer to her home. She had few connections or close friends. Hill was the closest.

'He also had a rather elegant cottage for a man who allegedly skimped by on a practically unworking country doctor's earnings. The painting in his study, the Titian – you must have noticed it, Valerie – was no part of his wife's dowry, for I happened to know it was sold only two months ago from Sotheby's in London. St Regis put a bid on it, a bid for a thousand pounds, which was too low to take the work. Ergo, the doctor had more cash hanging around than he let on. When Hill cashed my draft for five pounds for me, what should turn up on the bills but the mark I had put on the money Pierre lent Lady Sinclair. I arranged Peter's funds for him, got them from the bank, and took the precaution of marking the bills in an inconspicuous way.'

'You were not telling me this, Cousin,' Pierre objected. 'I too can mark bills. I am very good at marking bills. What mark were you using?'

'Green dots, Peter,' I said, causing Sinclair's head to spin toward me.

'You are exceptionally observant,' he mentioned. 'Next time you can mark your own bills, Peter. You remember I mentioned to Hill that the deSancy library on archaeology was for sale in

London? When a letter was promptly sent off to Lombard Street, I took the liberty of opening it, and. . . .'

'Yes, I can deduce what you found. Hill was putting in an offer to buy it, but what you have skipped over rather lightly is how the letter fell into your hands.'

'The clerk at the post office was very obliging. St Regis gave me a letter of introduction, covered with all manner of impressive seals, and the fellow took the notion I was a sort of inspector from Bow Street, I believe. I may have mentioned the name of Townsend, the Chief of Bow Street, but I assure you I did not actually say I was in his employ.'

'Thoughtful of St Regis,' I said, in a burst of annoyance at being outdone at every turn.

'I have mentioned to you before that he has always been kind to me,' Sinclair answered mildly. 'As I was saying, this confirmed that he was rolling in Lady Sinclair's money, and it remained only to find out what hold he had over her.'

'Also rolling on my monies,' Pierre interjected.

'It had to be something underhanded,' Welland went on, ignoring the interruption, 'not bare-faced blackmail, for the two of them were on the best of terms throughout the whole thing. Peter and I decided to follow him when he took his jaunt to the sanatorium, feeling, at the time, that it was some former lover of Sir Edward's that was involved. I, as you may recall, was required to return rather suddenly to see a lady about a horse,' he said, glowering at me.

'You *thought* you were required, though in fact the lady managed the horse very well till you arrived. So how did you discover the lady in the sanatorium was letting on to be Alice, or that Hill was letting on that at least? More important, who the deuce is she?'

'She was not aware of Hill's deception at all. She was really, and I am indebted to Miss Brendan, the local seamstress, for the information, the female who caused Hill's rather abrupt abandonment of his Harley Street practice. Her name is Rogers. He very nearly killed her with an overdose of medicine, administered some strange combination, I believe. She has been dotty ever since, was staying with her sister till the sister died, supported by Hill, then he put her in his friend's sanatorium. It was how he prevented the family from suing him for malpractice, by looking after her. Rumors of his incompetency still linger in the village. Practically no one will go near him. His extra burden in supporting the woman, added to his miniscule practice, is probably why he needed money in the first place. I think it was the Franconis, all unintentionally, who put the idea in his head of letting on to Loo that the Rogers woman was Alice, by mentioning a lady who had been wronged. They were a pair of dupes, just plying their trade of holding séances and reading fortunes, making a meager living from it. Under Hill's suggestions, discreet you know, but strong, they realized any mention of mysterious ladies and injustices went down very well, and occasioned more séances and readings, all at a guinea a shot. Hill confirmed that he and they rigged the ropes for the ghost to walk, but the Franconis were only Hill's instrument. He gave the show away that he knew of the panel in the feather room when he jumped up and opened it when the ghost of Alice visited us.'

'So the whole thing began after the Franconis came?'

'It may have begun a little before, but it stepped up then. Some idea may have been forming in Hill's head that Loo was ripe for plucking, I mean, and their coming facilitated it. He suggested rather strongly to them that they leave once you and I began making troublesome inquiries.'

'Yes, he planned then to marry her, have her sell out her rights to Troy Fenners, and get her whole fortune in his hot little hands at one go. But how did you know Alice was the mysterious lady, and that Hill was pretending she was still alive?'

'Deduction, induction, all that clever stuff. I knew Hill had the blunt, and realized when Loo said it was 'impossible' for Alice to haunt Troy Fenners, despite her tragic death, that Loo thought she was not dead at all. At least that made sense to me. If she was thought to be alive, she was surely a woman wronged, her case requiring justice. But where could she be, sending out her demands for money? Hill had been off to the sanatorium, where Peter found out he was footing the bill for Miss Rogers. I arranged this last séance to try to shock someone into blurting out the truth, and sure enough, Loo did.'

'Good luck, and good guessing on your part,' I complimented.

'*I* am the one who is inventing the ghostess,' Peter claimed, smiling proudly. 'Evelina is *my* mis – Miss Talbot.'

'What does he mean?' I asked Sinclair.

'Just what he says. Miss Talbot is his particular friend, from the village here. Pray do not inquire too minutely as to her trade. A discreet uncertainty is best in some cases. Of course she was not plying her customary trade this evening, nor wearing her own gown or face either.'

'I expect the obliging Miss Brendan supplied the copy of Alice's gown; but do tell, who supplied her face?'

'Alice's portrait, plus about five pounds of newsprint. It was a paper mache mask, doused with phosphorescent powder, to emit a nice ghostly glow. The hair was Miss Talbot's own, coiffure by Mr Sinclair,' he said, bowing to accept some imaginary accolade.

'And the fortune teller, Ethelberta?'

'She is who I said she was, a gypsy fortune teller from Barrow Woods, at Alton. The Franconis told me of her. We arranged for her to come. She does not usually do séances at all but was willing to act the part, for a stipend of course. Now, why don't you ask me what you *really* want to know?' he said, with a sly smile.

The image of Mary Milne darted into my head. 'What do you mean?'

'How did I make her disappear?' he prompted me.

'Oh, that – I can think of half a dozen explanations. It was dark.

She might have hidden under the table, or behind the curtain, or. . . .'

'No, you looked in all of those places, Valerie. I did a spot of mind reading on my way across the park while securing Hill. Don't you want to know?'

'You obviously want to boast of it. Go ahead.'

'Oh, well, if you're not interested,' he said, shrugging his shoulders. 'How about more sherry, Peter?'

'How did you do it, then?' I asked, as though it were a matter of very little interest.

This scanty show of enthusiasm was enough to bring forth the story, for he was bursting to show off. 'You remember the trapdoor in the ceiling that we decided was not a trapdoor, but only a piece of poor carpentry?'

'Yes, I remember it. Was it a trapdoor?'

'It was, and it led to a passage that fed into the other secret passage, the one to your aunt's chamber from the saloon. I did not actually see much point in that panel in the feather room, so I decided to investigate it further last night.'

'You dropped your glasses.'

'Ah, it was *you* who recovered them. I made sure it must be the case and have been wondering why you did not quiz me as to their being there. I have half a dozen pairs on standby, so it was not important. I am afraid we gave your aunt a bit of a fright. She set up screaming to wake the dead. I was planning at the time how I would have Alice appear and disappear, and thought if there was even a crawl space above the trapdoor in the feather room, it would be helpful. I never looked for such luck as the two passages joining, but once I saw the passage went somewhere, of course I had to follow up and see where it debouched. I had hopes it would be in *your* room, Valerie.'

'Sorry to disappoint you. How did Miss Talbot get into the passage and out again?'

'The butler, who I had to take into my confidence, let them in through the saloon entrance. They hastened along to be ready on cue.'

'Who is involved in this "they" you speak of?'

'Miss Talbot and Napier, my valet. He stood by at the ready with a rope to haul her up after her performance and return the trap-door to its place, in case any curious young females should decide to investigate. Apparently all the young females were too uninter-ested to bother looking. They had the devil of a time getting out. Some damned fool nailed the door shut in Lady Sinclair's room, but they found their way out by the saloon exit. Our friendly butler went to their aid.'

'My Miss Talbot is got down safe and sane,' Peter assured me. 'She is much a good actress, *hein*?'

'Very good. You might have told me this, Welland. I told you everything – showed you the secret passages, got the papers from the scriptorium for you, and you kept everything a secret from me.'

'I had every intention of telling you,' he lied amiably. 'I most particularly invited you for a curricle drive for the very purpose, but you preferred to hear a reading of *Tenebrous Shadows*, so there was no opportunity to include you in our more interesting doings.'

'What did you steal from the carton, incidentally? It was several pounds lighter than when you took it away.'

'Oh, really? I must have misplaced some of the stuff. I'll have a look for it.'

The speech was reasonable, the tone highly suspicious. 'You could have given me a hint what you were up to. I would have gone for the drive if you had.'

'True, but I have never made a habit of *begging* ladies to drive out with me. Before the words *St Regis* jump to your lips, I would like to have a private talk with you.'

Peter poured himself another dollop of sherry, not hearing, or not understanding, or not caring that he was being hinted away.

'Why you don't go home, now, Welland?' Peter asked, swishing his drink around in his glass, while casting lecherous glances at me.

'Why don't you?' Welland countered.

'I am home, me.'

'Miss Talbot is still at the gatehouse, waiting for a drive home.'

Pierre considered this, but 'a bird in the fingers' was always preferable to him. I was right within hand's grasp, whereas Miss Talbot was a park away. 'You take her home,' he suggested to his cousin.

'Oh, very well,' Sinclair said, arising with an impatient jerk. 'One of us had better. We'll have that chat tomorrow, Valerie.'

'*We* will be having our chats now, this night,' Pierre said, inching closer, his hands coming out, all fingers, while his sherry glass teetered on the edge of a table, hastily set aside.

'In a pig's eye we will. Hold him till I get away, Welland.'

'Why don't you be good, and take Miss Talbot home?' Welland asked, in a wheedling way.

'That Miss Talbot, she is not amenable for kissing,' Pierre complained. 'Many trinkets I have gived her. Bonbons, a ring of garnets, many flowers. Maybe she is liking better the money. . . .'

'You never want to underestimate the power of money,' Welland urged, while I waited with bated breath to see if the bird in the bush was becoming more desirable.

Pierre dug into his pockets. 'I have got only these little pieces of money,' he said, fingering over a few shillings and pence. 'I think it is not enough. Folding paper monies are better, no?'

Welland reached into his pocket, till he intercepted my shocked, disapproving face. 'I'm fresh out of folding money,' he said to Pierre. 'About St Regis's plans for my future, Valerie,' he went on, turning to me, 'I have written him. I expect to see him any day, probably tomorrow, and I'll speak to him then.'

'I am not interested in his opinion, or in a man who lets his decisions be made for him by another. Try your luck with Miss Talbot,' I suggested.

'Peter, go to bed, please,' Welland said, obviously wanting privacy with me.'

'I am fresh out of being tired,' Pierre replied happily.

'I'm not. I am for bed,' I said, and swept from the room.

'Maybe I shall be trying my lucks with Miss Talbot,' Pierre said as I left, jingling his few shillings in his hand.

Chapter Twenty-two

While I was at breakfast with my aunt the next morning, Dr Hill came up to Troy Fenners, hat in hand, to seek an interview with Lady Sinclair. When he was announced, Loo turned an imploring eye toward me.

'It would be easier for Walter if I see him alone, dear. You understand.'

I was not in the least eager to be present at the embarrassing meeting. I went to the saloon, thinking to see Welland waiting there. Surely he had not permitted Hill off the leash to come unaccompanied? He could easily have bolted, for all anyone knew. This was exactly what he had allowed, however. Welland was nowhere around. I toyed with the idea of going to the gatehouse, but decided it was time to sit on my thumbs and let him come courting me.

When Pierre ambled into the saloon some half hour later, he was showing the signs of a late night. 'I require monies,' he said briefly, without making a single lunge at my unprotected body. 'I shall be going at the bank alone. I now have much monies there after realizing funds. I require my monies now, today.'

I felt fairly sure the requisition had to do with Miss Talbot, but did not wish to hear it confirmed. 'Welland is not going with you?'

'No, I shall going alone from present onward. Welland is soon now leaving us, you comprehend.'

'Yes, I know.'

'I must stand up on my own feets from the present onward. I am to have conversations with Lord St Regis, who is not most happy I did not first be going to see him. He is to see over my monies and my houses I shall be purchasing.'

This sounded as if it was St Regis's feet he meant to stand on, but no matter. At least he would not be standing on mine. From all accounts there was nothing St Regis preferred to interfering in the family's dealings. He would have Pierre shackled to some fortune equal in size to his own in jig time. After another half hour's wait, Sinclair had *still* not come up to see me, but Pierre had let it slip out that the reason he sat in the saloon was to prevent Hill's untimely departure.

A reason for Sinclair's absence was soon discovered. Loo received a note informing her St Regis had arrived. He was coming to see her and Dr Hill, and was kind enough to add a post-script saying he wished to make my acquaintance. Loo came to tell me of the impending visit. 'You had better go and comb your hair, Valerie. And for goodness' sake don't say anything forward or bold. I tremble to think what he will do, but I won't have Dr Hill put into gaol, whatever he may say.'

'It is what he deserves.'

'The young are cruel. You cannot know what dire straits he was in, with those horrid Rogers people squeezing him for money. I should have married him, but I did not, and shan't do it now either, for he did not behave honorably in this matter, stealing my money and lying to me. He has promised to pay back all he can. He is to give me some Titian painting, and all the money he stole that he has not spent, but unfortunately he spent a good deal of it on books and things, as well as Miss Rogers's fees at the sanatorium. Some remains, and he is to try to pay back what is owing over the next years. He is going to sell up his cottage and return to Harley Street, or at least to London. He will not want to remain here where the story of his disgrace is bound to leak out, with that wretched St Regis coming to make a great scandal. Do you think it possible St Regis can press charges, Valerie?'

'I have no idea. If the money is returned, I don't see how he can, but I think you are letting Hill off *much* too lightly.'

'I know you do. Walter has been a good friend over the years, though, to Edward and to me. How should it be possible to have him put in prison, maybe even *hanged*? Having to leave the neighborhood he loves and go back to London will be punishment enough for him.'

'I doubt you will have a word to say in the matter. St Regis will take over the whole once he arrives.'

'I must go and make a fresh toilet before he comes. I shall wear a gown. A regular morning gown, I mean, instead of this contraption Miss Brendan made up for me. These things are nice and cool for the summer, but somehow I think St Regis will not like it.'

'St Regis may go to the devil. You can jump to his tune if you like. *I* plan to go riding.'

'Oh, Valerie, I wish you will not!'

I did not do it, but neither did I sit waiting like a tame bunny for the great St Regis to come and size me up, and see if I would make a suitable mate for his errand boy. He would only ask horrid questions about dowries and things that were none of his business. I went for a walk through the park.

When I returned more than an hour later, St Regis was still closeted with my aunt. I was hoping I had stayed away long enough that he would have to wait for me. There were sounds of scraping chairs and general movement in the scriptorium, indicating the more important meeting was over. I darted down the hall, to be sitting in state in the saloon, telling the servants where I was to be found, in case his lordship wished to see me now. Uppermost in my mind was the question of Welland's whereabouts in all this morning. I assumed he was with St Regis, which turned out to be the case.

St Regis was every bit as pompous, overbearing, and hateful as I had so often pictured him. He was of medium height and build, but held his shoulders back in such a self-consequential way, while looking down his nose at me through a pair of pince-nez glasses. 'This would be Miss Ford,' he said, making a slight gesture toward bowing.

'How do you do, my lord,' I said, reaching out to grip his hand. He looked quite startled at this unladylike freedom on my part.

'Fine,' he said, blinking his surprise to Welland, who stood biting back a grin behind him. He was without his green glasses on this occasion. 'Just fine, thank you.' Then he released my fingers and turned to his cousin. 'I approve,' he said. 'I heartily approve of Miss Ford. She will suit you admirably.'

'Thank you. You can leave us now, Sinc. I just wanted Miss Ford to meet you, since she has heard so much about you. Most of it untrue.'

I turned a warning stare on Welland, shocked that he would treat his patron so cavalierly. 'Very well, then,' St Regis said at once. 'I shall be at the gatehouse waiting for you. Mary will want to talk to you. Very happy to have made your acquaintance, ma'am,' he added to me before leaving.

'You see, I told you it would be all right,' Welland said, stepping forward with an easy smile.

'Why on earth did he bring *Mary*?' I asked, disliking the proximity of the fiancée at such a critical moment. I feared St Regis hoped to rekindle a romance in that corner.

'He could not like to be separated from her on the honeymoon.'

'You mean St Regis married her *himself*?'

'Not exactly,' he said, hunching his shoulders in a way there was no trusting. His forehead too was all wrinkled up, denoting some double dealing. 'The fact is. . . .' He stopped, tilted his head to the side, and laughed at me. I swallowed a couple of times, while I did some rapid thinking. 'Did you not tumble to it? I made sure when you mentioned my overbearing way, so unsuited to a secretary. . . .'

'That was Welland Sinclair in those pince-nez glasses!'

'Yes, and you know who that makes *me*. The odious St Regis at your service, ma'am,' he said, sweeping me a bow.

'I should have known! If there is *one thing* in this world, Welland. . . .'

'The name is Hadrian. Like the wall, you know.'

'. . . one thing that could make me hate you more than I always have, it is knowing you are that busy-body, interfering, penny-pinching little. . . .'

'Six feet tall. I only seem little to *you*.'

'. . . little *toad* of a St Regis.'

'I still want to marry you, Valkyrie.'

Oh, joy! What a relief it was! As he was so busy to find fortunes for his kin, I naturally feared he would be after one for himself. I wanted to revile him more for the looks of it, to pay him back for his deceit, but I emitted a shaky laugh all unawares.

'On the tenth of July,' he went on. 'It is my parents' anniversary. I decided long ago to hold my own wedding on the same day, if I could coerce my bride into it. I am a romantic, when I am not being an odious little toad. Why don't I kiss you, and see if I turn into Prince Charming?' he suggested warily.

Sure enough, he did. He did not have far to go in my opinion. The more alarming transformation occurred in me. I felt strangely uncertain, shy of him, *feminine*, possessed of some weakness that was not at all characteristic of me. I wanted to be small, dainty, to come up to his chin, instead of his eyebrows. And had I not taken the precaution of wearing my lowest heels, I would have gone a little above even the eyebrows.

'Mmmm, I certainly *feel* like a prince,' he said when he released me. 'Shall we try for king?'

'Let me get used to a prince first. You were only a secretary when you left last night, you know. All these promotions take some getting used to.'

'There's no better way to get used to anyone,' he said, pulling me back into his arms, where his kinship to Pierre St Clair was most forcibly demonstrated, and most thoroughly enjoyed.

I expected to see Pierre land in on us, as he usually did at the worst possible times. On this occasion, it was Aunt Loo who interrupted the seduction. 'He has left, Lord St Regis,' she said, stiff with disapproval, but I think it was for the man's name, not his present activity.

'That is all right. Welland will follow him.'

'Did you let Hill off scot-free?' I asked.

'It is known as giving a dog a second bite. If he keeps his promise, sends over the Titian, and returns what part of Lady Sinclair's money he has not squandered, then we shall assume his intentions to repay the rest are good, and not call in the constable. If he doesn't. . . .' The shoulders went up in a shrug.

'It is a shabby trick,' Loo said.

'You think he'll bolt, in other words,' St Regis remarked.

'Certainly not. I haven't a doubt in the world he intends to repay it all to me, every penny.'

'We shall see,' he answered skeptically.

He soon saw as well by hostile glances, impatient head shakings, and a general lack of conversation from the hostess that he was about as welcome in her saloon as frost in July. He took his leave. Lucky St Regis. *I* was left behind to hear all her angry disparagement of 'that wretched man, coming dressed up in green glasses so I would not recognize him. He *knew* what a chilly reception he would get if he came as himself, whereas Edward was always fond of Welland, and he thought I would be too, but I ain't. He is even worse than St Regis for stiffness.'

'Is that why he wore them?'

'Yes, and I would not have recognized him in the least. I only met him once. I found him perfectly forgettable. And he was not writing up anything on ghosts at all, the rogue. Doesn't know a thing about them really.'

'You should be grateful to him, Aunt Loo. Hill was a criminal.'

'Nobody is perfect. He was driven to it by necessity.'

'The necessity of buying fancy paintings and books. You are incurably generous, foolishly so. But I shan't say another word. It is your life, not mine.'

Her sniff and lifted nose told me how completely she agreed with me. It was not the proper moment to announce my betrothal. I had to tell someone, so I told Pinny.

'You too, miss?' she asked, smiling fatuously.

'Oh, Napier told you about Mary Milne and Mr Sinclair?'

'He did, but that wasn't what I was referring to, miss. Marriages come in threes, they say. I'm to be the third – me and Napier.'

'Oh, Pinny! I'm so happy for you! When is it to be?'

'As soon as ever we get back to Tanglewood. Napier wants to be married at our new home. Do you think I might be able to go on doing for you, miss? His lordship told him I could work upstairs or down or in the kitchen, just as I liked, but if *you're* to be there. . . .'

I was too wrapped up in my own glory to have thought of this perfect solution, but when it was brought to my attention, I gave it my hearty approval. There was nothing more I could ask for from life. Except perhaps a phaeton and pair for myself, and a hunter from St Regis's stables. Maybe a few dozen new gowns and a sable wrap, and of course the use of the family jewels while I was mistress of Tanglewood. . . . Quite a few other prerequisites occurred to me as well, but mostly I thought of the exquisite joy of having hunted down such an unexceptional husband for myself, all fair and square and without the aid of dowry or family managing. How they would gape at home when I told them!

Chapter Twenty-three

*T*he remainder of the day was neither comfortable nor enjoyable, except that I had my success in nabbing a husband to hug to my bosom, and also to impart to my family in a letter. Marie and Elleri would be green with envy, since they are too foolish to see how my advancement will work to their benefit, throwing them in the way of better gentlemen than they meet at home. Aunt Loo was in the boughs throughout the whole time, sulking, complaining, banging doors, and chewing out the servants. All the young gentlemen – St Regis, Welland, and Pierre – disappeared and stayed disappeared throughout the afternoon and early evening. I assumed they were taking turns spying on Hill to see if he tried to leave without telling anyone. I did not think it was his intention to do so for the simple reason that Nancy was still in my aunt's stable. Had I been the doctor, I would not have left such a mount behind.

It was during dinner, a solemn meal taken with only my silent aunt for company, that she gave over being sulky. The soup had come and gone, likewise the fish, fowl, meat, and vegetables. Dessert on that occasion was fresh strawberries, enough to put a smile on the sourest face.

'Delicious,' I complimented, looking to see if she could be coaxed into a word.

'Ingenious!' was her unlikely reply, given with such force and enthusiasm it could not possibly refer to berries.

'What is that you are talking about, Aunt Loo?'

'Hill, the rascal.'

'I thought you had forgiven him.'

'Forgiven him? I should go down on my knees and thank him. Tell me what you think of this notion, Gloria. I mean, Valerie. I am finished with Gloria. I am weary of her awful strength and forward behavior, if you want the truth. I finished her up today, and shall hire someone to write up the fair copy, for I have a much better idea for a novel. My villain will be a trusted family physician, privy to all the dreadful secrets of a wicked family, only of course the heroine will not be wicked like the others. She will have escaped *The Curse of the St Clairs*. Maybe I ought to make it St something else.'

'I would, if I were you.'

'They take an oath, you know, doctors, not to be telling about the countryside what they have learned in the sickroom – Hippo-something it is called, but little will Hill care for his oath. Of course I cannot call him Hill either, though it would serve him well if I did. I know a great deal about medicines from my dealings with Walter. I shan't repeat the black drop, for I have already used that in *Search for the Unknown*, but he could be killing someone off by any of a dozen slow poisons Walter has spoken of. Lead poisoning or arsenic or deadly nightshade, only I don't think it is one of the *slow* ones.'

I was happy to see her thoughts diverted in this harmless direction. 'Who will your new heroine be?' I asked.

'Marie,' was her unhesitating answer. 'She is *by far* the prettiest of my brother's gels,' she went on, heedless that one of her brother's girls sat under her nose. 'She is nineteen – the very best age a girl can possibly be. They reach their peak at nineteen, with all the gaucheness and awkwardness of youth worn away, without yet beginning to fade. The ugliest female in the world is at least slightly attractive at nineteen, but Marie is a beauty. I wanted to have her be Gloria, but she had not the required strength. She will do excellently for my new heroine. No great feats will be required from her. Hill has a hold over her mama, you see, some secret from her past, and he is making the mama allow him to marry Marie, for she is so outstandingly beautiful. Not a great overgrown weed like Gloria. I am not entirely happy with Gloria. She seemed to get bolder and less ladylike as the novel progressed. I don't know what can account for it.'

'I cannot imagine,' I answered ironically.

'She was too capable; that was her main fault,' she explained, in an effort to smooth my ruffled feathers.

'Have you selected a hero for Marie?'

'I think it is time for an army man,' she said, cocking her head to the side and trying to narrow her eyes. 'St Regis is always trying to send some colonel down to visit me. He will be too bold for the hero, but he will give me authentic background for military matters. He will be company too. I shall miss Walter.'

'We don't know for sure that he won't be back.'

'Ah, it will never be the *same*, Gloria. My confidence in him is gone. I even begin to wonder why he was always giving me laudanum. Do you think he was trying to befuddle my brain? He *did* say more than once that I should have a full-time medical man in the house. He hinted I need looking after, imagine!'

As we finished our strawberries, there was a caller admitted in the hallway. 'Bring tea into the saloon,' Loo told the servant. 'I think Walter has come with my painting.' She did not look particularly pleased about it.

It was not Hill, but St Regis and Pierre, who awaited us. 'I have bad news,' St Regis told Lady Sinclair.

'If it has to do with that wretched Dr Hill, it will come as no surprise to *me*,' was her answer.

'It has to do with him. He loaded up his traveling carriage with every valuable thing from his cottage and headed up north. We were watching him, in case of this stunt. He has been turned over to the constable, Lady Sinclair. You were overly kind to have given him another chance. He has proven beyond any doubt that his character is black. It will be prison for him.'

'Serves him right, the villain. Tell me exactly how you caught him, St Regis. I like to get all the details accurate.'

St Regis lifted his brow to me, demanding an explanation for her change of feeling with regard to Hill. There was a book on the sofa table. I lifted it and nodded toward my aunt, while making writing motions with my other hand.

He understood me at once. He smiled, settled back, and began composing a chapter for her. 'It was very exciting. Worthy of a novel, but no one writes those really good, frightening ones nowadays. The shadows were just deepening, etching a tangled, intertwining pattern on the ground. There was fog settling on the floor of the spinney where we hid in wait for him.'

'We are waiting till he has all the good things piled in the carriage,' Pierre added.

'Let St Regis write – *tell* – it, Peter,' Aunt Loo directed. 'I shall just get a pencil and paper, if you will wait a minute. I want to set it down for – for my diary,' she explained hastily.

She scratched away, seeking details of how it felt, waiting in the fog, how the carriage team behaved when the pursuers' shouts rang out, what actual words Hill uttered – all very factual, or at least very well invented by St Regis.

'Much good funs,' Pierre concluded, when the last word had been jotted down.

'Before you go, I expect you will want to speak about those few heirlooms that I sold,' Loo said, with a wary eye to her caller. 'When Hill's funds are turned over to me, there ought to be enough for me to pay you for them, and without having to give him so much money, I shall have plenty to run Troy Fenners again.'

'The gatehouse needs some work,' St Regis said. 'The upstairs of it is going to rack and ruin. Now that the barns are in good shape. . . .'

'Why do you not let it to that widowed colonel, Auntie? His rent can look after its repair, and you mentioned this might be a good time for him to visit you.' She did not look averse.

St Regis smiled serenely, but it was Pierre who spoke. 'There will be enough to give me back my monies also too?'

'Yes, over a year or two,' she told him. 'You are rich as a nabob, Peter. You are in no hurry, are you?'

'St Regis is buying me the properties near Tanglewood. How much monies do I need?' he asked St Regis.

'We'll sort all the details out tomorrow. I see Lady Sinclair is tired now. We shall leave, and let her get to bed.'

'Yes, I am exhausted,' she agreed, and arose to leave.

I had still not told her of my pending wedding, and wished to do so before she retired. 'You never mean it! Why, Valerie, what do you see in him?'

Her reaction was so unexpected I hadn't a word to say. 'Hmph, serves him right is all I say,' she concluded. On that thoughtless remark, she strode into the scriptorium and closed the door.

'Hadrian,' I said when I returned to the saloon, 'there is just one thing I am still unclear about. What did you take from my aunt's carton of papers?'

'What do you think?'

'I can't imagine.'

'Letters from Welland's mother to Sir Edward. Love letters that Sinc would not like to see when he eventually takes over here at Troy Fenners.'

'You're going to give it to him?'

'Let him have the use of it, later on. He's a good worker, but not actually my most favored relative. I can think of people I would rather have at our doorstep, in the dower house.'

'Sherries?' Pierre asked.

'Are you not feeling tired, Peter?' St Regis asked, in a meaningful voice.

'Not at all one bit. I am very much not tired.'

'You are very much insensitive to the tang of romance in the air; for a Frenchman.'

'I am English, me. We English do not have the flair for romance.'

'Speak for yourself,' St Regis said, arising and taking him by the elbow, 'There is another English custom you must learn, my friendly cousin.'

'Kissing of the bride?' he asked hopefully, with a look over his shoulder.

'No. Removing yourself from a room when a lady and gentleman wish for some privacy.'

'I am too much, you mean,' Pierre said.

'Definitely *de trop*.'

'If you are a good boy, Peter, I shall ask my sister to visit us at Tanglewood,' I bribed. It must be Elleri. Marie would be busy describing to Auntie the effect of various poisons on her body.

'She is beautiful, like you?' he asked.

'Much prettier, and *smaller*.'

'Me, I like the grand Valkyrie,' he told me, offering some last bit of resistance as St Regis dragged him determinedly to the door. He was shoved out, the door closed firmly behind him, then Hadrian turned back to me, his brown eyes dancing.

'Me, *I* like the grand Valerie too,' he said, advancing toward me at a rapid pace.

Also by Joan Smith
and soon to be published:
PERDITA

TWO INNOCENT LADIES
MATCH WITS WITH AN
ALL-TOO-KNOWING LORD.

Governess Moira Greenwood's beautiful young charge, Perdita Brodie, is a high-spirited chit. Indeed, she rebels against her stepmama's choice of mate and manages to get Moira and herself positions in a not quite shabby travelling acting troupe.

While Moira cooks, her lovely cousin sings, attracting the very insistent attentions of the cold, handsome rakehell Lord Stornaway – who takes the pair for lightskirts!

Although Moira explains the truth, the self-satisfied lord believes not a word; he's positive the two are ladies of ill repute. Moira finds him the most rude and uncivil of men and tells him so. Still, there is something about him she can't quite define that is not *completely* loathsome. . . .